Highlander
Avenged

ALSO BY LAURIN WITTIG

Charming the Shrew
(The Legacy of MacLeod—Book I)

Daring the Highlander
(The Legacy of MacLeod—Book II)

The Devil of Kilmartin
(A Kilmartin Glen Novel)

Jewels of Historical Romance, an anthology

The Winter Stone, three novellas

Highlander Betrayed
(Guardians of the Targe—Book 1)

HIGHLANDER AVENGED

GUARDIANS OF THE TARGE

BOOK 2

LAURIN WITTIG

Published by Montlake Romance, Seattle

www.apub.com

Amazon, the Amazon logo, and Montlake Romance are trademarks of Amazon.com, Inc., or its affiliates.

ISBN-13: 9781477823309
ISBN-10: 1477823301

Cover design by Anne Cain

Library of Congress Control Number: 2014900811

Printed in the United States of America

For Flora and Kinta
I wish for you your very own happily-ever-afters!

CHAPTER ONE

Scottish Highlands, Late Spring, 1307

"HOLD!" JEANETTE MACALPIN GROWLED HER FRUSTRATION AT her cousin Rowan, who glared back at her from her perch on the end of her bed. The Highland Targe, a grey, palm-sized stone that had been in the keeping of the MacAlpin women for generations, lay in Rowan's lap on top of an open ermine sack. "How am I ever to train you to be a proper Guardian if you cannot even master the simplest of blessings?" Jeanette knew her voice was strident and her words harsh but her patience had long since died. "The symbols must be made together with the words." She floated her hands through the air in graceful arcs and swirls, just as her mother had taught her, repeating the rhythmic chanting that completed the protective blessing. "I was able to do this when I was but eight winters old!"

Rowan was staring at her now, a look of fury in her pale green eyes. "And how many years before you were eight did you get to practice this? More than a fortnight, I am sure."

Rowan's fury brought Jeanette up short. The two of them rarely disagreed, and never argued. She closed her eyes and tried to find the calm reason that had always been her way, but the danger that loomed over her beloved clan, a danger only a trained Guardian could protect them from, had smothered any calm she might still harbor.

"You are right, of course," she said, wishing that she could rid her voice of the edge of her own rising anger. Jeanette had been trained almost since birth to take her mother's place as Guardian, and yet the power of the Targe had chosen Rowan for that position, ripping itself from Jeanette's mum against both her will, and Rowan's. The new Guardian should have been Jeanette, or even, perhaps, her younger sister, Scotia. Never in all the lore she had studied had a Guardian not been a direct descendant of the MacAlpins of Dunlairig.

Until now.

Rowan was her cousin on her father's side—not from the female MacAlpin line. Rowan was a MacGregor.

With a resigned sigh and a hard swallow to ease the constriction of her throat, Jeanette forced herself to unclench her hands.

"Again," she said as nicely as she was able to say.

Rowan scowled at Jeanette, then rubbed the spot between her auburn brows before pinching her eyes closed, scrunching up her forehead as if she were in pain, and mumbling the most basic blessing a Guardian needed to know. The beautiful, sometimes guttural, words of a language no one had understood for generations were almost right, though when spoken without the gentle spirit of Jeanette's mother, they sounded harsh and angry. Rowan's hands gripped her knees as if she dared not let go.

"Stop," Jeanette demanded. "You must use the hand signs at the same time. Do it again, and focus on what you are doing this time."

"Enough!" Rowan wrapped the sack around the Targe stone, cinching it closed with a hard tug on the drawstring, and stood abruptly. "I have told you more than once that the things you insist I must do worked for your mum's gift. They do not work for mine."

"But it is the way of the Guardian—words and symbols. It is the way the Guardian calls upon the power of the Targe stone."

"Not for me."

Jeanette blinked and pinched her lips together hard for a moment as she searched her memories of everything her mother had taught her and everything she had read in the chronicles left by past Guardians. Irritation with herself this time had her muttering her father's favorite curses under her breath. She could not remember any mention of another way to train a Guardian.

"You must be trained, Rowan." Her words strained against her clenched teeth. "I promised Mum I would train you to be a proper Guardian. I promised that I would prepare you as she prepared me. If I do not, you will not be able to protect the clan, as is your duty now. We need you to put Mum's protections back about this castle. I will not let her down again."

The ire drained from Rowan's face, leaving behind an odd blend of sympathy and irritation. She sighed and reached for Jeanette's hands. It was all Jeanette could do not to pull free of her cousin's grip. She'd rather have Rowan's ire than her pity.

"Is that what all of this is about?" Rowan asked. "Cousin, you have not ever let her down."

Jeanette yanked away and turned from the sorrow in Rowan's eyes.

"I did not protect her from that English spy." The horror of that moment when he had plunged his dagger into her mother's heart would never leave her. "I was not chosen by the Targe to be the Guardian, as she wanted, and now I seem unable to help you take up her place. I let her down, and now the entire clan is in danger because we have no true Guardian."

"We what?"

Jeanette could hear the coldly quiet anger in Rowan's voice and she immediately regretted her rash words. She squared her shoulders and faced her cousin. "We have no trained Guardian."

"You said 'true' Guardian."

Jeanette looked at her feet. "Aye, I did."

"Jeanette, I know it was a blow to you when I was chosen, but I *was* chosen. I am the true Guardian. I did not ask for it, nor did I want it, but it has fallen to me and I have accepted the responsibility. You have tried to train me in the ways you were trained but they do not work for me and my gift. Perhaps it is because I am not a MacAlpin? I do not ken, but it does not mean you have failed and it does not mean I am a false Guardian." Now it was Rowan who was pacing the room.

"I ken that you are the true Guardian, Rowan. I do. But it has left me unmoored. Whether you have intended to or not, you have taken my purpose away. If I cannot train you—"

The heavy oaken door swung open without so much as a knock and Scotia, Jeanette's dark-haired younger sister, stood there, glowering at them, as she had done every day since her mother had been laid to rest barely a fortnight ago.

"You are summoned to the chief's chamber," she said.

"Both of us?" Jeanette asked. As Guardian and as wife to the new chief, Nicholas, Rowan was always included in the chief's meetings, but no other women.

"Nay, only the Guardian. We are not called."

Jeanette sighed. "We will begin again after the midday meal," she said to Rowan.

"Nay, we will not," Rowan said, a new firmness to her voice and her bearing. "Nicholas will help me learn to use my gift with the Targe. He is the only one who has been able to so far."

"But—"

Rowan cut her off with a raised hand. "I promise to speak the words of the blessing every time."

"And the motions." It was not a request.

"I will endeavor to remember the motions as well, but I do not promise that."

"'Tis a start," Jeanette said.

Rowan stared at her for a long moment, as if she could not decide what to say next. Finally, she shook her head. "'Tis all. For now at least."

"Nay—"

Again she was silenced by Rowan's hand in the air. "I will ask for help when I am ready for it—that I promise, but for now I must discover how to use my gift in my own way."

" 'Tis not the way of the Guardians."

" 'Tis the way of *this* Guardian," Rowan said as she left the chamber.

Scotia looked over at her sister, her dark eyebrows drawn down over the same green eyes Rowan had. "At least she gets a say in how we destroy the English," she said, venom making her voice raspy, "if they dare show their faces here again."

Jeanette shook her head at the sister she barely recognized anymore and sighed. The English spy had killed more than just their mother. With one swift stroke of his blade, he had killed Scotia's innocence, too, filling her instead with hate and an unquenchable thirst for vengeance.

"Aye, she gets a say, but she cannot seem to learn even the most basic blessing, and if she cannot do that, she will never be able to protect this clan or this castle, as is her duty. Time is running out. The castle and all who abide here are vulnerable. None of us will be safe when the English return for the Targe."

Jeanette strode out of the tower and into the bailey and stopped, shocked, as always, by the destruction that had befallen her home, Dunlairig Castle, in just a few weeks.

She pressed the heel of her hand to her chest, where the ache of all her losses seemed to gather like a hot stone. To her right, the entire north side of the curtain wall was nothing but rubble, revealing the rich woad blue of the loch and a vista of craggy mountains in the distance. They still did not know why the wall had fallen, but that mystery had been set aside in the face of more pressing problems. To her left lay the blackened remains of the great hall. Most of the clan's supplies and the hall itself had been burned by the same English spy who had killed their Guardian, her mother, taking her from them just when she was most needed. Jeanette squeezed her eyes tight, as if that would reverse the disasters that had overrun the small clan.

It did not.

She needed to get away from everything and everyone, if only for a short time. She needed to find that calm center within her that had always been there but that had disappeared the day her mother had died, or maybe even before that, when Rowan had been chosen by the Targe.

She crossed the small bailey and went through the deeply shadowed gate passage. She didn't know where she was headed, but she knew she needed to get out of the castle. When she came out of the passage and into the sun, Denis, the guard, pushed himself off a small cask he often sat on just outside the gate.

"Where you be going this fine day, mistress?" he said to her as she whipped past him.

"For a walk." She flung the words back over her shoulder.

She could hear short bursts of breath wheeze out of him as he jogged to catch up. A surprisingly strong hand on her arm stopped her.

"You cannot leave the castle alone, Mistress Jeanette," he said, holding her in place with a light but firm grip. "The English could be anywhere," he said in a loud whisper, as if they could be standing just behind her.

She looked down at his hand, then up at the watery blue eyes of the old man. "None have been seen since that murdering spy was killed, have they?"

"Nay, but that does not mean—"

"I will be fine on my own."

"I cannot allow that."

She pulled out of his grip and stood as tall as she could, which meant she was actually looking down at the bandy-legged guard.

"I can take care of myself," she said. "I will be alert." She placed her hand on his arm this time and softened her voice. "I promise."

He looked unsure but it was a rare thing that Jeanette, once considered the future Guardian, was gainsaid anything she really wanted. She had learned not to misuse that privilege but she also knew how to subtly apply it when she needed to. And even though it was clear she was no longer the future anything, the clan had not yet lost the habit of treating her as if she were.

Denis sighed. "You shall not be gone long, then?"

"Nay, not long." She gave him a quick smile, even though she did not feel like smiling, and took off for the forested ben that rose behind the castle.

Leaving the morning sunshine for the cool shade of the tree-sheltered path was the closest thing to peace she had felt since her mother had taken ill last fall. She tried to pull both the coolness of the air and the peace that floated on it into her, but shame over her failures, grief, and fear for what the future held shoved it away. She could not draw enough air into her lungs for a deep breath, but she could not stop moving, either. Peace was not within her grasp and might never be again.

She needed to go, to leave, to escape all the pain that seemed trapped as much within her as within the broken castle and clan. But she knew that wherever she went, she would always carry the pain with her—the knowledge that she had not lived up to her birthright—like a scar on her heart.

A tiny wren trilled in the trees above her head, filling the wood with a song full of joy and life so at odds with Jeanette's black thoughts that she grimaced. She might not be the Guardian, but that did not mean she needed to wallow in self-pity. She was sick of it, sick of herself. She would find a way to be of use to her clan.

Morven, the clan's aging healer, had trained Jeanette for years now, telling her that she would one day be the clan's healer when Morven could no longer fulfill her duties. The death of Elspet, Jeanette's mum, had hit the auld woman even harder than the rest of them. She'd brought Elspet into the world, helped her birth her bairns, and had fought to find a cure for the illness that had all but wasted Elspet away before the spy had killed her. Before all this, in spite of her frailty, Morven had held on to her place as healer. Since then, she had withdrawn into herself and left all healing work to Jeanette.

Jeanette knew she would have taken Morven's place eventually, even if she *had* become the Guardian, but now she could step into that position without reservation. That would serve the clan and it would keep her busy, even once Rowan decided she did need Jeanette's help with her training. If she ever did.

The wren fluttered in a nearby holly tree, fussing at her now, as if to chide her for lingering in its territory. Jeanette looked about her to get her bearings and realized that she was very near the one place that had always been peaceful, had always reinforced her sense of calm—the sacred wellspring where she used to watch her mother make offerings and prayers to the power of the Targe. Tears she refused to shed clogged her throat. Visiting the wellspring would not be the same without her mum, but at least she might feel closer to her there and might be able to draw some small comfort from that.

She quickened her pace up the rocky trail and soon made it to the top of the path, where it turned left around the shoulder of the ben. She stepped onto an almost imperceptible track to the right that she knew wrapped around a large moss-covered stone outcropping. From there it ran a hundred feet or more to the shallow cave that sheltered the wellspring where crystal-clear water poured forth from a crack in the mountain, splashing into an icy pool before it ran down the benside to the loch.

Anticipation had her rushing down the track even faster than she had climbed the ben. She came round the last curve, hopped over the water that escaped down the ben, and skidded to a stop in the small cleared area just outside the cave.

It took a moment for her to understand what she saw there.

A man knelt in profile next to the pool of water. A shaft of sunshine cut through the shadows, turning his bare torso golden, and picking out strands of almost-white-blond hair on his head. He stopped, just as he was about to pour water over his right arm, and looked over his shoulder at her. He smiled and it was dazzling.

Jeanette blinked, and blinked again, as she started considering what she should do. Here was a stranger. Should she run or stand her ground? She slowly let her hand settle over her sgian dubh, her small knife.

"Are you mute, then, lass?"

His voice, deep and laced with humor, shocked her out of her thoughts. She couldn't help but watch as he reached for the tunic laying by his feet, and pulled it over his sun-kissed skin before rising and facing her, grinning at her now. His shirt stuck to his wet skin, drawing her attention to his chest and rippled stomach, drawing her eye—

She gasped and snapped her gaze back up to meet his. He didn't look English, with his shoulder-length dark blond hair, braided at the temples, and his well-faded plaid that he wore with ease. But neither had Nicholas, their new chief, looked English when first he came among them. Yet, somehow, Jeanette had always known Nicholas was an honorable man and that had proved true. She couldn't say exactly why, but she had the same sense about this man.

And then she remembered what her mum had always told her: "You are a fine judge of character, my sweet Jeanette. I do not understand how, but you always seem to ken the truth of someone when first you meet." The memory was both sweet and melancholy.

"Lass?" he asked, his grin even wider now, lending a twinkle to his green-and-brown hazel eyes.

Instinct warred with recent experience and instinct won out. He might be an honorable man, but that did not mean she trusted him. Not yet.

"What are you doing here?" she finally snapped, setting her fists on her hips. She would find no comfort here in the company of a stranger and she wanted him gone. "Who are you?"

"I could ask the same of you," he said.

"Nay, you could not. This is my family's land and you do not belong here. I ask again, Who are you?"

The man folded his arms across his chest and cocked his head at her, his grin firmly in place as if he thought it disarming. Which it was.

Jeanette notched her chin up and waited for him to answer her questions. He was the interloper here. He was the one shattering the serenity of the place with his skin and his smile and his eyes.

"I am Malcolm MacKenzie," he said finally.

She nodded. "Where is your home?"

"In the north, west of Inverness. Now, who are you, and whose land is this?"

"Come away from the pool." She desperately wanted him away from her mother's place, and motioned for him to join her outside the sheltering rock, but as he passed her, the almost-transparent damp linen of his tunic revealed a large festering wound on his upper right arm. She grabbed his arm at the elbow, stopping him. "What happened?"

Malcolm looked down, a swear hissing from his lips.

" 'Tis nothing," he said, but when he went to pull away from her, she held him fast, already pushing his sleeve up, exposing the long, oozing gash on his upper arm.

She could tell, from the faint marks around the edges of the wound, that it had been inexpertly stitched at one point. But the stitches were gone now, and yet it still oozed and there were faint red lines leading away from it.

She looked up at him. The grin had been replaced with a scowl, the twinkle no longer in his eyes.

"You were here to heal this."

He stepped away from her touch and jerked the sleeve down. "'Tis none of your concern, lass."

She would be damned if it was not. This she could do something about. This was something she was still useful for and she might as well embrace her healer duties right away. She dug in the bag of herbs and salves that always hung at her waist but realized she must have left the salve she searched for back at the castle. She did have a small linen pocket full of moss with her. It was good for dressing a wound like this, but also good at drawing the fester out. She looked about them, trying to spy anything else that might help his wound heal, but there was only the wellspring.

"Did you pray?" she asked.

"Pray? For healing? Aye, every day."

"Nay, that is not what I mean. The water will not heal you without a prayer, a chant really, and even then 'tis not immediate. Come, let me show you."

She grabbed his hand and pulled him back to the little pool of clear mountain water.

"Take off your tunic," she said.

"Lass, do you seek to take advantage of me?"

"Advantage?" Confused, she looked up to find him grinning again.

"You demanded I take off my clothes." He winked at her but she just rolled her eyes.

"I am a healer. Take your tunic off—only your tunic. That wound is in a bad way. 'Tis trying to send out poison to your blood. You are lucky I came upon you when I did. A few more days and it might not be within my skill to heal you."

His expression turned serious again and he took off his tunic, scowling a little as it pulled away from the wound.

She took his elbow once more, stunned for a moment by the warmth of his skin and the golden hue of it next to her pale hand. But she had a task to do, so she turned him so that his arm was illuminated by the sun, and began to press around the hot edges of his wound, bringing the greenish ooze to the surface.

"How long has it been like this?" She was aware that she had fallen into her "healing voice," as her mother used to call it. A soft, reassuring voice, showing concern but not fear.

He did not speak, and when she glanced up from her work, she found his eyes fixed on his injury. He did not look to be in pain, but there was something in his face that told her he was as concerned as he should be.

"How long?" she asked again softly, as if he were a bairn she did not wish to frighten.

"It has been a while."

"A battle?" She had seen similar injuries in her kinsmen after a battle. Swords sliced clean and deep and if the wounds were not tended properly, they did not heal well.

"Aye."

She worked the wound a bit more, pleased that he did not make her stop, nor did he complain over her attentions, as some warriors were wont to do. The wound showed signs of partial healing. The stitches had been removed some time ago, from the looks of it, which meant his injury had not happened recently.

"This happened before winter set in," she said.

"Why would you say that?"

"No one battles in the Highlands in winter."

He raised an eyebrow as if he challenged her conclusion, but Jeanette held firm in her opinion.

"Aye, before winter set in," he said.

Jeanette tried not to smile at his admission. It was almost summer, now. She thought back and determined the wound could be no less than six or seven months old, and still it was not healed. He would be in no shape to battle this summer, the high season for that sort of activity. She looked at the wound and his arm closely, then looked down at his hand. The muscles were weak from disuse. Even if she could heal his injury, it would take even longer before he could wield his claymore, the large two-handed sword she had noticed leaning against the wall of the cave.

'Twas too bad. He looked to be a braw warrior and her clan could use a few more of those if the English really did send more soldiers, as the clan expected. Jeanette shuddered at the thought of what it would mean to her beleaguered clan if they were set upon again before they could rebuild the castle wall.

If they were set upon . . .

She stilled and looked up at him. Here she was, with a half-naked stranger who claimed to be a MacKenzie but whom she knew nothing about, regardless of what her instincts said. She did not know his loyalties, nor his true reason for being on MacAlpin land, for she doubted he had come so far from his home just to wash his wound in the wellspring. Why would a Highlander be wandering alone in the wilderness with a wound such as this anyway? Why would he not have gone to his home to be nursed back to health, or have asked for help from any chief he might encounter? He would not if he was hiding, and he would only be hiding if he should not be here.

"Did you fight for the English?" Though she tried to hold it in, all the hatred she felt for the English rolled out with her words, along with the disgust she felt for those Scots who fought with them against their own countrymen.

"I fought with Robert the Bruce at Methven and Dalrigh." He once more pulled free of her grip, thunder in his eyes. "There are Scots who would fight with the English devils, but I am not one of them. Are you?"

"I have more than one reason to hate the English king and the men who fight for him." She glowered at him.

"Then we have that in common," he said.

She watched him, gauging the truth in his words by the evidence of his body. He met her eyes without hesitation. His feet were planted firmly on the ground, as if he held fast to his assertions.

His hands were unfisted at his sides and he seemed genuinely insulted that she called his loyalty into question.

Jeanette let out a long breath.

"Come, kneel down by the pool and let me finish caring for your arm, Malcolm MacKenzie."

Malcolm couldn't help but smile at the beautiful woman. The turn of events this morning was stunning. He had heard there were healing wells in this area, though he'd only stumbled across this one, following the nearly hidden path on a hunch. And then an angel had found him. He wondered at his own excessive language but it was apt.

"Will you kneel?" She motioned for him to resume his place by the pool of water, then she knelt beside him and began to move her hands in the air over the wound as she whispered something. The words meant nothing to Malcolm, nor did the fluid motions of her delicate, long-fingered hands. When her hands stilled, she closed her eyes and kept whispering, and he took the opportunity to look at her more closely.

She was perhaps twenty years old, no more, with flaxen hair and, though they were closed now, her eyes were the color of a clear midsummer sky. When first he saw her, the sun had outlined her gentle curves for a long moment, and then she'd spoken— nay, commanded. There was no shortage of confidence in her as she stood there, her hands on her hips, demanding answers to her questions.

And she was a healer.

Saints be praised.

When her whispering was finished, she took a small wooden cup from the fold of her arisaid, dipped it into the icy water, and poured it over his wound as she returned to her whispering again. Malcolm's skin prickled against her hand where it cradled his elbow, but the numbing water was a welcome respite from the pain that had seared through him when she had poked and prodded at his arm. As she poured the water over his arm, again and again, he was captivated by the way it flowed down his skin, rippling over and around the angry wound, then running off his elbow and her hand and splashing back into the pool.

"Why did you not return to your home when you were injured?" she asked, breaking his reverie.

She released his arm, shook out the cup, and put it back where she carried it, then grabbed his tunic and used it to carefully dry the area around the injury.

She looked up at him and raised her eyebrows. It was only then that he realized he'd been so busy watching her graceful movements, he hadn't answered her question.

"I . . . I was too ill, and then winter set in." He sat back on his heels and reached for the tunic in her hand.

"Do not don that yet." She pulled a handful of dried moss out of her healer's bag. Deftly, she arranged the moss into a thick layer that would cover the length of the no-longer-oozing gash. She dipped it in the water, squeezed it out, and laid it over the site. "Hold it there a moment."

He did as she asked while she pulled a rolled-up strip of linen from the bag and used it to secure the moss in place.

"You must come to the castle with me," she said, rising and brushing sandy grit from her skirts. "You will need that arm seen to for a fortnight at least, maybe longer."

"The castle? What castle would that be?" He tried not to smile as she watched him don his tunic. He also tried not to wince when he raised the arm she had just tended to slide it into a sleeve. He refused to let pain keep him from doing anything— well, anything but training with his claymore. His will, it turned out, was stronger than his arm, or his hand. But if she could heal his wound, finally, then it would not take long before he was back in fighting form. As he tucked his tunic back into his plaid, she seemed to realize she'd been staring and she pushed past him, out of the sheltered area and back out into the sunshine.

"Dunlairig Castle," she said. "This is Ben Lairig." She raised her hands to indicate the mountain they stood upon. "The valley that runs from its foot, west toward the sea, is Glen Lairig. This is the home of Clan MacAlpin of Dunlairig."

"And you are?" he asked.

Her breath hitched as he stepped into the sunshine next to her.

"I am the one who will bring a warrior, trained to fight the English, to a clan who desperately needs one."

"Why would your clan be fighting the English? I have heard that King Robert clashes with them in the south of late."

She looked at him, her bottom lip caught between her teeth. "Suffice it to say, they have attacked us once, and we expect they will attack again. Will you lend your experience to us, and your sword, in exchange for my care for your wound?"

"You say 'twill take a fortnight to heal my arm?"

"Aye, maybe more."

He looked away and considered her request. Clearly he needed a healer's care since neither the old man who had tended him after the battle and sheltered him through the winter, nor he himself, could keep the thing from festering again and again. But he would not promise more than he could deliver.

"I will gladly share whatever I can from my experience fighting the English, in payment for your healing care, but I cannot offer you my sword." He held out his right hand and did his best to make a fist but his fingers would not obey his command. His hand closed only halfway, making it impossible to grasp the two-handed claymore.

She looked from his hand to his face and back, nodding a little.

"Then we shall have to work on your hand, too."

He laughed at her confidence. "Aye, that we shall."

"So we are in agreement?"

"There is one other thing," he said. "My duty is to return to the king's army as soon as I am able. When my arm is healed and I can once more wield my sword, I must take up that duty."

"So you will help us until your arm is healed and strong enough to fight and I will do everything I can to make it so as quickly as possible. Are we in agreement now?"

"Aye, we are. Shall we seal our agreement with a kiss?" He grinned and waggled his eyebrows at her, charming a smile out of his angel.

She shook her head as if he were a naughty lad, then headed down the same trail he had taken to the spring. He quickly looped his travel sack over his shoulder, grabbed his claymore with his good hand, and hurried to catch up with her.

After they had been walking quickly down the ben for a while, he began to wonder how far the lass had come from her family all alone. He looked down the trail, hoping to catch sight of this castle she was taking him to but the trees crowded close, their thick leaves and the underbrush of holly and juniper obscuring any view beyond the next curve.

"Tell me about Dunlairig Castle, lass." He caught up with her, walking by her side in spite of the narrow path. "How far away is it?"

"Not much farther."

"What is the best thing about it?" he asked, hoping for something more than a terse reply.

"It still stands," she said quickly. "Mostly."

He laughed, well acquainted with the never-ending maintenance required for castles of any size. The Highlands themselves seemed to lay siege to any structure men had the temerity to build.

As they reached the bend in the path where it curved around a huge lichen-dappled boulder, the sharp snap of a branch had him reaching for his companion, even though he could not grasp her arm as she had his earlier.

"Wheesht!" he whispered when she started to complain. "Stay here." He merely mouthed the words but she nodded once to show she understood. He handed her his claymore, as it was more of a hindrance than a help right now, then motioned for her to move into the thicker brush of the forest as he drew his dirk, a long thin dagger, crept up to the boulder, and peered around it.

Hellfire and damnation!

There, just stepping out of the wood to stand in the middle of the path, looking directly at him, was an English soldier, his sword drawn and a grin slashed across his face.

CHAPTER TWO

LONG HABIT HAD MALCOLM REACHING FOR HIS CLAYMORE, BUT the sharp pain of his wound speared up into his shoulder and stopped him just as he remembered that he had given his sword to the woman.

"Who are you, ye feckin' bastard?" The English soldier scowled at him and waved his scrawny weapon around as if he knew what to do with it. The soldier glanced all around. "Where'd the bitch get to?"

"I saw a lady, but no bitch," Malcolm said, correcting the man, earning himself another scowl. He dared not look behind him, but he hoped his angel had slipped off the path and into the wood. If she was smart, she would be on her way down the ben to her castle. At least there she might be safe if he could not best this man. His task now was simple: he needed to kill this soldier, as he'd killed so many before. He missed the weight of his claymore in his hands but he'd make do.

"'Tis a poor excuse for a sword, you have," Malcolm said. He grinned at the soldier as he slid his dirk back into its sheath, then flipped a branch up from the ground with his foot, deftly catching it in his left hand. It wasn't his claymore. It wasn't even the cheap sword the soldier had, but it was better than his dirk, if only because his reach with the branch was longer than the soldier's with his sword.

The soldier smiled broadly, showing a dark gap where his two front teeth should have been. "'Tis better than yours."

Gaptooth advanced up the path toward Malcolm, the light of victory already gleaming in his eyes.

Malcolm judged his position: The large boulder on his left would block the swing of the soldier's sword. He took half a step backward to give himself more coverage from the boulder, then held the branch as if he planned to swing it like a sword, though his right hand upon it was all show and no grip.

"You think you can best me?" Malcolm taunted the soldier. "Malcolm of MacKenzie, son of the greatest chieftain in the Highlands and favored warrior of King Robert of Scotland? I have killed a score of your lot single-handedly"—the irony of his words was not lost on him—"on a bad day, more on a good one." He knew his boasting would bring the man closer and raise his ire. An angry man was not a good fighter.

"Aye. I know it for a fact."

The man advanced slowly as if he toyed with his prey, his confidence lending him a smug air. Malcolm waited, holding his position, conserving his strength.

Another step, two steps, and the soldier was in Malcolm's range. He lunged for Malcolm, his sword work hindered by the boulder. Malcolm swiftly shifted the branch in his good hand and, using its greater length, shoved the broken end of it into the man's unguarded belly like a pike.

The soldier staggered back just as Malcolm's angel erupted from the wood behind the man, screeching like a banshee, Malcolm's claymore in her grip, but upside down so that she held the sheathed blade. The soldier swung around to face his new assailant and the woman swung the sword like a war hammer, hitting him solidly on the side of his head with the thick pommel. Gaptooth grunted and crumpled onto his side, his sword clattering to the ground at the same time.

"I am so sick of smug Englishmen thinking they can best a Highlander," she said.

Blood gathered on the soldier's temple before spilling down his face to puddle on the ground. Malcolm approached the woman slowly, not wanting to startle her into swinging the heavy pommel at *his* head.

"Is he dead?" she asked.

Malcolm tossed the soldier's sword out of the man's reach in case he wasn't, then turned him over and listened for his breath.

Malcolm smiled up at his boon companion. "Nay, lass, he is not, but I doubt he'll come around anytime soon."

Consternation clouded her face. "I meant to kill him."

"You did?" he said, surprised by her reaction. "Why did you not swing with the blade if you wished him dead?"

As if she just realized what she had said, her face went white and she shuddered. She shoved the claymore toward Malcolm and he took it from her, laying it next to Gaptooth's sword.

"Lass? Are you well?"

She shook her head slowly, side to side, staring at the unconscious man as she put more distance between herself and him. "I have never wished to kill anyone before."

"I can believe that. 'Tis not something healers are wont to do."

"Aye, 'tis not, unless they have been driven to it by dire circumstances." She looked at him then and the rosy glow of righteous anger, mixed with a sadness that weighed heavily in her eyes, replaced her pallor. She squared her shoulders as if remembering who and what she was. "Still, I would have him alive so he could be questioned."

"Better to have him dead." Malcolm rose to his feet and grabbed the man's much lighter sword, surprised at how heavy it felt, despite its inferior size and quality. He had lost more strength over the long winter than he had realized. It did not matter. It did not take control to drive a blade into an unconscious man's chest. "I doubt he will tell us anything, even if he were to awaken. Better to end him now." He placed the tip of the sword over the man's heart, just where it would slide between the ribs.

"Nay!" The woman leapt up and wrapped her hands around his that gripped the pommel, pulling him away from their captive. "Any information about the English's plans for us, even something small and seemingly inconsequential, might be the key to divining our best defense against them. We need to get him back to the castle."

She knelt beside Gaptooth and began going through the leather sacks that hung from his belt just as Malcolm heard something . . . voices.

"We must go, angel," he said very quietly. "Others approach."

"English?"

"I cannot say, but we will not wait to find out. Leave him." He handed her the soldier's sword, picked up his claymore, and urged her off the trail and into the deeper shadows of the wood.

"We should stay close and discover who else is trespassing on MacAlpin territory this day," she whispered to him when they were out of sight of the trail.

"Nay, we need to get to the safety of your castle as quickly as possible."

THE SHAKING SNUCK UP ON JEANETTE AS SHE AND MALCOLM made their way down the thickly wooded ben. First her hands began to tremble, and then it seemed her whole body was racked by trembling as if she shivered from a fever.

But 'twas no fever that took hold of her.

The fury that had gripped her when she had seen the English man standing there sneering at Malcolm, and calling her a foul name, had blinded her to anything but making the man shut his mouth. She had not so much as thought about what she was doing beyond choosing which way to hold the claymore. She had wanted to hurt the man, to take his life, just as the English had hurt her family.

Now, as the fury subsided, the danger of the situation, the folly of her actions, took hold of her thoughts. She gave thanks that she had only injured the man, not taken his life, though honestly she could not say if she would regret it if she had. Perhaps she was more like her impulsive sister than she believed. Nay, Jeanette was not a prisoner of her emotions, as Scotia was. Jeanette was the thoughtful sister, studying all sides of a thing before reacting to it.

But not this day. She had sought calm and instead she had helped a strange man because her instincts told her he was no danger to her. This day she had attacked an English soldier because she was angry at his king. This day she had acted from her grieving, angry heart, not from her head, and she did not understand why.

She did know she was lucky, that no harm had come to her or her companion from her rash actions . . . so far. It did not appear that they had been followed by whomever Malcolm had heard, but they still had to get back to the castle and warn her family that the English were back. At least one of them was.

But she could see that Malcolm was nearing the end of his strength, and it would take them longer to return home through the wood than by the trail. Though he was not admitting such to her, he had started to stumble over tree roots and let his arm hang, weighed down by the claymore, rather than holding it more closely to his body to keep it from damage or tangling in the wood. His right sleeve showed speckles of blood where her dressing should have protected his wound.

Jeanette knew a burn ran down the mountainside not far in front of them. If the man's pride, or stubbornness—she didn't know him well enough yet to judge which—kept him from admitting he needed to rest, she was not so encumbered.

"I AM THIRSTY," MALCOLM'S COMPANION SAID FROM BEHIND him, her voice still wisely quiet, but it held a tremor he had not heard before. He stopped to let her catch up with him. "There is a burn not far ahead. 'Twill not delay us long to quench our thirst," she said. She looked pointedly at his injured arm. "'Twould appear I need to re-dress your wound, as well."

"'Tis a good idea," he said. The idea of sitting for even a few minutes, and slaking a thirst he had not been aware of, sounded like a reprieve from the lethargy that was quickly overtaking him. "Why do you not lead the way?" He motioned for her to pass, giving him the opportunity to see if she was as fatigued as he.

She clearly wasn't fatigued as she strode by him. She was pale, though, even for her, and her hands trembled. He recognized the signs of the shock of battle settling over her. He had seen it many times with lads after their first battle was finished and the surge of battle lust subsided, leaving trembling limbs and queasy stomachs in its wake. She was a brave one, this lass whose name he had yet to learn. Strong, steady, and the look in her eye when she had felled the soldier was no less satisfied than any warrior's he had seen taking down a foe. Until she'd realized what she'd done.

It was clearly not in her nature to hurt anyone, yet she seemed to feel no remorse over felling the English soldier. There was much to this woman he did not understand and he found that remarkably intriguing.

Before long they came to the burn, which was still rushing with spring runoff between steep banks. His companion looked at him, then back at the burn and sighed.

"If we follow it down a little ways, it comes to a clearing where the banks are much more gentle," she said, and she headed almost straight down the ben now, following the burn so quickly it was as if she raced it.

Malcolm had to push himself even harder to keep up, losing sight of her in the thick foliage now and then, until he almost ran her over when she stopped suddenly.

"Angel, what is wrong?" he whispered near her ear.

She was standing statue still, her breath hitching as if she could not draw air into her lungs, still trembling like a leaf in a summer gale. A beautiful clearing opened up before them, the burn running strong on his left, but with a bank so gentle, he knew the clearing must flood at times. When he glanced at her again, her eyes were fixed upon a set of three large boulders to her right and her blue eyes were filled with a misery he did not understand. Was she suddenly taken with remorse over the soldier?

He touched her shoulder lightly, earning him a startled look as if she had forgotten he was there.

"What troubles you?" he asked.

She shook her head. "Nothing." She walked into the clearing, knelt beside the burn, then began to wash her hands, using the coarse sand she found along the edge of the water to scrub them clean. Malcolm looked at his own hands and discovered they were blood-splattered and dirty from their scuffle with the English soldier. He joined her at the burn, scrubbing as best he could with a hand that did not function well. Each movement pulled at his wound, making it ache even more. He clenched his teeth and finished washing, determined, as always, not to let the wound get the better of him.

When he was done, the woman pulled her cup out of the fold of her arisaid and filled it with the crisp clear water, and offered it to Malcolm without a word.

"I thank you," he said, letting his fingers brush hers as he lifted the cup from her hand, hoping, as his touch had done a moment ago, the contact would pull her out of whatever evil thoughts held her hostage. He drank deeply, then rinsed the cup out, refilled it, and handed it back to her. She took it and drank, but the haunted look in her eyes did not fade, though the trembling had mostly subsided.

Perhaps distracting her would help her break free.

"I still do not ken your name, angel, and after what we have done together this day, I feel it only fair that you share it with me."

She sighed and sat back on her heels. She gave him a formal head bow. "I am Jeanette MacAlpin, daughter of Kenneth."

"It is my great pleasure to make your acquaintance, Jeanette MacAlpin, daughter of Kenneth," he said formally, returning the head bow with an ill-concealed grimace and a small adjustment of his right shoulder.

"I need to tend your arm," Jeanette said.

He pulled off his tunic without a word and turned so his injured arm was close to her, the linen bandage fallen to his elbow and the moss now on the ground. He could not stop the sigh that escaped him when she laid her hands on either side of the wound, calming the ache with just her touch. He looked down at her and was pleased to find the haunted look now completely replaced by one of deep thought. At least some good had come of his damned wound.

"Have you had this fever before?" she asked, her voice once more that soft but firm tone he had heard when first she'd seen his arm.

"Aye, off and on for months, though it seems stronger now than it has been in some time."

She nodded and caught the side of her full bottom lip between her teeth. "Sometimes the fever works with the wellspring to burn out what cannot be washed away." She dipped another cupful of water for him. "Drink. You need to drink a lot when you have a fever lest it burn right through you."

He took the cup from her, but she deftly avoided his fingers this time. He drained it again, while she wet more of her moss and used it to gently wash the greenish mess speckled with pink droplets of blood that oozed from his wound. When it was clean, she bade him to stay where he sat by the burn. He was glad to comply. As she moved away from him, he couldn't help but admire the way the end of her pale braid just brushed the small of her back, drawing his attention to her gentle curves, and the graceful way she moved, as if she were in her element here in the forest. He'd thought her an angel but perhaps she was more of a wood sprite, or one of the fey, the fairy folk, lulling men into her underground world where everything was beautiful and no one ever died.

She leaned down to gather some newly greening moss from the forest floor and glanced back at him, catching him staring at her. Their eyes locked and he could not look away. Curiosity and concern showed in her crystalline eyes and then she gave him a shy smile as if to ask why he was staring at her. He dared not think what she saw in his eyes while his imagination had been heading in directions it should not. She was just a beautiful lass in the greenwood, and he an injured warrior with fever dreams catching him even while he was awake. He looked away, unsettled by the powerful pull this woman he'd only just met had upon his thoughts and his body. He needed to stay focused on healing his arm so that he could return to the king, and eventually so he could return home to take his place as the next chief. A beautiful woman would only be a distraction from his duty.

She startled him when she laid a large portion of the moss over the wound and bound it in place with the long strip of linen she had used before. She had him back in his tunic almost before he knew what she was up to. When she stepped back from him he immediately missed the feel of her hands, even though there had been nothing even slightly flirtatious in her touch.

"We should away," she said, and he was glad to notice that the trembling was completely gone and only a ghost of the haunted look was left in her eyes. She was truly a strong lass.

"Aye, you are surely missed by now." He awkwardly tucked

his tunic back into his belted plaid. "Does your family always let you roam the bens by yourself?"

The last wisps of sadness left her eyes, and were replaced now by a snap of temper. He grinned at her, which won him a scowl.

"Aye, they do. Until lately there has been no danger to us on our own land."

"And yet they let you wander by yourself now that things are indeed dangerous?" He could not stop himself from asking, any more than he could stop the spurt of anger at her kin for not protecting her better. It was a good thing he was with her when they'd met that soldier. He did not want to think what might have happened to her if she had been alone upon that path.

And then he remembered the screech she had let out as she felled the man. The woman . . . Jeanette . . . was stronger and more cunning than she looked. His anger was replaced by a warm feeling that had him smiling at her. He stood, a little more wobbly on his feet than he was comfortable with, but he held his good hand out to her. She looked at his hand, then placed hers in it, palm to palm. He closed his fingers around hers and gently pulled her up to her feet, holding on to her for just a moment longer than was necessary.

"Let's away, then," he said.

The lass had her lip caught between her teeth again and Malcolm had to stop himself from reaching out to touch her. He tried to fist both hands, and pain shot through his arm, reminding him forcefully of where his attention needed to be.

"Do you think it safe to take the trail again?" she asked, looking across the clearing at a small path. "It will take us far less time to reach the castle that way than it will by cutting through the forest."

He considered how far they had come from where they had met the soldier, but those other voices he had heard made him uneasy that the soldier Jeanette had felled was not the only one nearby. "Let us go to the trail, but we will listen and watch before we step out of our cover, and we must be ready to abandon it at the first hint of anyone else about."

She nodded and led him down the path, stopping just before they reached the main trail again. He edged out, looking up and down the trail and listening for long moments. Finally, he nodded and they silently set out on the trail.

Not long afterward, they came to a spot in the trail that opened up, revealing a long, narrow loch, a deeper blue than the late-spring sky, and, sitting before it, the battered remains of a ruined castle.

"That is not—," he said, stopping in his tracks.

Jeanette stopped beside him and, for a moment, stared into the distance, though whether she looked at the ruins or somewhere else, he couldn't tell. He took a moment to look more carefully at the place. One whole side of the curtain wall, nearest the loch, was gone, though he could not see the foot of it to tell if it was a rubble pile, or was removed completely. And on the left, inside the wall that still stood, were the burnt-out remains of a large building—probably the great hall. A single tower stood opposite the burnt building and it at least did not appear damaged, but closer examination might prove him wrong in that estimation. There was no way this castle could support anyone, let alone keep them safe.

"That cannot be your home," he said, keeping his voice low.

She turned her back to the devastation and faced him. Her eyes were filled with sadness, but her raised chin and stiff posture spoke loudly of anger, if not rage.

"Aye, it can be," she said, challenge now burning the sadness from her gaze, "and it is." She abruptly turned back to the castle and strode down the path.

He pushed himself to catch up with her. There were too many questions raging in his head.

"Who did this?" he asked.

"The wall?" She shrugged but did not slow down. "We do not ken why it fell. But the fire, that was set by an English spy. He killed my mum, too. Murdered her in front of me as she lay in her sickbed."

She looked back at him then, and he suddenly understood why a woman such as she, a healer dedicated to saving lives, would have attacked that English soldier so fearlessly. Vengeance was the strongest of motivators, even for a woman like Jeanette MacAlpin.

"I am surprised you did not slice that Sassenach bastard's head off today," he said, meaning every word.

"I would have, if I could have managed the sword better."

His gaze snapped to hers and he could feel a rage that matched hers, rolling off of him like storm-driven waves on the loch. Here was something he could give her, something he was well schooled in after more than a year in the king's army. Once his arm was fully healed, he could give her vengeance against her enemies.

"Next time, I shall do it for you," he vowed.

CHAPTER THREE

As they drew closer to the castle, the nearest part of the curtain wall obscured the devastation Malcolm had seen from higher up on the ben. If not for the strong odor of burnt wood, far stronger than those caused by the usual fires kindled within a castle, he might doubt what he had seen. They veered around the castle to the west and still all looked well, until they neared the gate.

An old, grizzled guard yelled over his shoulder, back into the castle, "She is here!" Then he strode toward them, his eyes narrowed and his hand upon his dirk, Malcolm clearly the target of his gaze. "Who is this, mistress?" he demanded.

"I am Malcolm, son of John, chieftain of the MacKenzies of Blackmuir."

The guard glared at him. "What business have you with us?"

"He is injured, Denis," Jeanette said. "He is in need of my help. Let us pass."

"How do you ken he is not an enemy to us? He could be another English spy."

Jeanette looked over her shoulder and gave him the slightest shake of her head as if to say he should not react to such a question, but Malcolm would not let his honor be smeared with such an implication.

"I am a Highlander, a Scot. My home is west of Inverness and my clan is sworn to fight for King Robert. I fought with the king at Methven and Dalrigh and I shall fight with him again as soon as this kind lass mends my arm. I am no bedamned English spy!"

"I believe him," Jeanette said to the guard, whose dirk was half-drawn now. She turned and glared at Malcolm. "You are not making this easy, Malcolm MacKenzie."

"Aye, you are not," the guard added.

"Denis," she said to the old man, "there *are* English soldiers on the ben. At least one, maybe more. We did not linger to find out. I need to speak to the chief and I do not think it wise for any of us to stand about in the open like this."

Denis looked from Malcolm to Jeanette and back several times, not budging from his spot between them and the gate.

"Denis?" Jeanette prodded. "'Tis of great import I speak to Nicholas immediately." Malcolm could hear the strain threading through her words, though clearly she tried to hide it.

"Did you not understand her, man?" Malcolm said.

The old guard grumbled but turned and led them to the gate, then through the short passage. Just as they stepped into the bright bailey, a tall auburn-haired woman strode toward them.

"Oh, thank the heavens," the woman said, "you are returned."

"Aye, I am returned. Did you think I would not?" Jeanette asked.

Malcolm noted the tension that sprang to life between these two as they spoke. He had the urge to touch Jeanette again, as he had when they had entered the clearing by the burn. That time she had visibly relaxed. Would it happen again?

He reached forward and laid his hand upon her shoulder, but this time she shrugged it off and stepped quickly away.

"We were worried," the woman said, stopping just in front of Jeanette.

"I needed some air, Rowan," Jeanette said.

"Aye, is that not what I told you?" the guard said to Rowan.

"'Tis," Rowan said, "but still, you were gone too long and though I made the men leave you be, I was worried."

As if seeing Malcolm for the first time, she met his gaze. Jeanette quickly made the introductions to her cousin, this time stressing his experience in the king's army.

"He is in need of a healer. We can offer him shelter, such as it is, while I care for him, can we not? And in exchange, he can give what assistance he can as we prepare to fight the English again."

Rowan did not respond right away, nor did she give her thoughts away. After a long moment she nodded. "Denis, you shall wait with them while I find Nicholas."

As they waited, Malcolm got a better look at the damages he had glimpsed from the trail. The length of curtain wall on his left was nothing but rubble, offering up a spectacular view of the loch and the distant mountains but leaving the castle vulnerable to any attack that might be launched against it. Men toiled there, clearing the rubble away. To his right he could now clearly see the source of the smoke stench.

The blackened and broken remains of a large building lay like a corpse rotting in the sun. The women and weans working to clear the remains were like insects cleaning the body. Scorch marks on the curtain wall surrounding the blackened heap gave testimony to the intensity of the fire.

Questions spun through him, but he set them aside for the moment, too intent on assessing the strategic impact of such destruction.

He glanced now at the outbuildings scattered along the edges of the bailey. All of them showed evidence of fire damage, too, though most suffered only blackened patches to their thatched roofs. The single stone tower he had seen from the trail stood across the way, the only defensible structure from the looks of the place, and it was not large. The devastation to this small castle hit him like a punch to the gut, as his mind spiraled through all the dangers such wreckage presented.

The only good thing he could see was that the English had left the castle in such ruins that there was no way they would want more from this place or these people, though he did wonder what the clan had done to merit such destruction. And then he remembered the English soldier skulking about in the wood not far from this very spot and his questions multiplied.

"There is no hospitality to offer," the guard said just loud enough for Malcolm to hear. "You will have to earn your way if you intend to bide here."

Malcolm nodded absently, for his mind was still busy solving the problem of how to defend such a broken castle. No matter how many ways he looked at the problem, there was only one conclusion he could reach: the castle could not be defended.

A rumble of men's voices rose from the crowd working on the rubble heap and Malcolm saw several men separate from the workers and head toward him, Rowan leading, hand in hand with one of them.

He turned his attention back to Jeanette, who stood a few feet away from him, watching the approaching group. Her shoulders were lifted just enough to betray the tension she must have felt and that made him wonder exactly what her place was in this clan. Her cousin Rowan was clearly the chatelaine, but that said little about Jeanette's position.

Three men arrived with Rowan, and Malcolm only noticed another woman when she stepped out from behind the youngest of the men. She was shorter than the willowy Rowan, with dark hair and eyes snapping with distrust.

"I am Nicholas, chief of the MacAlpins of Dunlairig," the dark-haired man who had been holding Rowan's hand said, that same hand now resting on his dirk.

Before he could continue, Jeanette spoke. "We encountered an English soldier on the trail to the wellspring, just at the big boulder. I do not think he is dead and we are not certain if there are more, but Malcolm heard voices and it seems unlikely one would be here alone."

To his credit, the chief did not question any part of Jeanette's statement. "Duncan, take a few men with you and see if you can pick up their tracks." The youngest of the two men standing just behind the chief nodded, then headed for the rubble pile again, shouting names as he went.

"You said you do not think he was dead?" Nicholas asked Jeanette. "Did you find him that way, or were you responsible for his injuries?"

"*We* are responsible for his injuries," she said. "Malcolm engaged him and I hit him on the head."

"She knocked him out cold," Malcolm said. "You should have seen her."

"You should have killed him," the dark-haired woman said, her words like a snake's hiss. "If he is English, he deserved to die."

"She could not kill him, Scotia," Rowan said to the lass. "Jeanette could never do that."

"I could," Scotia said.

"I doubt it not," the chief said, shaking his head. "Perhaps one day soon you'll have no choice but to prove you are so bloodthirsty." He turned his attention back to Malcolm. "My wife says you are a warrior in King Robert's army."

"I was until I was injured." He shrugged his right shoulder to indicate where. "I will be again when Mistress Jeanette has healed me."

"As you can see," Nicholas said, raising his hands to indicate their ruined surroundings, "there is little we can offer you for hospitality, but you are welcome to stay here and partake of what little we have in exchange for any information or insight you can give us about the English and their tactics."

"I thank you," Malcolm said formally, though he thought it odd that a chief would not be well versed in such things. "I will

35

share what I can, though why they would return here when they have already done so much damage, I cannot fathom."

There was a look that ran through all the people gathered around him but he could not tell what it meant.

"Suffice it to say that we are certain they intend to return and soon, given your meeting with one of their soldiers this day so close to the castle. Defending the clan is paramount."

Malcolm felt his eyebrows rise. "Defend?" Was the man daft? Was the entire clan daft? "If what you believe is true, and the English are returning here soon, there is no defending this place."

"If we were to defend this castle," Nicholas said, "I would ask your opinion of how that might be done."

"There is no defending. The curtain wall will trap you in an attack by anyone coming over the broken part of the wall. You have only the tower to retreat to, and it does not look big enough to keep many safe within." He shook his head. "There is only one thing you can do if you wish your clan to survive another English attack." He paused, knowing what he was about to say would not sit well with these proud Highlanders.

"If you stay here, you will all be caught like birds in a cage, easy prey for your hunters. I can see no other outcome. You must abandon this castle."

EVEN THOUGH THEY HAD BEEN PREPARING FOR THE NEED TO abandon their home for almost a fortnight, Jeanette knew she was not the only one who had been holding out hope that their efforts would not be necessary. But the English were back and the MacAlpins could not defend the castle without the curtain wall being repaired unless Rowan could call upon her gift to raise a barrier, as Jeanette's mum, the previous Guardian, had done. Yet Rowan could not perform the simplest of blessings, as she'd demonstrated just this morn. She could not protect the entire castle.

"Denis, keep our guest company," Nicholas said as he turned and headed for the tower, Rowan by his side and the older man in their wake. "Have Duncan join us when he can," he said over his shoulder.

Malcolm started to argue but Jeanette pressed her hand to his arm.

"You are not wrong. It is just that we have been hoping it would not come to this," she said to him.

"I thought you wished my assistance."

"And you have given it."

"Jeanette, Scotia!" Rowan called over her shoulder. "You, too!"

Scotia's eyes went wide, then narrowed with suspicion.

"Why now?" she asked her sister.

Jeanette had no idea, but she would take advantage of the opportunity to press Rowan to take up her training again. Her cousin could not refuse in front of others, especially under these dire circumstances. She would not.

"I suspect we shall find that out anon, sister. Denis," she said, turning her attention quickly to their guest's comfort, "see that Malcolm gets something to eat and have Mary make up a sorrel tea for him." She looked at Malcolm. "'Twon't be much to eat, I'm afraid, but the tea will cool your fever."

"No need, lass," Malcolm replied. "I shall partake of my own rations until they are gone, and the fever will pass on its own, as it always does."

"We are not so bad off that we cannot feed a guest and offer him a simple tea." She cast a determined look at Denis. "I shall come find you when we are finished. I want to check your wound again," she said to Malcolm, though she knew it was only an excuse to seek him out.

Jeanette and Scotia hurried after the others and when they were all standing in the confines of the chief's small chamber, one floor up in the tower, silence settled over the five of them.

Nicholas sat in the only chair. He glanced at Uilliam, the black-haired, heavily bearded bear of a man who stood at the back of the room near the door. Nicholas said, "It would seem we can no longer stay in Dunlairig Castle."

Uilliam's voice rumbled over them: "Unless Rowan can raise a defense."

Jeanette nodded at his assertion.

Rowan bristled, but Nicholas nodded. "She cannot *yet*, and we dare not allow ourselves to be—how did Malcolm put it?—'caught like birds in a cage'? The time has come to evacuate the clan."

He looked at each of the women, Rowan, Jeanette, and Scotia. "The caves are ready?"

"Ready enough," Rowan said. "Peigi and her sisters returned from the Glen of Caves two days ago and reported that the necessities are in place, though it will not be a comfortable home and more work will be required once we arrive."

The Glen of Caves was hidden away in a deep fold of the mountains, far enough from Glen Lairig to be safe, but close enough to get there in a few hours' time on foot.

"Uilliam, you have sites chosen for the warriors to camp?"

"Aye. With only a score of us, and some of those needing to keep watch over the women and weans at the caves, it will be easy to move the camp as needed. And we shall be plenty close to keep watch in the glen for the English. Once we know how many, and where they are, we can plan our attack."

"Duncan told me just this morning," Nicholas said, "that almost all the livestock have been moved up into the mountains. We shall have to leave behind those that have not been moved yet, for now at least."

"Good," Uilliam said. "Shall I start sending word up and

down the glen, carefully of course, for everyone to leave their homes tonight?"

"Aye, and we will begin sending out small groups from the castle as soon as 'tis dark," Nicholas added. "With luck we shall all be away before dawn and before any English soldiers are the wiser."

"Is there any word from my da?" Jeanette asked. Her father, the previous chief, had been sent to ask for help from their allies.

"Nay," Uilliam said, moving from his spot by the door to her side. He frowned down at her, which might have scared some people, but he was like an uncle to her, her father's best friend, and champion when her father had been chief. "But he would want to know why you left the castle this morn when you knew 'twas dangerous. I could have expected as much from Scotia"—a gasp burst from her sister—"but not from you. Your da would have my hide if anything happened to you while he was away."

Jeanette looked at Rowan, the row between them this morning still humming in the air. "Rowan and I had been working and I needed to get some air. We had no reason to believe there were any English vermin lurking so near." 'Twas the truth.

"And where did you come to meet this Malcolm Mackenzie?" Nicholas took over the questions.

"I found Malcolm at the wellspring trying to heal a wound on his arm."

The room filled with voices but Rowan, bless her, quieted them with a glare.

"Go on," she said.

"I bathed his arm at the wellspring—"

Uilliam started to object but Rowan once more silenced him with a look.

"I am a healer. 'Twas nothing more than that. When that was done, we had started down the ben to return to the castle when Malcolm heard something. He handed me his claymore—he cannot wield it until his arm is better—and I went to hide in the trees. An English soldier stood in the trail. Malcolm started to fight him off with a branch, but 'twas clear he could not keep that up for long, so I came up behind the soldier—" More spluttering from Uilliam. Another glare from Rowan. "—I came up behind him and swung the sword handle at his head. I hit him so hard, he collapsed to the ground and moved no more."

Scotia gave a raucous whoop but quickly quieted, folding her hands in front of her as if she were a demure young lass, but the feral look in her eye told the truth of her feelings.

"The rest I have told you. We returned to the castle as quickly as possible. And we dare not linger here any longer unless Rowan will let me teach her how to raise a barrier," Jeanette said, looking her cousin square in the face now.

A heavy silence fell over the gathering.

"You ken well that I cannot do that yet," Rowan said, her voice low and tight.

Nicholas reached out and touched Rowan's elbow for just a moment. "You will, love, soon."

"Or not," Rowan said, her glare now targeted at Jeanette. "So far I can only reliably call upon my gift defensively."

"Which is why, for now, we must move everyone to a safer place. I want Rowan and the Targe stone with the warriors. She is"—he made a point of looking at Jeanette—"our best weapon. Jeanette, you and Scotia will go with the rest of the women and the weans to the caves."

Scotia started to complain but stopped when Uilliam cleared his throat and put his large hand on her shoulder.

"So I am not to continue her training," Jeanette said, not bothering to make it a question.

"Not for now," Nicholas said, but he looked at his wife. "Not for now."

"And what of Malcolm MacKenzie?" Jeanette asked. "If he goes with the warriors, I will not be able to take care of his wound. I gave him my word I would see to its healing."

Nicholas pondered her question, then pushed out of his chair with a sigh. "I will go and speak with him, and then I shall decide if he will be of better use to us as one of the warriors, or as one of the men assigned to the caves."

It was not the answer Jeanette wanted. Regardless of his decision about Malcolm, she would not be allowed to train Rowan.

MALCOLM SAT IN THE BAILEY ON A LARGE STONE THAT HAD clearly once been part of the demolished side of the curtain wall. He'd eaten, had the tea Jeanette had made up for him, then sat, keeping his eyes on the door at the foot of the tower, waiting to see what would happen next. He had not expected the chief to closet himself away when action was called for. It certainly wasn't what Malcolm would have done.

The tower door opened and Nicholas stepped out into the noonday sun. As soon as he spied Malcolm, he strode across the bailey to him.

"Come with me," he said, and made his way to the stair that led up to the wall walk.

"Is the wall stable?" Malcolm asked.

Nicholas shrugged. "It was all stable, right up to the moment when it was not," he said over his shoulder.

When they reached the top, Nicholas stopped and stared over the bailey, toward the loch and the mountains beyond. Malcolm let his eyes roam over the terrain that was easier to see from here. There was a steep drop-off between the castle and the loch and it looked as if much of the fallen wall had tumbled down that way. The forest was kept well back from the rest of the wall. He saw several men stationed around the wall walk, their eyes trained outward, and he saw plenty of industry inside the wall, where some people were still clearing rubble and others were working hard to set up a palisade wall of small tree trunks to close the space where the wall had once stood. It was clear they would not get the work done soon enough to protect them if the English came here in any numbers.

"What would you do?" Nicholas asked suddenly.

Malcolm was surprised by the question. "Me? I would remove everyone from the castle and find a safer place for them until I knew more about my enemies, their numbers, their position, their likely plan of attack."

Nicholas nodded. "And the wall? What would you do about that?"

"Exactly what you are doing now. Clear it, put up the quickest defense I could until a proper wall could be rebuilt."

Nicholas was quiet for a while. "You fought with King Robert's army." It was not a question.

"Aye."

"Battles against the English forces?"

"Aye, though at Dalrigh we were caught between the English, who were dogging our heels after Methven, and those traitorous MacDougalls who fight with the English."

"And that is where you were injured?"

"It is. I fell there and was left for dead. I am told, by the crofter who found me, that it looked as if I had managed to crawl off the field and into a thicket of bushes. He cared for me until I was strong enough to leave, which was not long past now. I owe my life to the man." He flexed his arm and tried to fist his hand, despite the hot pain that shot from fingers to shoulder. "It is my hope Jeanette can finish what he started and make my arm strong and whole again."

"If it is possible, Jeanette has the skill for it. What service can you provide in exchange for her skill and our shelter, such as it is?"

"I . . ." He realized it was a question to which he did not honestly know the answer. "I have experience fighting the English and have seen their tactics in battle, though this is not a place those tactics are likely to be used. They prefer to fight on open land, not forest-covered bens. I can train the warriors." He tried to clench his fist again and shook his head. "Nay, I cannot do that, at least not now." He held up his right hand for Nicholas to see. "Perhaps I could train the lads with their dirks? And I can certainly act as lookout, or scout if you have need."

Nicholas was nodding his head. He looked sideways at Malcolm and he appeared to be making a decision. "I appreciate your honesty and I will take the services you offer in exchange for Jeanette's healing care."

"It would do no good to lie about my abilities, good or bad. In battle it would be evident I had lied."

Nicholas laughed quietly. "Aye. I am not used to honest men, though, so it always comes as a surprise to me."

Malcolm could feel his brows lower and his forehead furl. "Why are you not used to honest men? Surely a chief must trust the men who fight for him."

"So I am learning."

Malcolm waited for a better explanation. Nicholas folded his arms over his chest and leaned back against the wall but still he was silent.

"If you are to help us protect the clan from the English," he finally said, "you should know that my father was English. My mother was Scottish. I had to leave my home with my mother's clan when I was ten and two. I made my way to my sire's lands in the borders, and rather painfully discovered myself unwelcome there. Eventually I found my way to London. I have a great talent for mimicry and gathering information, and I eventually came to the attention of one of King Edward's courtiers who employed me in the king's household as his spy, and from there I came to be among the king's spies. I was sent to Scotland to find a relic he desires to obtain, a relic I discovered was in the care of the MacAlpins, so I made my way here and it was not long before I remembered what it meant to be a Highlander and how much I missed this land. It was also not long before I fell in love with Rowan. I forswore my fealty to King Edward, married Rowan, and, according to the customs of this clan, became the chief when we wed."

He looked at Malcolm as if he expected some sort of reaction but Malcolm was too busy taking in what the man had said.

"You never fought in battle for Edward Longshanks?" Malcolm asked.

"Nay, before he attacked a place, I was often sent in to gather information about how many armed men were gathering there, or whether the sentiment of the people was to fight or make peace, but I was always pulled out before the fighting began and I was sent ahead, often as a refugee from the war. I learned to protect myself on the streets of London when I first arrived there, and killed a few men in service to the king, but the little training I received in warfare I learned here in the Highlands, when I was a wean." He looked away. "I have been training with a sword, but it does not come naturally to me. I am far more comfortable and adept with a dirk."

"That explains much," Malcolm said. "And the relic? Did you find it?"

"Aye. I cannot be sure if King Edward knows that or not, but he knows where I am and he's sure to know by now that I have left his employ. I know his temper well, and he will not take such a traitorous act lightly, which is why I was sure English soldiers would turn up here sooner or later."

"If they are after you, then why do you not just leave the clan and draw the English away?"

"I have considered that, but circumstances dictated that I stay and we fight the English together as a clan."

For a man who revealed so much of his past to Malcolm, Nicholas talked his way around things he did not wish to speak of with all the slipperiness of the spy he had been.

"Why do you tell me all of this?" Malcolm asked.

"Because you were honest with me about your weakness and I thought it only right that you know what everyone else does about my weakness before you decide if you are really willing to join our cause."

Malcolm found he liked Nicholas, in spite of Nicholas's time spent in service to King Edward. The man was forthright, yet cautious. He was willing to fight for a clan that had not even been his for long. And though Malcolm knew anyone trained as a spy was adept at gaining the trust of people, he did not get a sense that Nicholas was being anything but himself.

"I will join your cause in whatever way I can serve, but only until my arm is healed enough to return to King Robert's army. My first duty is there."

Nicholas pushed off the wall and faced him, a smile on his face. "Good. We are all leaving the castle tonight. The women and weans are heading into the bens with a few of our younger warriors. You will go with them so Jeanette can continue to tend your arm. Train the lads as best you can and help to keep watch over everyone."

"I thought you would want my advice on strategy and tactics," Malcolm said, both glad Jeanette could fulfill her promise to him, and irritated that he was being sent away from where any fighting would be.

"When the time comes, I will. For now we do not even know how many English have made their way to Glen Lairig, nor if more are on their way. For now we need trackers and scouts to discover what they can, and you need to get your arm back to fighting strength, then the time will come for making plans."

CHAPTER FOUR

JEANETTE PUT THE LAST PLAID BOUND FOR THE CAVES IN A large basket fitted with straps, so it could be carried on a back, and rolled her aching shoulders. All around her the bailey was filled with women packing baskets. A few men were readying anything that could be used as a weapon. Weans, lads, and lasses carried the full baskets into the bolt-hole, a hidden tunnel that ran from beneath the tower out into the forest, where its exit was well concealed. They were staging the supplies in the tunnel and each person would take what he or she could carry as they left their home behind them. Whatever they couldn't shift to the caves tonight could be fetched when possible, without their ever being seen entering or leaving Dunlairig Castle. She arched her back, trying to loosen the kinks that had taken hold there. She gazed up at the sky and realized it was later than she'd thought. It would not be much longer before the sun set, an hour at most. As soon as full dark descended, they would begin to leave the castle and the glen.

She closed her eyes and pushed away the new layer of grief that threatened to take hold. They would all be leaving their homes this night, whether they lived in the castle or in cottages up and down the glen. It was not right that the very thing that should be protecting the MacAlpin clan from the English was the reason all these troubles were descending upon them. She was still disappointed that Rowan would not let Jeanette continue training her, but she could not stay mad at her cousin. Jeanette knew that Rowan would do anything within her power to protect her family; it was only that she did not know how to manage her very real power yet.

But she would. Jeanette was sure of it. The obstacle was how?

There were the chronicles of the Guardians, scrolls written by many of the Guardians that had come before. They might offer a clue.

Jeanette looked up at the top of the tower, at the window that opened onto the chamber where her mother had died. She would have to enter that room to collect the chronicles before she left here this night, but not yet. She could not face that room just yet.

Malcolm's deep laugh pulled her attention across the bailey where he'd been working with the men for hours. He had not stopped since he descended the stair from the curtain wall with Nicholas, though she knew he must be tired and his arm must pain him. To look at him, though, one would never know he was injured at all.

She watched as he lifted a small ax with his left hand. He nodded, as if in answer to a question, then took a fighting stance and, with a loud shout that startled the young lads watching him, he moved as if dancing, if the dance was meant to be in battle, lunging at an invisible foe, slicing with the ax, whirling away again. She couldn't take her eyes off him as he lunged and swung and whirled again and again. His strength was clear, and she couldn't help but wonder how much stronger he would be once his arm was well. The thought of his arms, strong and whole, also made her wonder what it would be like to be held by him. Would he be as gentle as he was strong?

"It is hard not to watch such a braw man, is it not, lassie?"

Heat rushed through Jeanette as she turned to find Peigi, one of the oldest women in the clan. Remarkably, she was still strong, if a bit more bent, and slower, than she used to be. It was Peigi and her two sisters who had been setting up the caves and they would leave tonight with the first group from the castle.

"Aye," Jeanette said.

"Who is he?" the auld woman asked as they watched him hand the ax to a small towheaded lad that Jeanette knew to be the imp, wee Ian, showing him how to set his feet and grip the weapon. "He must be someone special to draw your attention away from the task at hand." Her familiar cackling laugh was hard to resist.

"Malcolm MacKenzie." She watched as he talked Ian through a few moves with the ax. Ian's carefree, childish laugh floated on the air and she realized even the weans had not been spared from the clan's troubles of late. She had not heard such a happy sound in far too long. "His arm is injured and I agreed to tend it until 'tis well. He will be coming with us to the caves."

Peigi grinned and danced her version of a jig, though she stopped as quickly as she began. "These old bones do not move as easily as they used to," she said with a momentary frown. "'Twill be nice to have someone new about to admire."

Jeanette laughed quietly and hugged the auld woman, pleased at the reprieve from her unhappy thoughts.

"Now he's watching you, lassie," Peigi said, waggling her eyebrows. "Och, this might be just the distraction we need!"

"Do not get the man in trouble, Peigi," Jeanette said, shoving one more plaid into the overstuffed basket before a lad took it away to the tunnel.

"Oh, 'tis not I who will trouble the man, I think." The auld woman actually waved at Malcolm. He grinned back and returned the wave just as Peigi's sisters came through the gate, a line of weans trailing behind them, carrying cookpots and baskets.

"Ah," Peigi said, "the evening repast has arrived." She clapped her hands together so hard that Jeanette was afraid she would crack every bone in them, but Peigi was as tough as any other Highlander, as she was so fond of saying. "Move all the baskets near the tower!" she shouted. "You"—she pointed at a group of lasses chattering together—"get the tables set up!"

A MUSICAL LAUGH DREW MALCOLM'S EYES TO THE WOMAN HE had been watching all afternoon. Jeanette stood next to a stooped, auld auntie, smiling down at her. Even from across the bailey he could see a glint of mischief in the old woman's eyes as she waved a gnarled hand at him. He grinned at her and returned her wave, certain that she was responsible for Jeanette's pink cheeks and that brief lovely laughter.

The next thing he knew, there was a parade of auld women and weans carrying dinner into the bailey and a flurry of activity to clear the remaining baskets away to the foot of the tower. Two long tables went up quickly—simple planks on top of anything that would serve to hold them up—and the pots and baskets of food were spread along them. There was a scramble for seating so Malcolm grabbed a bench near him and crossed the bailey.

"I've a seat for you, Jeanette," he said as he drew near, indicating the bench he easily carried despite his injury. "But you shall have to share it with me." He heard that same cackling laugh he'd heard earlier and looked behind him to find the old woman.

"Och, looks like Jeanette has found herself a braw warrior at last."

Malcolm got a glimpse of Jeanette's flaming cheeks and couldn't help but be amused, even if it was at Jeanette's expense.

"Peigi, he is a friend, 'tis all."

Peigi patted her on the cheek as if she were a wee bairn.

"'Tis the best way to start," she said, winking at Malcolm.

Charmed, Malcolm grinned back at the old woman. "Malcolm MacKenzie, mistress," he said, giving her a brief nod of his head in greeting.

Peigi stepped forward and ran her hand down his upper arm. Malcolm tried to hide a wince as she ran her hand over his injury, but the canny woman noticed.

"She is healing this, aye?" she said, nodding toward his arm.

"Aye, she is."

"Good. She shall need a strong man, that one."

Jeanette rolled her eyes and shook her head.

"Do not mock me, child," Peigi said without even looking at Jeanette. "You are a strong lass, and that needs a strong lad if you are to have any respect for each other. You are a strong lad, are you not, Malcolm MacKenzie?"

"I will be, as soon as this arm is healed," he said.

Peigi stared into his eyes so long, he became uncomfortable, but he could not seem to look away from the woman.

"I think you are stronger than you ken, even now, laddy," she said, bobbing her head as if she was pleased with what she saw. Without another word, she left them, calling orders as she went for everyone to begin the meal.

Malcolm made sure to guide Jeanette to a spot where the bench would fit at the end of one table, then he slid in beside her, sitting close enough that their hips touched.

"You need not sit quite so close, you ken?" Jeanette said to him, but she did not move away.

"Aye, normally that would be true, but seats are scarce and we must make room for as many as possible to enjoy this hot meal."

"Um hm," she said, ladling a savory stew that made his stomach growl into the wooden bowl that had appeared before them. "It looks like we shall have to share this bowl, as well as the bench," she said, a small smile lifting the corners of her mouth.

"I suppose we shall," Malcolm said, smiling back at her, pleased at her gentle teasing. He passed along a basket filled with horn spoons, and another with still-warm bannocks. Soon the crowd grew quiet, with only the occasional murmur of appreciative words and sounds for the meal.

After the stew had been passed around a second time and the bannocks were gone, Rowan stood up from her place near the head of the other table, her auburn hair glinting like copper in the light of the setting sun.

"I speak for all when I say this meal is a great gift to us. Our thanks to Peigi, Aileas, and Teasag"—she nodded at the three old ladies—"and their army of helpers"—she nodded at the weans who had settled on a plaid spread on the ground for their meal—"for bringing it to us."

Fists banged on the tables in agreement, joining voices shouting the names of their benefactors.

Peigi rose from where she sat at the far end of the table from Rowan along with the other two and raised her hand for silence. Eventually she succeeded in gaining enough quiet to be heard.

"Each does what he or she can. This was our gift to the clan this day in the hopes of sending everyone off with a full belly this night. Safe journey to us all!" She raised her small wooden cup in a toast, then drained it like she was a warrior.

Cheers went up and Peigi blinked her eyes, her cheeks suddenly pink. Malcolm leaned in to Jeanette and whispered into her ear. "That one must have gotten into lots of trouble when she was a lass."

Jeanette leaned into his shoulder, ever so slightly, and he took that as a good sign.

"Aye. The stories of those three are legend in the clan." Her voice was wistful.

"And you thought to be a legend in the clan, too?"

She chuckled. "I suppose, but not in the same way." The humor drained from her face, leaving her once more deeply thoughtful. "I thought I would be the next . . ."—she leaned away from him then and looked across the tables at her cousin Rowan—". . . wife of the chief."

He was certain she had been about to say something different but whatever it was, she kept it to herself. An unexpected stab of jealousy curled in his belly as he realized that would mean she, not Rowan, would have been Nicholas's wife. Did the lass love him? He glanced at Jeanette but did not see a lovelorn lass there. Indeed, if anything, she looked sad, the lovely smile he had seen earlier now replaced by lowered brows and a tightness about her pale blue eyes.

"So Peigi was notorious in her younger days?" he asked, hoping to pull her back out of her dark thoughts. He might not be able to lift whatever burden she carried, but he could help her relax and forget her troubles for an hour or two.

Jeanette glanced over to where the three old women were holding court, clearly telling stories on each other in view of the laughter coming from those gathered around them and the mock indignation of one of them.

"The three of them, sisters, you ken, were notorious for being great beauties, drawing men from far and wide to woo them. They've each been married more than once." She leaned close again and whispered, her breath heating more than his ear. "'Tis said they wore their husbands out—and not from nagging." Now she raised her delicately arched pale brows at him and he could not help but smile back, pleased at her pink cheeks and playful comment.

"Now that is a legend worth striving for," he said, glad to see a twinkle of mirth in her eyes.

Three boys approached, two of them hanging back behind their leader, wee Ian, all of five winters old.

"Malcolm," Ian said, reaching up and pulling on Malcolm's right arm, his small hands gripping just above the elbow, "will you show us how to fight with the ax some more?"

Malcolm couldn't stop the wince that came even with the lad's easy grip. He'd worked hard this day, even as his arm ached and burned.

"Not now, Ian," Jeanette said before Malcolm could respond.

"We've still a lot of work to do before we can leave the castle tonight, but Malcolm will come to the caves with us."

"Aye, and I'll need strong lads like you and your friends to help me keep watch over the women and bairns," Malcolm said, looking Ian in the eye. "You lads will have to be trained. Do you think you can do that?"

All three little boys nodded at him, their heads bobbing with enthusiasm.

"Go find your mums now," Jeanette said. "You'll be leaving with them, soon. We'll see you at the caves on the morrow."

Jeanette and Malcolm watched the lads scamper away.

"That was very nice of you," she said. "You have managed to turn leaving their homes into an adventure and a challenge."

"I only wish I could do the same for you," he said, looking over at her.

She looked around at the people gathered in the bailey. Some of the women were already up and clearing the table. Lasses were at basins of hot water, washing out the bowls and pots, while others dried them and one of Peigi's sisters directed the packing of the dinnerware that they were to take with them.

"I have only ever lived here, in this castle," Jeanette said quietly. "I find it hard to imagine that I will not wake up here in the morn, that I may never wake up here again."

Malcolm leaned his shoulder against hers. "Do not give up, angel. The battle is not yet joined and from the looks of this clan, you all are determined to return to this glen and this castle. In my experience, those defending their homes are much more dangerous in a battle than those hired to fight."

He looked about at the people of Dunlairig, most of whom he hadn't properly met yet, and saw a spirit and strength that spoke of a pride and love for their home, but he also saw only a few warriors and wondered if they would be enough to protect this clan, and not just this night as they left the castle behind them.

He wondered if he would make any difference in their battle.

As soon as it was full dark the first group left the castle through the bolt-hole. Several warriors went with them to keep them safe as they traveled, just in case there were English soldiers about. It would take each group several hours to get to the caves, for they would be walking in the dark over sometimes difficult terrain. Peigi and her sisters went with the first group so they could help organize everyone as they arrived. Jeanette would go with the last group. Forced to sit quietly lest the castle was being watched, she found herself envying those who had already left, not because they were the first to go, but because they did not have to wait for the inevitable with only the melancholy thoughts of all she had lost and all she was leaving behind to occupy her.

Malcolm sat nearby, flexing his hand and fisting it as best he could, but even in the dark she could see it pained him.

There was something she could do besides just sit and wait through most of the long night. She pushed up from where she sat on the cold ground and crossed over to him.

"Come with me," Jeanette said. "I need to tend your arm while the torches still burn enough to see by."

She led him to where a torch was set into a sconce on the curtain wall near the tower. "Roll up your sleeve," she said, sorry that she would not get to see all that tawny skin the man had.

When he did, she unwound the binding and handed it to him, and gently pulled away the moss padding to reveal what was still an angry gash on his arm, but was already better than it had been this morning. The red streaks that had begun to reach out from it were gone. She laid the back of her hand next to it, feeling the fever that was still there.

"This must hurt a lot," she said.

" 'Tis nothing I cannot bear, lass. 'Tis far better than when 'twas new."

She nodded, well believing that, for this was a wound that had clearly been very deep. "You are lucky the bone was not broken by this blow."

"Aye." His voice was tight and when she glanced up to see if she was causing that tightness by hurting him, she saw not pain, but anger in his normally cheerful eyes.

"How did this happen?" she asked, her curiosity suddenly flaring as she dug out the salve Morven had given her to keep wounds from festering. She was hoping it might also aid in treating a fester such as this man had.

"I had a moment's distraction during the battle of Dalrigh and one of the English bastards got lucky."

"Your kinsmen must have been distracted, too." She'd seen her father and Uilliam train the warriors of her clan often enough to know they seldom fought alone if they could help it. As the son of their chief, Malcolm would have the warriors who would become his advisors and his champion when he himself became chief, fighting with him no doubt, as Uilliam had always fought beside her father.

Malcolm grunted as he handed her the binding and, without prompting, held the moss in place. Jeanette whispered the healing chant she had used at the wellspring as she once more wrapped the strip of linen around his arm to hold the moss in place. When she had tied off the wrap, she laid her hand gently over the covered wound and once more whispered the chant.

"Why were you not taken home?" she asked. "Surely they were not so distracted—"

Malcolm's arm went tight beneath her hands and when she looked up, he was staring out toward the inky loch, his mouth set in a hard line as if she'd said something that angered him. She thought back, and realized that if his kinsmen had not taken him home after he was injured, it was likely they had not lived. Perhaps it was grief she saw in him, not anger.

"Oh, Malcolm." She rolled his sleeve down for him so she could stand close to him for a little longer. "I am sorry," she said, genuinely ashamed that she might have opened another wound in the man, for the loss of his close kinsmen could not be easy to bear. "My curiosity sometimes outruns my sense."

"Nay, angel, 'tis only that the battle was very nearly a rout of our army and though I do not remember it, I got myself off the field and into a thicket. Someone bound my arm—I do not ken who, perhaps it was even me—but it kept me from bleeding to death. I do not know if my kin survived or not, but I suspect they did." He did not say why he thought that and she did not want to press him to reveal things he did not wish to reveal.

He touched her hand, holding it gently against his arm for a moment. "My arm feels better already."

He took a deep breath and she could feel him relax as he slowly backed her out of the bright circle of torchlight and into the deep shadows where the tower and the curtain wall met. He ran the back of his fingers over her cheek, then leaned in and laid a gentle, chaste kiss where his fingers had been.

"I thank you," he said.

The touch of his kiss on her cheek lit a yearning deep within her and for once Jeanette did not think. She acted, capturing his face in her own palm before he could move away. She turned to meet his lips with her own. Still, he was tentative, careful, as if he thought she might break if he dared more. And she wanted more.

She took his face in both hands and whispered against his lips, "I will not break if you kiss me." Truly she did not understand her own actions, but in this moment she did not care. Later she could figure out what had driven her to such boldness, for now, she just wanted him to kiss her.

And he did.

He wrapped his strong arm around her waist, pulling her close. He tilted his head slightly, and the kiss went from careful to . . . more. So much more.

Heat poured into her, starting where her lips met his, then cascading through every part of her, over her skin, and deep inside where the yearning grew into wanting. A rushing, tingling sensation flowed from her feet to where he nibbled at the corner of her mouth, and then laid a trail of kisses to the hollow behind her ear. Wanting grew into needing. He pulled her closer, or maybe she pulled him closer. Their lips met again, hungry, so hungry, and suddenly his tongue slipped inside, twining with hers in a dance she'd never danced before. Her mind was overwhelmed with sensation—with glorious, powerful . . . desire. Her body hummed, as if she vibrated from the inside out. Malcolm pulled her closer still, and though she'd never been with a man, she knew enough to recognize that his desire was just as powerful as her own.

And then he stopped, his forehead leaning against hers. Her body still melded to his. But his lips were too far away. She stopped the whimper that wanted voice just before it slipped out of her.

"Jeanette, angel, we must stop," he said, but now there was a different sort of strain there. "We must stop," he said again, as if he spoke the words as much for himself as for her. With a sigh, he released her, steadying her with a hand on her hip until she proved stable on her feet. When he dropped his hand at last, the need within her writhed.

Every nerve in her body was alive and very nearly painfully so, and yet she did not mind. She was sure she would regret her impulsive actions in the morning when she had to face him in the light of day, but in this moment she could not. In the past few hours he had made her remember that there was more to life than fear and grief, with his easy grin, and gently teasing words.

And just this once, he'd made her stop thinking, and taught her how to feel.

"I will not apologize for kissing you," she said.

"I would be offended if you did." Laughter lit his eyes in spite of the deep shadow in which they stood. "I will not beg your pardon for kissing you, either. Indeed, I intend to do so again, if you would not mind." He reached for her hand and pulled her just close enough to place one more chaste kiss on her cheek. "I do not think you will mind," he teased.

"I do not think so, either." She was suddenly shy with this golden man who seemed bent on making her smile.

He looked out over the bailey and they both realized that the next group was readying to leave the castle.

"Do you think we were seen?" she asked, suddenly aware that they were not in as private a place as it had seemed to be.

"I am sure we were not. Someone would have been over here long before now if we were."

"Uilliam, for certain. He is my father's eyes and ears, even when Da is not here."

The truth of that hit her. If her father were here and had seen them, he would have stopped them, might even have required Malcolm to wed her, though his leniency with Scotia's trysting made that unlikely. But, still, for the first time, she realized that no longer would the man she wed be required to renounce his own clan and become the Guardian's Protector. No longer would the man she wed be required to become the chief of the MacAlpins.

Jeanette looked out over the broken curtain wall toward the dark loch that reflected the starlight. For the first time, she considered that her future might not be here in Dunlairig after all.

CHAPTER FIVE

Jeanette alternated between sitting and dozing, and pacing the bailey, as she waited her turn to set out from the castle. The first group should have arrived at the caves by now, and three more groups had followed since, each taking a different route to their sanctuary. Only the final group was left and it was not long before they, too, would abandon their home. She had delayed one last task as long as she could but the time was short and she could put it off no longer.

Malcolm looked her way from his perch on one of the stones that were still strewn through the bailey from the crumbled wall. She smiled at him, remembering the joy and abandon she had felt in his arms when they kissed, and tried to pull those feelings around her as if they could shield her from what she must do now.

She took up a lantern that burned nearby and made her way to the tower. She trudged up the stair, passing the landing that would lead her to Rowan and Nicholas's chamber. Was it really just this morning that she and Rowan had argued there? It seemed much longer. She continued to the top floor, where she shared a chamber with her sister. But that was not her destination.

Jeanette turned to her right and stood before the closed door of her mother's solar, a sunny room with windows that looked east and west. A room that had held such happy memories until it had been turned into a bedchamber when her mother took ill last fall. A room that now held only the memory of her mother's murder at the hands of a spy for the English king.

She hadn't set foot in it, or even looked into it, since her mother's body was taken for burial. She did not wish to go in now.

But she must. The scrolls that held the chronicles of the Guardians of the Targe, the collected lore of a long line of women, all Guardians in their own time, could not be left behind. Some were so old, the chronicles were pictures only. And there were many gaps in the lore. She did not know if there were missing scrolls, or if there was simply no one from those periods who knew how to write. Her mother's own tenure as Guardian would have gone unrecorded if Jeanette had not begged her father to find a tutor to teach her reading and writing.

And the end of her mother's years as Guardian had yet to be added. Neither had the beginnings of the newest Guardian, Rowan.

Shame slithered in Jeanette's belly. Grief stole her breath. But she could not make herself reach out and lift the latch.

"Angel?"

Jeanette jumped. Malcolm stood next to her, looking down upon her with concern and questions in his hazel eyes. He reached out and ran a hand down her upper arm, a soothing motion like that of a mum quieting a bairn.

"We are ready to leave as soon as you are," he said, his voice as gentle as his touch.

"I have to get something."

"From within this chamber?"

"Aye." But still she did not reach for the latch.

"What is this chamber?" he asked.

She swallowed, started to answer, and then had to swallow again, her throat suddenly clogged with tears she would not shed. She gripped her hands together, hoping he did not notice their trembling. He did not press and at last she thought she could speak.

"'Tis . . . 'twas my mum's chamber."

He was silent for another moment, then sighed. "She died here?"

"She was murdered here. Aye."

She waited for him to say something, but he simply pulled her into his embrace and while there was no heat to it this time, there was comfort, understanding, and a peace she had not felt in far too long. She wrapped her arms around his waist and leaned into the warmth of him, resting her cheek against his chest, her ear just over his heart where it thumped a slow, steady beat.

She did not know how long she stood there, taking comfort from this man who was still a stranger, and yet was not, but eventually she opened her eyes and noticed the moon was setting, just visible through the window at the end of the corridor. She knew they must leave soon, before the sun could rise. She really could put it off no longer.

"I must get . . . There are things that must come with us for safekeeping," she said.

He pressed a kiss to her forehead, the sweetest kiss she had ever received. He opened the door, then took her hand and led her into the room.

"Where are these things?" he asked.

Jeanette dared not look at the bed where her mother had been stabbed. She dared not look at anything but Malcolm, who held her gaze as if he knew exactly what she needed of him in this moment. She knew she should not reveal the secrets of this chamber to someone not of the clan, but she did not think she could do this on her own.

"You must promise to tell no one what I am about to show you—" She stopped. Nay. She might not be the Guardian, but she was no weak lass. She was Jeanette MacAlpin, daughter of Elspet, brought up to be strong, resilient. She would do this on her own.

And yet her hands were trembling again.

"I will get whatever it is you require, Jeanette. I will tell no one."

"Nay. I will retrieve them, but I must ask you to close your eyes and promise me you will not open them until I say so."

"Do you wish me to wait outside?"

He really was an honorable man. "Nay. I think . . . I need you to stay in here with me, but I will fetch what I came for." She handed him the lantern.

He nodded and, without another word, closed his eyes.

She steadied her breath, drawing strength from his solid form and silent acceptance, then moved to the tapestry that hung between her mother's bed and the hearth. She drew back one corner of the heavy tapestry, letting it rest over her back, hiding her from the room and the room from her. In the darkness she reached unerringly for the stone she'd removed many, many times. When the heavy block was free, she set it on the ground, then reached into the cavity and pressed a lever. A cleverly disguised narrow door, just high enough for her to step into if she bent nearly double at the waist, swung into what most believed was the tower wall.

Jeanette knew better. This was where she stored the chronicles, but it was also the entrance to the hidden stair that allowed an escape in a time of need, leading right down to the bolt-hole under the main stair at the bottom of the tower. Once, not long after Rowan had come to live with them, Jeanette had shown this place to her cousin and the two of them had followed the tunnel all the way out into the forest, where the exit was hidden behind a massive boulder.

When they had returned the same way, they couldn't get the hidden door open again and had finally, hungry, tired, and a little scared, had to retrace their steps and find their way back to the castle through the forest. It was dark by the time they'd stumbled through the gate and discovered that people had been searching every part of the castle, including the well, looking for them for hours.

Elspet, Jeanette's mum, had scolded the girls, forbidding them from ever doing such a thing again, and extracting their tearful promises that they would never tell a soul outside of the family about the tunnel. She then had put them to task mending everything she could find in the castle that had even a tiny rip in it. But she had also showed them the hidden interior latch so that the next time, if there was one, they could let themselves back in.

Jeanette frowned. She hadn't been down those stairs since then. If only she'd hidden her mum in here that fateful day . . .

Her mind refused to relive that day, skittering away from the sharply painful memory. She lifted the six hard leather tubes that protected the scrolls and backed out of the doorway, once more pushing the tapestry away with her back as she closed the doorway and replaced the stone, pressing it even with the others so it would not be obvious should someone look at this section of wall.

She came out from behind the tapestry, her hair in her face and the leather tubes cradled in her arms.

When she had moved back to Malcolm's side she said, "You may open your eyes."

When he did, he grinned at her. "Your secret storage, 'tis clearly in need of cleaning."

"You looked?!" Her heart was beating triple time, though at least now it wasn't from the fear of her memories, but from her fear that she had compromised the safety of her clan.

"Nay. Nay!" Indignation puffed out his chest, and seemed to make him even taller. "I gave you my word. Do you accuse me of breaking it?" He did not give her time to respond. "I kept my eyes closed, but I could not close my ears, angel. Somewhere in that wall"—he pointed to the tapestry—"is a piece that moves. The hinges are in need of oiling, though the sounds are not loud. And you"—his indignation settled into something softer as he pushed her hair away from her face, then ran his thumb over her cheek, showing her the dirt that came away on it—"are not as clean and neat as you were but a moment ago. A MacKenzie never breaks his word, but neither does he shut down his mind."

Quickly, he gathered the tubes from Jeanette's arms with barely a glance at them.

"We need to be away," he said as if she had not doubted his honor. He nodded toward the door, then followed her out, taking care to close the door behind them, closing off her mum's chamber, perhaps for the last time.

THE TRIP TO THE GLEN OF CAVES HAD BEEN UNEVENTFUL, though they had hurried to get there before the sun rose over the horizon. Thankfully, by the time they arrived, the old women had porridge prepared for everyone, and quickly shooed the late arrivals into the large cave, where they could sleep. The next several days were a blur to Jeanette, filled with discovering more caves, cleaning them out, and moving families into them in an effort to clear out as much of the main cave as they could, for storing their supplies and as a "great hall" for the clan. The old men and boys who had come to the caves were busy keeping watch at the passes into the glen, or training with Malcolm and the handful of warriors who had been assigned there.

Jeanette had barely seen Scotia at all, and had only seen Malcolm at meals, and they both looked as tired as she felt. She could not remember if she'd even tended Malcolm's wound since they arrived there, but she thought it likely she had not. As soon as the evening meal was done each day, she had dropped onto her pallet in the main cave and slept, only to be awakened again and again in the night by strange dreams and nightmares, and then to rise with the sun and repeat the work until she could barely think clearly.

Today, she had spent most of the morning organizing their supplies in the cave, and when she finally came out into the bright sunshine, she could hear people in the distance, but no one was in the cleared area just outside the cave where the cook-fires had been set up. She closed her eyes and turned her face up to the sun, letting the heat and the quiet soak into her. This was just the sort of day her mum would take her, Rowan, and Scotia into the kitchen garden and teach them about planting things so they would grow strong and delicious, or she'd take them into the wood and teach them about the plants and animals they saw there, where to find them, what they were useful for, and what the best time was to harvest or trap them.

She rubbed the heel of her hand over a spot in the middle of her chest, pressing against the ache that blossomed there anytime her thoughts turned to her mum.

When she opened her eyes, Malcolm was standing across the clearing, staring at her, a soft smile on his face, and his arms filled with deadfall for the woodpile.

"You are not training the lads this morning?" she asked as they walked toward each other.

"I gave the wee lads the morning off. They need to explore their new home a bit and I"—he dropped the wood on the pile, wincing as he did—"I decided a bit of different work would be good for me, too."

"I am sorry I have not seen to your arm as I promised." Jeanette wished she could make his arm better immediately, returning it to all the vigor she was sure he'd once had in it, but in truth she feared he might never have full use of it again.

"May I look at it? I fear there has been no time to tend your injury properly since we left the castle."

"'Tis fine for now, angel. There is much to do and I will do my part to help."

"You will not be much help if it festers again. If that happens, you shall be a burden upon me." She surprised herself with her teasing, but was rewarded with a smile.

"I would not wish to be a burden."

"Exactly. Take off your tunic. Let me see how your wound fares."

Now the smile turned to a grin. "As you wish, lass."

He fumbled with the pin that held the ends of his plaid at his shoulder. Jeanette stepped close, pushed his hand away and unfastened it, letting the fabric fall behind him.

"I dinna think I can take off my tunic without help," he said, his grin nearly splitting his face in two now.

Jeanette's cheeks heated, and a little thrill ran through her at the thought of undressing the braw man, but she stepped back, set her hands on her hips, and shook her head.

"I have seen you take off your tunic with nary a trouble, warrior. You do that. I shall fetch my bag of simples." She turned her back on the grinning man with the twinkling eyes and tried to settle the swirling sensations gathering low in her belly by turning her mind to where she had left her healer's bag.

When she returned from the cave, Malcolm was leaning against a large boulder not far from the mouth of the cave. His face was turned up to the sun, eyes closed as hers had been, but he looked much more at peace than she had been, and it came to her that he was content with where he was in this moment. She could not ever remember a time when she had been as content as he appeared. She was always looking ahead to the next challenge, the next need of those around her, the next problem to come her way.

But here was a warrior, calm, focused, content. How did he do that?

She studied him. His tunic lay on the ground at his feet. His broad, heavily muscled shoulders were relaxed, and she could see his chest rise and fall slowly. His brow was smooth, his feet were spread and braced him easily against the boulder. The breeze caught his golden hair, tossing it in his face, but he did not push it back or try to control it at all. He just smiled, a small smile that played over his perfect lips. Kissable lips.

The memory of their kiss hit her hard and fast, and she found herself wanting to go stand between his legs and kiss him again.

"Are you not done looking at me yet, angel?" he said, cracking one eye open to look at her.

She opened her mouth to deny it, but nothing came out. She tried again, but still, no words. "Aye," she finally managed and the man beamed at her. "I see you had no trouble with your tunic," she said, not meeting his eyes.

"Only a wee bit. 'Twould have been much easier had you assisted me, Jeanette."

"Aye." Her breath hitched at the image in her head of pulling his tunic up, slowly revealing all that honeyed skin covering the rippling muscles of his stomach, his chest, his arms. She wanted to reach out and touch him, run her hands over him, fall into his kiss again. "Aye," she said again.

"Jeanette? Where are the extra—"

Jeanette gasped and whirled to find Teasag striding into the clearing, grinning at her.

"—Plaids?" the woman finished.

"Plaids?" Jeanette fought her way out of the sensual haze of her daydream, trying to understand what Teasag had asked. "Plaids," she said, focusing on that one word and wishing Malcolm still had his plaid draped over his shoulders, hiding some of that enticing . . . "Aye, plaids." She pulled herself back to the auld woman's question with an effort. She pointed to where a pile of them were stacked just inside the cave. "Shall I bring them to you as soon as I've seen to Malcolm's injury?" she asked, hoping she didn't sound as unsettled as she felt.

Teasag smiled, a knowing look in her eyes. "Perhaps Malcolm can help you," she said, turning around on the path and once more leaving Jeanette and Malcolm alone.

Malcolm was quietly laughing behind her. She whirled back to him, a finger raised.

"Do not laugh at me," she said, mortified that she had been so obvious in her distraction not just to him, but to the auld woman, too.

Malcolm quieted his mirth, but grabbed her finger, pulling her close, just between his legs, where she had moments ago imagined herself.

"If you will not laugh at yourself, angel, you leave it to the rest of us to do so." And then he kissed her . . . or maybe she kissed him. Nay, he kissed her, pulling her closer until he could hook his good hand behind her neck and draw her down to his mouth. Not that she put up much of a fight.

"'Tis sure I am his wound is on his arm," came Teasag's voice again from somewhere behind Jeanette, but Malcolm did not stop kissing her. The woman cackled, but Jeanette could not find it in herself to care, not in this moment when his lips were so soft yet so demanding against her own, when his hand both held her and caressed the sensitive skin of her neck. She cared about nothing except continuing the kiss, until men's voices filtered into her fuzzy mind. 'Twas one thing for the auld women to know she kissed Malcolm, but 'twas an altogether different thing for the guards to know. The women could be trusted to keep the gossip among themselves. The men would tell Uilliam, and he would tell her father.

She backed out of his embrace, blinking and running the tip of her tongue over her bottom lip.

"We have much to do," she said, forcing herself not to look at his mouth, but rather at the bandage she needed to remove.

"There is much we need to do, indeed, angel, but I think you should tend my wound for now."

She glanced at him and the look of raw desire upon his face must have matched her own. He ran a hand down her arm, hooking her hand in his, and she realized that though his words sounded teasing, he was completely serious.

SCOTIA STOOD JUST WITHIN THE SHADOW OF THE TREES, A bucket of water in either hand, and stared at her sister, nestled in the space between Malcolm MacKenzie's thickly muscled thighs, pressing her palms to the man's naked chest and kissing him as if they were lovers, as if they had known each other far longer than a few days.

Scotia's hands clenched around the bucket handles and a muscle twitched in the side of her face. How could her sister—calm, purposeful, steady Jeanette—be dallying with a man she barely knew when their world was crumbling to pieces around them? That was something they would all expect of Scotia, but she found the idea repulsive now. Dallying with lads was for kinder days, not for days when revenge was all any of them should want.

The bastard who had killed her mother had paid too easily for his crime. It grated upon her that she had not been the one to kill the man. Her father had taken all of their revenge for himself, leaving nothing for the rest of them. But there were other English who would be held accountable for the commands of their king. She had made a vow to herself, and to the memory of her mother, to see it so.

Though it would seem even that had been stolen from her by sending her away to the caves with auld women and her humiliated sister. 'Twas not a time to retreat and she wanted nothing to do with such a cowardly act.

She wanted to play a part in protecting the clan from the English that Nicholas was sure were on their way.

Nicholas.

She wanted to hate him, too, for his half-English blood and his years in service as a spy for King Edward, but the man had proven himself true to the needs of Clan MacAlpin. Rowan had chosen him. Kenneth, Scotia's father and the chief, had stepped aside to make Nicholas chief. And she could find nothing to hate in the man as hard as she tried.

Auld Teasag's voice broke into Scotia's spiraling thoughts, chiding Jeanette for her wanton behavior, though the woman did not seem serious. If it had been Scotia kissing any man, everyone would have scolded her. But Jeanette only got teased when they all should be serious.

They all should be serious . . .

Aye. Her mum would tell her to stop feeling sorry for herself and to do something useful, that it would make her feel better, stronger, and Scotia would like to feel both. Voices of the guards returning from their hunting turned her thoughts to what was being done . . . and what wasn't being done . . . for the safety of the clan.

Everyone was focused on getting the caves settled, finding food, hauling water. She looked down at the heavy buckets she held, loosening her white-knuckled grip on them just a little. They needed to find other sources of water, lest the burn nearby dried up in the summer. If that happened, they'd be constantly hauling it up the benside from the burn that ran along the bottom of the glen. She could search for other burns, and while she did that, she could look for ways to protect the MacAlpins while they lived here for who knew how long.

Tomorrow, at first light, Scotia would say she was searching for water, but she would be doing so much more. She would be doing something important, something that might turn the tide should the English find this glen—which is exactly what Jeanette should be doing. Not kissing the MacKenzie like nothing terrible had befallen her and her clan, like there was nothing to grieve over, and nothing to avenge.

Scotia would not sit by and let more grief befall them. She would do something even when Jeanette did nothing, *especially* when Jeanette did nothing.

CHAPTER SIX

That evening Malcolm was grateful that some of the lads had been successful in their rabbit snares this day, for he had quickly grown tired of porridge and dried meat three times a day. There was still porridge for dinner, but there was also rabbit stew.

He looked about at the large cooking area with its makeshift spit and iron pots nestled in the coals of several different fires. The men had managed to move large stones and a portion of a downed tree to circle the cooking area, serving both as a way to keep the bairns and weans away from the fires and as seats for some while they ate.

Malcolm closed his eyes and breathed in the crisp air and the relative silence of the night, hearing only the crackle of the fire and the sound of the wind in the trees. Every once in a while there would be a low murmur as someone spoke, or a bairn would fuss, but everyone was tired and seemed content to sit for a while before turning in for the night.

Night. It was inevitably the time when his mind, and his body, settled on thoughts of Jeanette. The knowledge that she slept not far from him invaded his dreams, making his sleep restless, and his waking hours a lesson in self-control. He found himself watching her move among her kin as she worked during the day, admiring her grace and the easy way she had with everyone. When she tended his injury, all he could think about was kissing her again, but inevitably they were not alone. If she didn't linger so over the care she gave his arm, he might think she arranged for others to be about, but it seemed she was as distracted by him as he was by her.

The lass in question chose that moment to leap up from her spot opposite him across the fire.

"I shall see the last of the food is put away," she said.

Scotia yawned. "I shall let you, though 'twas my task this evening." She rose and took her leave. Malcolm watched as she disappeared into the main cave, followed by a few others who had lingered after the meal until it was only Malcolm and Peigi by the fire, while Jeanette crouched across it, scrubbing a pot out with sand. A pleasant silence settled over them all until Peigi rose and moved to sit near him on the log.

"Go to her, my braw lad." She patted him on the arm with a hand twisted by age. "Jeanette has always been fixed on duty, has always put the needs of others before her own. Even now when she grieves over the loss of her mother and her home, she does not think to reach out for comfort, yet she seems to find it with you, Malcolm MacKenzie."

He glanced at her, finding mirth glittering in her eyes.

"Go and help her in her task, then steal another kiss or two to send her to sleep with sweet dreams, not the nightmares she has been having."

"Nightmares? I have heard naught from her in the night."

"Even in that she would hide her own need. She has not slept well since before we came here." She nodded toward the cookfire where Jeanette was now busy banking the embers. "I think she does not wish to sleep but she will not speak about it."

That explained the circles under her eyes better than the work she had been occupied with these past days.

Peigi gave his arm a squeeze. "I think you were sent here for a reason, lad, and not just so our Jeanette could heal your arm. The lass needs a bit of fun in her life, especially now when all is doom and dread. You seem just the lad for the task. This life is too short, and all too often too hard, not to take what pleasure you may when you can."

Malcolm stared at the woman. Was she suggesting . . . Nay, surely not, but she winked at him as she rose.

"I was never one to miss a bit of fun when I was younger and prettier. It is what makes life worth living, especially in hard times." She looked down at him. "Go. Show the lass that it harms not to have some fun. Duty will always be waiting for her."

Fun? 'Twas not exactly how he would describe the quick passion that rose between himself and Jeanette whenever they touched. He looked over his shoulder and found the auld woman standing in the mouth of the cave watching him. She leaned her head toward Jeanette, then gave him a shooing motion with her hands. He nodded at her, not knowing if being alone with Jeanette was a good thing or just a test of his will.

"Can I help you with that, angel?" he asked, not waiting for an answer before taking the heavy lidded iron pot from her hand. He grabbed another, leaving the largest for her to prepare the morning porridge.

Without a word he took the pots, both now clean, into the cave and deposited them along the wall. He grabbed the plaid he'd been using for a bed and returned to the cook circle. Jeanette had filled the remaining pot with oats and water and was settling it into the embers to cook slowly overnight. He put the lid upon it, then grabbed her hand and led her to the log Peigi had sat upon.

"I am not done banking the fire," she said, even though she showed no resistance to being pulled away from that task.

"Aye, lass, you are." He wrapped his plaid around her, taking a moment to pull her braid free of it as an excuse to stand close to her, then he tugged her down to sit next to him on the ground, the log at their backs trapping some of the fire's heat about them.

"Peigi says you've been having nightmares," he said quietly, staring into the fire. He knew this was not what Peigi had in mind, but he needed the distraction of conversation until he could overcome the instinct to pull her into his lap and kiss her until he'd had his fill, if that was even possible. Besides, if he could get Jeanette to talk about what bedeviled her, it might help her sleep better. "Is that why you become so busy in the evening? So you do not have to dream?"

She gave a long sigh and leaned her head on his shoulder. He smiled as the scent of her, like a breeze off a loch in springtime, settled over him, but he kept looking at the fire pit, hoping to give her a sense of privacy in the dark of the night so she'd talk to him.

"Peigi is a busybody," she said quietly.

"Aye, a spunky auld woman she is, but she means well." He needed to touch her, so he took Jeanette's hand in his and let them rest on his thigh, their fingers twined together.

"I dream, but I do not remember much . . . just a feeling of panic, of grief, and anger. So much anger."

"You have much to be angry about."

"You have no idea."

"Nay?" The pain in her voice pulled at him in a different way than her scent or her touch did, making him want to soothe her hurts, and right whatever wrongs had been done. "Tell me, lass. Perhaps that will help keep the dreams from tormenting you."

She was quiet for a long time and he thought perhaps she had gone to sleep, but she sighed again and began to speak.

"You ken what happened with my mum, her murder?"

"I know only that she was murdered, not why, or by whom."

"There was another spy," she said. "He came here with Nicholas, but he was a very different sort of man. When Nicholas's loyalties shifted to Rowan and our clan, his partner decided to finish the job himself. He thought my mum could help him do that and when she couldn't . . . she was so ill . . . He . . . I . . ." It was as if she could not push the words out into the night air.

Malcolm gave her hand a squeeze, but kept his eyes trained on the glowing coals of the fire, hoping she would continue. He heard her swallow hard.

"I could not stop him. I could not help her. And then Rowan was the one . . ."

The one? Questions. So many questions plagued him, but he did not want to push her when she was just beginning to open up. His questions would hold and perhaps she would answer one or two without him even asking.

"Rowan went with the men to find the spy. Rowan turned the tide in the fight. Rowan became . . ."

"Became the Lady of the castle? Should that not have been your place as the eldest daughter?" He silently cursed at his inability to hold all his questions in. The spark of anger he felt over her rightful place having been taken from her made that difficult.

She hesitated. "That is not how it works in our clan. Rowan was . . . chosen. Then she chose Nicholas and now my father is no longer chief and my sister and I . . . we are unneeded."

" 'Tis not what I have seen." He lifted her hand and placed a kiss on her knuckles where they twined with his. "You are much loved by your clan, and much trusted to take on this task of providing safe haven for them."

"Peigi and her sisters are the ones providing safe haven. I was sent here so I would not press Rowan any longer."

"Press her for what, angel?"

Jeanette seemed to consider how to answer him. "There are duties she must perform as Lady of the castle, duties I have been taught, since I was a wee lass, in preparation for her position, but she resists my teaching them to her."

The urge to shake Rowan surprised him, but then her resistance to learning her proper duties also surprised him. "Perhaps she needs some time to adjust to her new duties?"

"Perhaps. In truth, we have never been at such odds with each other and I find it hard to accept. 'Tis why I came here, rather than staying with her at the warriors' camp, to give us each some time to accustom ourselves to the changes in our destinies."

Malcolm mulled over all the things she'd told him, understanding now why there had seemed to be such tension between the two women, though his instinct was still to protect Jeanette and reprimand Rowan for causing her cousin such distress, but that was not his place. He and Jeanette had shared a few kisses, though that was hardly enough to make him lay claim to her and her troubles as his own, and yet, just as much as he ached for more kisses, he wished to ease her heartache. Jeanette shivered and Malcolm wrapped an arm about her, pulling her close and arranging the plaid to better shelter her from the damp night air. They sat quietly together for a time, staring into the crackling fire that was starting to burn low. After a while, she turned enough to rest her cheek in the hollow of his shoulder and pulled part of the plaid across him as she rested her arm across his waist. Her breathing slowed. She tucked her hand under her cheek and Malcolm found himself living his own dream. Only this time, instead of her making him restless, he pulled her even closer to him, breathing in the scent of her, and slipped into sleep.

JEANETTE WANDERED HIGH UP ON THE BEN, PICKING HER WAY along a rocky path between huge pines, silvery birch, and the occasional rowan tree. A stag with one jutting antler, and one bent at an odd angle, stepped out of the shadows into the path before her and stopped, turned to stare at her for a long moment, then continued on his way, disappearing quickly and silently back into the forest shadows. She tried to follow him, but the trees were too densely packed, the underbrush too full of thorns, and so she turned to see where he had come from.

In that direction the trees seemed to open for her, displaying a breathtaking view down the benside, laying out the glen below her. It was thickly blanketed in shades of springtime green, broken by the darker green of the pines that had yet to shed their winter needles. She could just make out a wisp of smoke drifting up through the tree cover and she knew that marked the cook-fire outside the main cave.

The thought drifted through her mind that they must be more careful to keep the fire small so no one hunting them could find them by its telltale plume. But as quickly as the thought came, it drifted away from her and she found herself farther up the ben, standing on a barren shelf of stone. The stag stood once more before her, as if he had been awaiting her arrival. He looked at her, then looked at the massive stone next to him. It jutted from the face of the mountain, broken by a slash of darkness that beckoned her to step into it.

And then the stag was gone.

Jeanette approached the place where he had stood, but she could not see him anywhere. She looked down the ben again, but the glen was much farther away, as if she'd climbed twice as high as she had been the first time the stag crossed her path, though she did not feel tired, nor could she remember traveling so far. The cookfire smoke was still visible, but only if she looked hard for it, and it was off to her right now.

She turned to look at the massive boulder behind her and found a picture of a resting stag incised into the stone. She ran her fingers over the curve of the stag's antlers and over the back, and then remembered the slashing cleft in the boulder. She tried to slide into the break in the stone but could not. Again and again she tried. Each time she could smell fresh air wafting through the darkness, a coolness floated over her heated skin, taunting her with the mystery of what was within.

"Lass?"

A warm, callused hand stroked her face. A kiss feathered against her forehead. She whimpered, aching with her frustration. But she did not look away from the entrance to whatever lay beyond the stone. She knew she must get through that stone.

"Jeanette, angel."

A deep voice floated around her, surrounding her in warmth and an itchy sort of need akin to, but not the same as, her frustration over being barred from whatever the stone held secret from her.

"Wake up, lass."

Someone shook her shoulder, pulling her away from the stone, and into his welcoming arms.

She snuggled even deeper into his embrace, sighing in contentment as a familiar masculine scent wound about her. Malcolm. She lifted her face and found his lips waiting for her, meeting her kiss with his own. She'd missed kissing him, even though she'd only done it twice before. These last days had been made even more difficult than they already were, due to her need to fight the urge to pull him into the wood and kiss him until she was sated. He slid his tongue against hers, pulling her out of her sleepy thoughts and back to him, to Malcolm, to his lips and his tongue and his hand sliding along her back, to his hand sliding up her ribs and cradling her breast in his palm, to her own need to press her breast into his hand, to her need to pull herself closer to him. But just as in the dream, her frustration grew, sending her heart hammering.

Dream.

Her eyes popped open and she scrambled to her feet, mortified at what he must think of her wrapping herself about him like a wanton.

He grabbed the plaid where it dropped, pulling it over his lap quickly.

"I promised I would wake you if you had a bad dream," he said, his eyes still soft with that flash of desire that had ignited between them.

"A bad dream?" she asked, pushing her tangled hair out of her face and brushing bits of leaves and dirt from her gown. "It did not feel like a bad dream." She gasped and covered her mouth, shaking her head. "I cannot believe I just said such a thing."

He considered her long enough to make her uncomfortable. "There is nothing to be ashamed of, Jeanette. We both were sleepy, not thinking. It was not unpleasant was it? It wasn't for me."

"Nay. Not unpleasant." She turned away from him and pressed her palms to her hot cheeks. It had been far from unpleasant. So far from unpleasant, she wished to continue what they had started. "I dreamed?" She busied herself stirring up the fire from last night's embers so she wouldn't have to look at him, for she was sure she'd throw herself back in his arms if she did.

"Aye. You were trying to talk, I think, and you did not sound happy. You thrashed about a bit, as well. I did not want you to hurt yourself."

She fed tinder to the fire and watched the flame surge up the twigs and dried leaves, aware of a similar heat that flowed just under her skin. "Thank you for waking me," she said. "I did not mean to fall asleep."

"Neither did I, but it seems we did." He pointed at the sky, which was streaked with the rosy pale light of dawn. He stood slowly, keeping the plaid wrapped about him like a cloak, though she did not see how he could be chilled enough to need it.

When he stooped to help her with the fire, carefully setting wood in place to catch the flame she kindled, the dream came back to her as if it were a memory of something real, not the nighttime rambles of her tired mind. And she realized 'twas not a dream, not in the usual way. This was like the dreams she had had as a child. Dreams that often became reality.

But what did this one mean? Would a stag lead her to a place of great frustration? Or was there something beyond the dark passage that she must find a way to get to?

She looked up the ben in the direction she must have gone in the dream. Up there, somewhere, was a stone jutting out from the mountainside, with the figure of a deer incised into it, and a deep cleft in the rock that she must figure out how to traverse.

She was certain of it. What she didn't know was if she should be afraid of what she found there.

MALCOLM WAS CAREFUL TO KEEP THE PLAID HE HAD SHARED with Jeanette wrapped about him, hiding the raging need that had awakened him. The lass had been pressing against him in her sleep, muttering and twitching her hands as if she tried to use them in whatever dream she was caught up in. He'd awakened her, as he'd promised, and then . . . It had taken every bit of strength he had for him not to push her on her back and have her then and there.

Of course they weren't far outside the mouth of the cave and the auld women were early risers, so that had fortified his constraint, but just barely.

He busied himself with the fire, letting the heat that the lass had kindled in him cool before anyone else joined them.

"Did you two spend the whole night out here?" Peigi walked toward them from the cave, her gnarled hands on her hips and mischief dancing in her eyes.

"Aye, mistress, we did," he said, but did not return her smile. He was just managing to get his body under control and he did not need that canny woman reading more into the situation than was true.

"Jeanette, will you check the porridge and make sure 'tis cooked through?" Peigi asked as she walked slowly into the wood. When she came back a few minutes later she was rubbing her hip. "I think 'tis time we turned our work to a little comfort," she mumbled as if to herself.

Jeanette looked up at the ben, then at the auld woman. "Scotia and I can find heather and sweet grass to stuff the mattresses with this day, so you dinna have to sleep upon the hard ground another night."

Peigi joined Malcolm where he was still tending the fire and turned her back to the fragile warmth it was at last casting into the chill morning.

"I think 'tis a good idea," she said, still rubbing her hip as if it ached. "My auld bones do not take kindly to hard rock for a bed. But do not take Scotia. I have another task for her this day. Take Malcolm." She winked at him, the auld troublemaker. "'Twould be good for his arm to do some work. Gathering the heather would not be too difficult for him, would it?"

Jeanette closed her eyes and Malcolm wondered what exactly was running through her mind. Did she wish to be alone with him as he wished to be alone with her?

Holy mother of God. He gripped the plaid about him as a new surge of desire took hold of him. If they were alone amongst the heather— An image of the two of them, naked, twined together amidst the fragrant heather, her skin heated by passion and the sun, filled his mind.

He tried to think of something else but could not. He made sure the plaid draped over him still where he crouched, yet tending the fire that no longer needed his care. He would need to work himself beyond fatigue to keep from reaching for her, kissing her, taking her.

He wiped away the sweat that beaded on his forehead with the back of his hand. Aye, working hard with his arm would be good for it. Working until it was sore might keep him from wanting what the lass had not offered.

"Jeanette?" Peigi said. "Will you and Malcolm stuff the mattresses for me and my sisters this day?"

Malcolm's mind turned her question into an innuendo and he had to stifle a laugh, even as the image of Jeanette, naked under him on one of those mattresses, took hold—her blond hair spread about her, head arched back in pleasure—made him ache with a need he could not slake.

Jeanette stirred the kettle of porridge, banged the wooden spoon against the side of it, and covered it once more. She looked up the ben again, then slowly nodded.

He could not stop the quiet groan that escaped him at Jeanette's acceptance. This day would be difficult for more than his injured arm.

Peigi chuckled.

CHAPTER SEVEN

JEANETTE LED THE WAY UP THE PATH THEY HAD TRAVELED INTO the Glen of Caves a few days before, determined to ignore the man who followed her. They each had a large, mostly empty, basket that they carried on their backs. At the moment all that the baskets contained was a little food for their midday meal and a short-handled scythe. They would gather as much heather as they could carry and take it back for the mattresses for Peigi and her sisters. Unfortunately, there were no large areas of heather within the Glen of Caves, so they were forced to retrace their journey out of the glen and almost to the shieling, the summer pasturage that was still high upon the ben.

Peigi had no idea what she had done this day, sending Jeanette and Malcolm off alone. 'Twas bad enough that Jeanette would not get a chance to look for the place the stag had shown her, but her heartbeat had tripled at the mere thought of being alone with the man in whose arms she had awakened. Her breath came faster than the exertion of walking merited and she had a hard time swallowing with her mouth gone bone-dry.

"I dinna think this is a good day for gathering heather," Malcolm said from behind her.

She almost agreed with him, then remembered that she was trying to ignore him lest she do something daft like throw herself into his arms. She walked on as silence sliced between them until his words sank in and pricked at her pride. Did he not wish to spend the time with her?

"Why do you not think 'tis a good day for this task?" she asked over her shoulder, chiding herself for not holding her tongue. She sped her steps. If she could not ignore his conversation, she dared not trust herself should he get within touching distance of her.

"If you looked up, rather than at your feet, angel, you would not ask." His voice was tight but she refused to look back to find out why.

Instead, she looked up to find a sky that matched her mood—dark with heavy clouds.

"Oh. Perhaps the rain will hold off long enough for us to at least get enough heather for Peigi. She is used to a feather bed and I fear she is not as resilient as she once was when it comes to where she sleeps."

"From what she tells me, I would say 'tis true."

His quiet laugh made her smile as she, too, remembered some of Peigi's bawdier tales. Peigi had been quite a wanton in her younger days and took no pains to hide that from anyone. She was, if anything, quite proud of her exploits with the lads.

"I think her tales have gone to Scotia's head."

"Scotia?" He drew nearer to her, but still stayed a step or two behind.

It was easier to talk to him, to pretend she wasn't drawn to him, when she wasn't looking at him.

"Aye, Scotia has kept us all on watch for her lest she do something she would regret with the lads."

"Your sister, Scotia?"

"Who else?"

"I have not seen anything like that with her. Indeed, she is grim-faced and taciturn every time I see her."

Jeanette suddenly realized that he was right. She had not had to chase after her sister, or reprimand her for her behavior, since . . . her mother had been murdered and the culprit executed in front of all of them.

"She has changed with recent events. I never thought to say this, but I miss her antics. They were annoying, but amusing."

"And what amuses you now, lass?"

She sighed and shrugged. "I do not ken. These days, there is little to be amused by, not even by Scotia."

"And so I have a task."

She looked back at his beautiful, grinning face, though she had promised herself she wouldn't, and she felt the dark clouds of her mood lift a little. "And what, pray tell, is that?"

"To find a way to amuse you, of course. I would hear you laugh. Laughter lightens even the heaviest of hearts."

He spoke the truth, yet she could not imagine laughing of late.

As they neared the shoulder of one of the sheltering bens, Malcolm stepped in front of her, making it impossible for her to keep her eyes, and her mind, off the comely man as he led her down a deer trail they had followed into the Glen of Caves a few days ago. Finally the forest opened enough to reveal glimpses of a hillside blanketed in heather. In the fall it would be shades of pinks and purples, but now it was green and while it would not make as fragrant a bed without the blossoms, 'twould still be better than most anything else in a mattress. And it would certainly be better than a plaid on the bare ground.

Which brought to mind the fact that that was exactly how she had slept the night before, though curled up against her companion . . . and she had slept well until the morning dream, and the part that wasn't a dream.

Heat burned in her cheeks and she was grateful Malcolm walked in front of her so he would not ask why she blushed so.

Malcolm signaled for her to stop just inside the cover of the forest. She set her basket down, unloaded the sack of food for their midday meal and the sickle-shaped knife she'd brought for cutting the heather, then she waited while he circled along the edge of the meadow. Eventually he waved her out of the shelter of the trees and met her in the heather.

"We should take care where we cut," she said, "so that it will not be obvious from a distance that this heather has been recently harvested."

He held out his hand for the sickle and she briefly considered not giving it to him. But then she reminded herself that part of why they had come on this task was to help with strengthening his hand and arm. The effort required to grip the knife would keep him busy and tire him out so that she would be able to better remember her role as healer for this man, and perhaps forget the feel of his lips on hers and his hand on her breast this morning. Her nipples tightened at the mere memory and she quickly handed him the knife.

It took him a few tries to figure out that he could not grip the knife hard enough in his injured right hand, but that he could manage it in his left, using his right to stabilize the branches instead. Once that was sorted out, he moved quickly from one bush to another, and another. She followed along behind him, collecting the cuttings as he liberated them, stacking them in the deep basket, while, all the time, trying her best to ignore the deep, yearning ache that built within her each time she found herself watching him work, admiring his determination, and the way he moved—the flash of his muscled calf or sinewy forearm as he worked.

He straightened to his full height, startling her out of her distraction, and shook out his right hand, wiggling the fingers as if they pained him.

"We should take a rest," she said as she picked up the cuttings and added them to her nearly full basket. "I need the other basket anyway."

He nodded, wiping his brow with his sleeve, and then took one side of the basket while she took the other. Together they moved quietly back into the cool dimness under the cover of the trees.

Jeanette pulled a waterskin out of the other basket and drank deeply before she turned to offer it to her companion. He was sitting on the ground, his back to a tree and his long legs stretched out in front of him. He arched what she was sure was an aching back and he smiled as she proffered the waterskin. Jeanette was transfixed by the man before her, his gold-streaked hair lifting and tangling in the breeze, his tawny skin that seemed to beg for her touch, and his smile . . . she remembered the feel of his lips upon hers and heat arrowed deep into her belly, increasing the ache there and leaving her restless and oddly out of sorts.

"How is your arm, and your hand?" she asked as he passed the skin back to her. She took another long drink, hoping the cool water would quench the heat that seemed to build within her.

When he didn't answer, she realized he was watching her drink, a look of hunger in his eyes that fanned the heat within her into flames.

"Your arm?" she asked again, annoyed at the slightly breathless quality to her voice.

"My arm is well enough. 'Tis my hand that will not do as I tell it." He pushed himself up to his feet and showed her his right hand.

Nothing looked wrong with it, but she was well aware that his grip strength was not anywhere near what it should be, what it had been. She feared he might never regain much strength in it, but she did not say that to him . . . not yet.

"Can you make a fist of it?" she asked, focusing on her healing lore to distract herself from how close he was standing to her now, and how the scent of fresh-cut heather mingled with a muskier scent that she was coming to know was Malcolm. She breathed it deep into her lungs.

He held his hand out, palm up, and curled his fingers but he could not make a fist. He pushed his fingers where he wanted them to be with his other hand, then grimaced as his right hand spasmed, contorting into what looked more like claws than fingers.

She dropped the waterskin to the ground and took his hand in hers, not so gently massaging his palm, then each of his fingers, loosening the cramping muscles. "You can do this yourself, you ken. 'Twould be good for your hand, loosening the muscles. When we get back to the caves I will fashion a ball out of cloth for you."

"Why would I want a ball, angel?" His voice was soft, as if he was lost in her touch.

"You must squeeze it as often as you think of it." She wadded up a corner of her arisaid and put it in his palm. "Try to squeeze that."

He did, the cloth giving just enough to exercise the muscles in his fingers and hand.

"The ball will strengthen your hand again and as you can close your hand more, you can remove the outer layers of cloth to make it smaller."

He tried it a few times, then dropped the cloth, holding his hand out to her. "I like it better when you ease my hand." He grinned at her, then he closed his eyes and let his head tilt back as she once more massaged his hand. "But I will do as you bid when you cannot."

When his hand finally relaxed, she pushed up the sleeve of his tunic, and continued her ministrations up his arm, working the tense muscles until she felt them begin to give way and soften.

"That feels good, angel," Malcolm said quietly.

"Why do you call me that?" she asked, still working on his forearm. "You have called me that almost from the moment we met."

He touched her cheek with his free hand, drawing her attention away from his arm and up to his face that was only inches from her own.

"Because the first time I saw you, you looked like an angel, a warrior angel, come to help me."

His touch was like spark to tinder, igniting a desire inside her unlike any she'd experienced before. No matter how much she tried to calm her heart, her breath, she couldn't. She licked lips gone dry, and he ran his thumb over her lower lip, tracing the path her tongue had taken.

She looked up and was captured by hazel eyes gone dark, intense, and hungry. His gaze was trained upon her as if she were the only thing in the world and she knew she looked at him the same way. What had started out as a way to lessen his pain had become a means for her to touch him, to touch his skin, to feel its warmth against her hands, to caress the hand that she wished was sliding over her skin.

"If you want to take off your tunic," she said, her voice just barely above a whisper, "I can continue working on your arm."

Without a word he whipped his tunic off and placed his hand back in hers.

"Sit down," she said. He complied before she had the words out of her mouth. She knelt and worked her hands up his forearm, then his upper arm, gentling her strokes over the now closed, but not yet fully healed wound, working her way up to his shoulder, knowing she had already stopped his muscle spasm and relaxed his arm muscles, but she did not want to stop touching him. Her hands trembled and an odd tingling flowed up from her feet and into her hands where she touched him. It was as if the feel of his skin under her hands called up a hunger she hadn't even known she harbored until he had come into her life.

Without thinking, she pressed a kiss to the top of his arm where it met his shoulder.

Malcolm groaned and hooked his injured arm around her, pulling her into his lap, leaning her back into his good arm as he covered her mouth with his in a kiss that was at once giving and taking, soft and demanding. She could feel the hard length of his desire against her hip and she could not help but press herself closer to it, nestling her bottom in the cradle of his lap in an attempt to ease the ache that had set up between her legs.

Malcolm kissed her jaw, then her neck, as she moved her head back. Jeanette ran her fingers into his hair, holding him close so he would not stop kissing her, would not stop touching her. His weak hand moved up and down her side as he kissed her, pulling her even deeper into his lap, tantalizing her with each upward stroke as he came nearer and nearer to her aching, swollen breast. He pressed his palm to her side, his thumb just grazing the bottom of her breast, and he stopped.

"Do not stop," she whispered, and he covered her mouth with his once more. At the same moment he swept his hand up to cover her breast, his thumb running over her sensitive nipple, the heat of him penetrating even through two layers of clothes.

And then he was lifting her with his good arm, guiding her to straddle him with his weak one, pressing the focus of all her need against the rough wool that separated her from the heat of him— and through everything he never ceased his kissing. She lost herself in the pressure of his lips against hers, their tongues dancing against each other, until suddenly his hands were under her skirts, drawing her attention to other parts of her that yearned for his attention. He slid his fingers along her calves, pressing, smoothing, much as she had done to his arm, though he did not linger as long, sliding his big hands now over her thighs.

Somewhere in her head there was a whisper that she should stop this, but the need, the inferno burning so hot within her shouted that quiet voice down, demanding more, more, though she could not say what more there was.

His hands slid between them, his fingers skimming over sensitive skin up and down, ever higher, his thumbs running along her inner thigh, stopping just short of the center of all her frustration. She wanted to cry out with her desperation.

And then he slid his hand all the way up her thigh, and his thumb skimmed over that most private, moist place and she knew.

Instinct took over as she pressed herself against his hand, pressed her aching breasts against his naked chest and rained kisses over his high cheekbones. She kissed his strong jaw, following it to the hollow behind his ear. He groaned as she squirmed against him and he slipped his thumb deeper into her cleft, rubbing a spot that had her dropping her head back and gasping.

"So wet," he whispered, and he shifted, giving his hand room between them to slip even deeper between those lips and with a surprised moan from her he slid a finger into her depths, his thumb still pressing and rubbing, driving her up to the edge of a chasm that begged to be leapt.

Thunder pealed all around them, but Jeanette didn't care. Nothing mattered but Malcolm and what he was doing to her body, drawing needs and sensations from her she'd never before known, driving her mad with want. She heard herself whispering "More" into his ear and "Do not stop, please, God, do not stop."

Her hips moved of their own volition, undulating against him as he thrust his finger into her and slid it out again, over and over, never stopping with the pressure of his thumb until she did not think she could bear such sweet torture anymore. Her breath rasped from her lungs, she pressed her thighs as wide as she could. She needed . . . she needed.

And then the world exploded around her. All the tension that had tightened and tightened within her shattered at once and she flew, she soared, she experienced what heaven must be like.

Slowly she became aware of her body once more, the burning need now transformed to a satisfied languor. She knew she was no longer the same person she had been this morning but she didn't care. This was a better person, a better place to be.

Malcolm slipped his hand free of her, wrapping his arms around her and holding her tight against him. She lay against his chest, her arms around him, listening to his heartbeat as her breathing calmed and her body slowly ceased its twitching.

"'Tis raining, angel," Malcolm said a few minutes later, pushing her wet hair away from her face.

Jeanette lifted her head, surprised to find it true. She turned her face up to the fat drops of cold water falling upon them from the leaves above and felt more alive in this moment, with this man, than she had felt . . . ever. She was a true dafty to have thought she could ignore him this day. She was doubly daft to have wanted to. She vowed she would not make that mistake again.

And from out of nowhere, all the joy she once had held within her bubbled up and she laughed.

Jeanette's laughter was like honey—sweet and golden—and Malcolm let it wrap about and settle into him. She smiled, her lips quirked up as if she had just learned something about herself and she was very satisfied with the lesson. Her sky-blue eyes were bright and, for the moment at least, free of worry and grief as she smoothed her hand over his cheek, watching its movement like a bairn's first discovery of a butterfly.

"I had no idea," she said, laying a sweet kiss upon his jaw. "I had no idea."

Malcolm could not help but grin as his angel kept running her soft hand over his face, tracing the path of a raindrop down his bare shoulder, and over his arm, then back, retracing her path with trailing fingers, so lightly laid upon his skin, they almost tickled.

She was glorious, sensual, unrestrained, and it had taken every fiber in Malcolm's being not to move his clothing out from between them and join their bodies as he wanted. But honor would not let him indulge either of them in such a way.

And yet, he wanted her, more than he should, when he had known her but a few days, and not just her body, though that was enough to captivate his attention. But there was so much more to his angel. Her laughter was magical; like a rare gem, it sparkled and delighted. Her intensity, whether tending his arm, seeing to the care of her clan, or giving herself up to passion, intrigued him, drew him.

But his destiny was elsewhere, and he realized that he would miss her when he left. Having her in his arms, hearing her sighs and moans of pleasure . . . that would make leaving her all the more difficult, but he could not regret what they had shared.

He kissed Jeanette once more, but neither of them held the desperation of a few minutes ago. This kiss was sweet, though not chaste. Arousing, but not to a state of frenzy, and this too he would miss when he left.

"We are getting very wet, angel," he said when she seemed to be losing herself in the kiss. He dared not let it go so far again, or else any thoughts of honor would not be enough to safe keep her virtue.

She sighed and leaned back, looking out at the rain hitting the heather, making the plants dance and shiver. She turned her face to the sky once more, closing her eyes and letting the raindrops splatter over her skin.

"I feel new," she said, still letting the rain fall upon her face. "Does that make any sense?"

"Aye," Malcolm said, realizing that he felt the same way, as if they had walked through a door into a new life, though he knew not what this life held for them any more than the last, but he did not care.

She looked at him then, her eyes wide. "Is it always this way between a man and a woman?"

He wiped the rain from her face, ran his thumb over her kiss-bruised lips, as he considered her question, realizing that nay, he had never felt quite this way with a woman before. He looked her in the eye. "It has never been this way for me."

"That makes me happy," she said, looking down, suddenly shy.

He lifted her chin with his finger so he could once more look into her beautiful eyes. "Me, also. But now we must find some shelter out of the rain so we do not ruin this moment with illness."

"Spoken like a healer," she said, with a smile and a quiet laugh as she reluctantly rose from her place in his lap.

He took a moment, while she was settling her sopping skirts over her lovely legs, to find his discarded tunic. He thought to wring the rain from it but his right hand did not cooperate, so he donned the soaking wet tunic, not bothering to tuck it back into his plaid.

"There are huts at the summer shieling, but I fear it is too exposed for us to take shelter there," she said, looking about her as if she was assessing exactly where they were. "If we go this way"—she pointed into the thickest part of the wood—"'twill offer some protection from the rain."

Malcolm considered the two options: a dry hut at the meadow where the clan grazed their animals in the summer; or under the trees, where they would still be exposed to the rain. No question, he agreed with her choice, and though her reasons were sound, his was more pressing.

He needed the cold rain to distract him from the desire that still coursed through his veins, and from the newly disheartening thought that soon his arm would be better and he would have to return to the king's army. He would have to leave Jeanette.

CHAPTER EIGHT

Jeanette almost crashed into Malcolm when he stopped suddenly in a small clearing and turned his face up to the sky, letting the rain cascade over him.

"What are you doing?" she asked. "I thought you wanted to get out of the rain."

"I did, but I find I need a wee bit of cooling off." He slanted a look at her so full of desire that he had heat rising to her cheeks and sinking to other parts of her.

Jeanette nodded slowly and joined him in the downpour.

"There's an auld cottage over there," he said quietly, pointing directly in front of them. "It looks like some of the roof may still be in place."

Jeanette had to squint against the raindrops and even then she could just make out a shadowed outline of a stone structure.

"Are you cooled enough?" she asked, wringing the cold rain from her braid.

His cocky grin split his face. "For now." He bent and gave her a quick kiss. "For now." He took her hand in his strong one and led her to the cottage, though when they looked closer, there was little to recommend it as shelter. "That corner looks dryer than the rest." He lifted his chin in the direction of the far corner.

There was a small section of roof left there, though it was hard to say if the original thatch remained or if it was now made only of layers of decaying leaves and pine needles, bright mosses, and assorted twigs and small branches that looked to hold everything in place against the gusty wind.

"At least the walls will stop the worst of the wind," she said, her teeth now starting to chatter as the cold seeped into her bones.

Malcolm squeezed her icy hand in his and helped her climb over the rubble of one wall and into the cottage, such as it was. They picked their way across years of windblown bits of trees that had thickly carpeted the floor until they made it to the corner and shed their baskets. Leaves had been gathered into that corner and arranged as if some large animal had made its bed there, though by the looks of it, not too recently. Jeanette moved a little away from the most sheltered area and began squeezing the water from her arisaid, skirts, and her hair. Malcolm did the same, hooking his plaid under his right elbow, while twisting it with his left hand.

When they both were done and as dry as they could be without a fire, they settled with their backs to one wall, hip to hip, knees drawn up to keep their feet under the sheltering remnant of the roof.

"I suppose 'tis just as well we cannot make a fire in this downpour," she said, by way of breaking what was becoming an uncomfortable silence between them.

"Why is that, angel?"

"If there are English keeping watch, the smoke would surely draw them to us. We need to take more care with the size of the cookfire back at the caves for the very same reason." Her dream came back to her, the thought an echo from it.

"I would risk a small fire if we could," he said, chafing her hand between his to warm it, but his skin was as icy as hers.

"I fear we'd only set our nest here afire if the rain didn't put it out first." She cast about for something else to talk about with this man she had already grown more than fond of, and realized she really knew very little about him. Now was her opportunity. "Tell me what I should ken about you, Malcolm."

"You ken what is important," he said, still intent on warming her hand. "What would you know?" he asked with a quick glance at her.

She thought about what he knew of her. "Do you have brothers? Sisters? I ken your da is alive. Is your mum?"

He laughed. "Three younger sisters. Da is alive. He is chief of Clan MacKenzie. And my mum died when my youngest sister was born many years ago."

"So you are the next chief."

"Aye. Though my da and I dinna see eye to eye on many things, on that we agree."

She thought about that for a while. "Do you want to be chief?"

He seemed startled by the question. "It is my duty and my destiny," he said. "I never thought about whether I wanted it or not."

"Duty and destiny do not always work out the way you think they will, not even when you do want them," she said, staring out at the falling rain. She could feel his gaze on her and oddly, it made what she had lost a little easier to bear. If she could not be Guardian, perhaps she could be content living out her life with a man like Malcolm. "If you could not be chief," she said, squeezing his hand that still enveloped hers, "what would you do?"

"As long as my arm and hand return to full strength . . ." He hesitated for the shortest of moments, as if leaving her time to say they would or would not, but she did not speak. She did not know. "As long as they return to full strength, then I will return to fight in the king's army, and when the time comes, I will be chief of the clan. There is nothing else I would want to do."

"But if they do not?"

He swallowed and shook his head. "They must."

She considered his hand in hers for a moment, his strong one, running her thumb over the back of it. The skin there was unusually clear of scars. For that matter, she now realized, so was the rest of his body. For a warrior, that was unheard of and bespoke a great skill on his part, and yet he'd sustained a terrible blow to his arm that could render him a warrior no more.

"You do not have many scars for a warrior," she said to him slowly. "How is it you got that one?" She nodded at his arm.

He released her hand and began rubbing the palm of his weak one, his eyes trained on his hands. He did not speak for a long time, though he shook his head slightly and his lips flattened.

"I do not ken exactly how it happened, angel." He sounded confused and a little angry. He kept rubbing his thumb in the palm of his weak hand and did not look at her. "My men did not follow me into the fray," he said. "'Tis the only thing I know for sure. When we fight together we are seldom overcome by the enemy, but alone . . ."

"Why did they not follow you? You were their leader, aye?"

He nodded. "My second, my cousin Cameron, argued that we should retreat, hide. He knew I never withdrew from a battle before it had even been fought. He knew I was determined to take down the traitorous Scots who fought against the freedom of their own countrymen. We argued. 'Twas unusual, for Cameron had never gainsaid my leadership before."

"Why did he argue against you?" she asked quietly.

He closed his eyes, his breath coming faster, his eyebrows drawn down over eyes clenched closed. Jeanette had the sense he was reliving that day, those moments.

"Our men were tired. Some were hurt, but that had never stopped us before. I remember yelling the MacKenzie war cry," he said, his voice hushed. "I flew into the fray, joining the battle before I ever realized my men weren't on my heels, as they were duty bound to be. Too late—I was engaged, cut off from Cameron and the others, surrounded by MacDougalls and English soldiers. The next thing I knew, I was dragging myself from the battlefield. I think I managed to bind my arm enough to stem, if not stop, the blood loss. And then I remember naught until a man from near where the battle was fought came upon me where I lay under thick bushes at the edge of the battlefield. He had to wait until the MacDougalls and the English had moved on before he could try to help any who could still be helped. He told me later it was two full days after the battle ended before he dared venture onto the field. His wife had died recently, so it was up to him to nurse me as best he could. I still cannot ken how he moved me to his cottage, for I was already ravaged with fever by then, and so weak from the blood loss I could barely sit, never mind stand."

He took a deep breath and seemed to pull himself out of the unpleasant memories.

"Why did you look sad when you spoke of duty and destiny?" he asked, clearly done delving into those memories.

Though she had many more questions for him, she would not push him now when he had told her so much already. Now it was her turn. She owed him at least some of the truth, now that he had shared some of his with her. But how much to say when it was no longer her tale to tell? Well, some of it wasn't hers to tell. Some of it clearly was; 'twas just a matter of tiptoeing through the parts she could share and those she had no right to share any longer.

"I was to be Lady of Dunlairig Castle," she began. "I have trained for it my entire life. It was my duty, my destiny, and my greatest desire to take up that role for my clan. But it did not come to pass."

"You were to marry Nicholas?" There was a harsh edge to his voice that she had not previously heard and his hand spasmed, the other one balled into a tight fist. She did not know if the harsh voice came first and the spasm second, or the other way round. She reached for his hand to massage it for him, but he pulled it away from her. "Were you?" he asked again.

"Nay." She almost laughed at the idea. Her cousin would not have brooked anyone else marrying the man, and he had never had eyes for anyone but Rowan. "'Tis not the way of things with the MacAlpins of Dunlairig. Nicholas is not a MacAlpin. Neither was my father, Kenneth, before him."

"I do not understand."

She sighed. "'Tis a MacAlpin woman who chooses her husband, and he becomes chief."

He stopped rubbing his hand, though the tiny movements of his fingers told her it yet hurt him. "A MacAlpin woman? But did not you say Rowan is your cousin and a MacGregor?"

"I did."

"Then why? How?" He looked over at her, confusion thick in his eyes. "Why are you not to be the Lady of Dunlairig Castle?"

She captured her lower lip between her teeth and rubbed the heel of her hand over her aching heart until she came to a decision. 'Twas not her tale to tell, but neither had it been Rowan's to tell Nicholas when she did. Rowan had led Nicholas to the secret of Clan MacAlpin. She could do the same.

"What do you ken of Clan MacAlpin?" she asked him.

"Other than that you are said to shield the Highlands from danger?"

She gasped, her mouth open in the shape of an O.

"Am I not supposed to ken this?" he asked, his whole attention turned to her now.

"'Tis supposed to be a well-guarded secret," she said, her hand once more to her heart. "How did you learn this?"

"Angel, 'tis all anyone could speak of in the castle while I was there, though they did try not to speak of it in my presence. With the curtain wall recently damaged, the great hall and most of your stores destroyed in the fire, and the sure knowledge everyone shared openly that the English were bound for your glen to wipe you all out, there was much conversation about how that protection that had been the clan's for centuries seemed to have vanished with the last Lady, as if she were responsible for it." He cocked his head and narrowed his eyes. "There is a tale I remember from my younger days—a bard told a tale of the Highland Targe. It was said to shield this way into the Highlands, repelling invaders. Is this the protection your kin spoke of?"

The man was astute. "Obviously it does not work that way," she said, "or we would not be hiding in caves."

"But I do not understand what that old tale has to do with why you are not to be the Lady of Dunlairig."

"What else did you learn from the tale?" Her desire to open herself up to this man, to share her story with him as she'd shared her body, shook her. She almost willed him to remember what the bard had recounted.

"There is a targe that has been passed down from one generation of keepers to the next—"

"Guardians," she corrected before she could stop herself.

"Guardians?"

"Aye, one at a time." She leaned toward him, dropping her voice, as if there were anyone else around to overhear. "Before one passes—"

"The next is chosen?"

She nodded.

"How? How is the next chosen?"

Jeanette swallowed and shrugged. She truly had no idea how Rowan had come to be chosen.

"Angel. Jeanette, Rowan was chosen?"

She nodded again, her throat suddenly clogged with anger. "She was."

"But it was supposed to be you. You were supposed to be the Guardian after . . . It was your mother, aye? She was the Guardian before Rowan?"

"Aye."

"Is Rowan of her line, too?"

"Nay. Rowan's da was the brother of my da. Her mother was no kin of any of us."

"Then why?"

She looked at him. "If I tell you, you must promise me never to speak of any of this to anyone, ever."

"You would trust me so much?" he asked.

She trusted him with her life, and perhaps with her heart. Was there more trust she could have for him?

"Promise?" she said.

"I do. I vow upon my honor to keep all that I ken of the Highland Targe and its Guardians between us alone."

She stared at him for long moments, trying to decide why she was telling him this secret. Was it to reassert her right to tell it? Or was it because she knew, somewhere deep inside her, that her destiny and his were inextricably entwined? If she was honest about it, it was both. She needed him. The clan needed him, and he would be of more use to them if he understood exactly what motivated the English to hunt them down.

"Each Guardian has a natural gift that is enhanced by the Targe when she becomes the Guardian," Jeanette said quietly.

Malcolm drew breath as if he already had a question, but he did not ask it.

"Rowan has a very powerful gift, one passed down to her by her own mother, though none of us realized it until she was chosen as the Guardian."

"Your mother chose her?" The question popped out as if he couldn't stop it.

"Nay," she answered. "Nay, my mum thought 'twould be me next and worked hard to make that so, as did I. Whatever power there is in the Targe chose Rowan and her gift for moving things with her . . ."—she looked at him, wondering if he would believe her—"with her mind. Whatever that force is, it took the Guardianship from my mum and forced it upon Rowan, though she fought it."

He was quiet for long moments. She held her breath, waiting for him to claim her daft, deranged, or simply a liar.

"You do not have such a gift?"

Giddiness overtook her at the simple question so at odds with what she expected. She shook her head. "We thought my aptitude for healing was my gift, but it seems not."

He rubbed the healing gash on his arm. "You do have a remarkable gift, regardless of whether you were chosen or not, my angel. It has only been a few days and my arm has moved from fester and pain to the gash closing quickly and itching." He leaned over and kissed her sweetly. "'Tis already more than I could have hoped for, and yet I have confidence 'twill heal fully very soon because of your gift."

"That healing came from the wellspring." She almost added "my love" but stopped herself before it came out. She was truly falling too fast for her golden warrior. She smiled a little. "Perhaps I have some skill, but not enough to be chosen."

"And 'tis usually the eldest daughter chosen?"

"Aye."

"Just as I have a duty and destiny, you did, too." He raised her hand and placed a sweet kiss on her knuckles. "We are alike more than we knew," Malcolm said quietly. "I, too, have trained my whole life to take up my duty and my destiny. If not for your gift of healing, I might never have been able to take up that mantle and become chief after my father."

"Are those all your questions?" she asked.

"Nay."

"But you do not ask them."

"You have shared more than you are comfortable with already this day."

As he had, she thought.

"If I need to ken more," he continued, "you will tell me when the time is right."

"Thank you," she said. "I have had no one to speak to about any of this and you have lifted a burden by listening, as I hope I lifted some of yours."

"You did, angel." Though he did not look unburdened. His brow was still furrowed and his eyebrows drawn down low. "I would not see you sad, Jeanette, nor worried if there was aught I could do to prevent it." He reached for her pale braid hanging over her shoulder, and ran his hand down its length before pulling her into his arms and holding her.

She wrapped her arms around his waist, tucked her head in the hollow of his shoulder, and peace settled over them. The rain was lessening now and she found, despite being cold and wet, she did not want to leave their rustic shelter just yet. Being held by this man, and holding him, was a different sort of intimacy than they had shared earlier this day, but its effect was every bit as profound on her heart, calming and settling her with a feeling that this was exactly where she was supposed to be.

A bark sounded from just outside the wall they leaned against, but Jeanette did not pay it much mind. The bark came again, but it was not a dog. It was a roe deer. Jeanette lifted her head, listening as the bark came once more, closer now, more insistent.

"'Tis a roe deer," she whispered.

"Aye." His voice was quiet as if he was drifting on the edge of sleep.

"I dreamed of a stag last night," she said, rising and immediately missing the feel of Malcolm's arm around her, his cheek resting on her head, but she had to look.

A stag with one bent antler stood—not ten feet away from the break in the wall that was once a small window—looking directly at her. Jeanette's breath caught.

"What is it?" Malcolm asked. He was immediately by her side.

"I have dreamed of that deer."

The deer gave that odd, almost doglike bark once more and looked behind him, then back at Jeanette.

"We must go," she whispered. "Someone approaches."

"The deer told you that?"

"Aye." But she was as puzzled by her words as Malcolm looked. She had no idea why she felt so strongly that the deer was here to warn her, but she was certain that that was exactly what he was here for.

MALCOLM AND JEANETTE CROUCHED WITHIN THE DEEP SHADOWS of the forest, not far from the tumbled-down cottage, listening intently. The stag had fled in the same direction as soon as they had begun to move, disappearing as easily as he had appeared. They had shed their baskets quickly when they made it into the wood and hid them in a thick copse of evergreen bushes.

"Perhaps your deer friend was wrong," Malcolm said quietly, only half in jest. Whoever or whatever came this way would not get past him if they offered any danger to Jeanette or her kin.

"Wheesht!" She looked over at him. "I dinna understand it either, but I know he was here to warn us," she whispered, her mouth so close to his ear, he could feel her breath upon his skin. "Someone comes!" Her words were very nearly silent now, but the tension in her body spoke loudly.

Malcolm was grateful for the need to focus on something other than the woman next to him. As they waited, distinctly English voices filtered through the trees, not close enough to make out their words yet, but moving steadily toward them.

"I tell ye, ye worthless bit of offal"—their words became clear as they neared Malcolm and Jeanette's hiding place—"the grazing area up here will not work for us. 'Tis too open, it is. And 'tis clear the blasted Scots bastards frequent the nasty little hovels regularly. They will discover us there far too easily, even for the daft likes of them."

There was another man, but all Malcolm could make out was a deep grunt, no words.

He and Jeanette held perfectly still, hidden by a thicket of prickly brambles between them and the path the English soldiers followed, and they watched as two men passed them, followed by four more dour-faced and dirty soldiers.

"We need to choose one of the deep valleys that run through these mountains," the first voice was saying just as the front two men stepped into a pool of dappled sunlight.

Jeanette gasped, but covered her mouth so quickly, the English soldier didn't seem to hear her. She grabbed Malcolm's arm with her other hand to pull his attention to her.

" 'Tis the English soldier we met on the ben," she mouthed at him, no sound accompanying the words.

Malcolm nodded, and quickly turned his attention back to the soldiers, his mind racing through attack scenarios. Instinct screamed at him to take these men out now.

"Nay," another of the soldiers said. "Valleys are traps, no matter how well hidden they are from our enemies. I'll not risk the king's men being cornered like rats in a trap."

All six of the battered and tattered soldiers hurried past Malcolm and Jeanette, five following close behind the soldier who appeared in charge, their gazes constantly shifting about them, as if they knew they were watched, or they feared attack, as well they should.

"Angel," he whispered, "stay here."

"Where are you going?" There was no fear in her voice.

"I will take them out one by one. We cannot have the English wandering these bens."

"Nay." She grabbed his arm to hold him by her side.

"I need to position myself nearer them before they move too far away," he said.

"I agree, but not to attack them." She looked pointedly at his right hand. "Your arm and hand are not strong enough to be of much use in a fight."

Anger rose in him like a dark tide. "I am a warrior," he hissed.

"I do not question that, but in truth you ken you are not ready to fight six English soldiers without a sword and on your own." There was no pity in her eyes, nor in the touch of her hand upon his shoulder. There was strength in both, revealing an iron will he had not thought the beautiful and dutiful Jeanette possessed. "But that does not mean we cannot turn this to our advantage." She raised a delicately arched, pale eyebrow at him in challenge.

"What do you have in mind?" he asked.

"You ken Nicholas, Rowan's husband, was a spy for the English when he came here?"

"I heard the tale, aye."

"He was able to accomplish much in his craft by simply listening. Perhaps these English curs will reveal something of their plans if we but listen for them?"

If any of his compatriots had said such a thing to him, he would have called them cowards, or worse, but given that the lass knew all too well that his arm was not ready for battle, much less a battle of six to one, he weighed her words with more consideration.

"Very well. Let us move close enough to spy upon these men and see what we can learn, though I do not like leaving them alive."

A hard glint in her eye told him she was as anxious for their demise as he was. "Their deaths will come soon enough."

CHAPTER NINE

JEANETTE'S LEGS WERE STARTING TO CRAMP AND HER FEET were falling asleep where she knelt behind a tree, but she refused to move. She barely breathed, which might have contributed to her discomfort. Nearby, four English soldiers stood, just beyond the tree line at the edge of the meadow that served as the clan's summer shieling. Its grasses were already lush with summer's onset. Malcolm was situated across the path the English had followed to the shieling. The two of them had been in these positions for nearly an hour, waiting for the two English soldiers—whom she thought of as the scout, the gap-toothed man they had confronted on the trail the first day she met Malcolm, and who seemed to know about the shieling before they got there, and the leader, who was clearly in command of this group—to finish their inspection of the huts and surrounding large upland meadow.

Her thoughts drifted back to that moment in the abandoned cottage when she had seen the stag and known, though she knew not how, that he was there to warn her. Chills raced over her skin, raising the hairs at the nape of her neck as she realized this was twice in less than a day that the stag with the bent antler had come to her—once while dreaming, once while awake. She had read of animals acting as guides in the chronicles of the Guardians but she could not remember which of the Guardians had them, nor what their particular gifts were.

Gifts. Was it possible? Was she finally manifesting a gift? Elation burst in her chest like the sun coming out from behind

109

stormy clouds, but she quickly tamped it down. It no longer mattered if she had a gift. Rowan was the Lady of Dunlairig. Rowan was the Guardian of the Targe. 'Twas too late for Jeanette to take up the role for which she had trained her entire life.

Still, Rowan's gift was important for the defense of the clan in this trying time. Perhaps . . . Jeanette refused to allow herself to hope, but it would not hurt to look to the chronicles to see if anyone who was not a Guardian had ever shown a gift of warning, for that was the only thing she could think it could be. Which would mean her dream was a warning, though it had felt more like the stag had guided her somewhere important.

She looked to where she knew Malcolm was hidden, though she could not see him. He had not questioned her when she said she'd dreamed of the stag, and he had not hesitated when she told him the stag had warned them to get them safely hidden in the wood . . . and just in time to escape being found by the English patrol. Would he help her find the place the stag had led her to in the dream? Perhaps she'd find some answers there.

Voices pulled her from her musings.

"Did I not say this would not do?" The gap-toothed soldier's voice was harsh, with just a hint of a threat in it. "You have wasted time. There is a better place, as I said this morn. 'Tis plenty big, and it is hidden from the usual travels of men in these parts."

The leader scowled at the man, and Jeanette could only wonder what they meant to hide.

"Show us," was all he said and they all turned to descend the ben.

When the English had passed by their positions, Malcolm rejoined Jeanette.

" 'Twould seem you were correct," he said under his breath, grinning at her. "There is much to be gained by spying."

She was surprised that he thought so, but pleased. Without another word they followed the English, determined to find out where they were bound this time. She would have to wait a little longer to find out exactly what her dream meant.

Malcolm followed along behind Jeanette as he had done for hours now. The pleasure of watching the sway of her hips no longer distracted him from the fatigue that weighed him down. They had left the caves early this morn and now it was nearly dark, which, this time of year, meant it was late indeed. The day, which had started out so promising, had ended up proving to him that he was no longer as strong as he'd once been. He'd lost more than the use of his hand and arm in that battle.

Irritation flared, breaking through his exhaustion long enough to remind him that the English were responsible for his injury, for the troubles that had come to Jeanette and her clan, and for spoiling a day that had gifted him with Jeanette all to himself. He watched her as she moved quietly, like she was more creature of the forest than woman of the castle, following a trail that was becoming increasingly difficult to see in the deepening darkness. Her pale hair almost glowed, as if she were moonlight itself. He remembered how soft it was, silky and fine, and wondered when he would get the opportunity to run his fingers through it again.

Damned English.

If he'd known 'twould take so long to discover what they were about, he would have been less open to spying on them and more insistent that they simply kill all the bastards immediately.

He rolled his right shoulder, imagining the bunch of his muscles as he hefted his claymore once more—the claymore he had left behind in the cave in spite of his instinct and habit to keep it ever with him.

But he could not wield it with only one strong hand. He tried to make a fist again, as he had been doing during this whole mad scramble after the English, but the more he forced his fingers to curl inward, the more they cramped. Frustration had him cursing under his breath. How could he be of any use to Jeanette if he could not defend her and her people, never mind his own? What sort of chief would he make with only one useful arm? What sort of husband, or father?

He used his left hand to force his right into the fist he needed but he could not keep that hand tightened.

Useless.

He was useless as a warrior so he was forced to play at spy. What had seemed a brilliant alternative earlier now rankled. 'Twas no way to be a chief, to Malcolm's way of thinking. A chief needed to be a leader in all things, especially war. He would have to work even harder than he had been to regain his strength. He would regain the use of his hand, and then he would once more be a warrior unsurpassed by any other. He would once more be worthy of his duty as future chief of his clan.

Jeanette stumbled in front of him, falling to the ground with a strangled cry before he could even reach out to her.

"Angel, are you all right?" He crouched beside her, helping her to sit up. Up close, he could see the exhaustion in her face and realized that she had been pushing herself as hard as he'd pushed himself. If he'd not been so wrapped up in his thoughts and injured pride, he might have noticed and used his own fatigue as an excuse to make her stop and rest.

"Aye," she whispered, pushing herself into an awkward sitting position. "I am sorry. I was trying to be careful but I think I tripped over a root."

The sound of men crashing through the wood caught the attention of both of them.

"'Tis the English," he whispered, pulling her quickly to her feet. "Can you walk?"

"I can." Her voice matched his in volume but with an edge of panic. "They must have heard me cry out. We must run!"

"If we run, they will hear us, and we shall both likely hurt ourselves. It is too dark for quick travel now." He looked about them but could see little in the almost complete darkness. The sound of men moving rapidly through the forest sent him into the same focused state of mind as when he enjoined a battle. But he was no longer a warrior rushing into the fray. He could not charge his foes, claymore drawn. Jeanette needed a warrior in this moment, not a sham of a spy. The need to protect her screamed through him, and yet he had never felt so powerless in all his life.

SCOTIA PLUNGED DOWN THE BEN JUST AS DUSK WAS BEGINNING to fall, following Myles, a castle guard not much older than herself who had been assigned to the caves. They ran as fast as they dared through the forest. She knew they were getting close to the warriors' camp when she started to hear the quiet *hur-er* of a tawny owl, the signal the clan used when they did not wish to reveal their positions. Myles responded in kind and no one stopped them.

As they skidded to a stop in the middle of a copse of trees, she saw a few tents, but little else. A scream built within her that someone should be standing guard, that someone should do something to stop this nightmare that had engulfed all of them, but she could not draw enough breath to speak, never mind yell.

"Scotia? Myles? What is it?"

She whirled to find Duncan, her childhood protector, now advisor to the chief, striding toward her from out of the wood. The relief that sliced through her at the sight of his familiar face made her knees weak and for a moment she wanted to throw herself into his strong arms and let him shelter her from all the pain that surrounded her, that pushed in on her until she thought she might collapse from the sheer weight of her grief.

But Duncan, who had been so sweet to her as a child, would now just chide her for acting like a wean and she'd not give him that satisfaction. Not now. Not ever again. She'd been through too much these last few weeks to ever let anyone hurt her again.

And yet her heart was aching with fear.

Nicholas, Rowan, and, it seemed, every warrior of the clan gathered around Scotia and Myles.

"Jeanette and Malcolm are missing," she said as calmly as her labored breathing would allow. "They left the glen this morning to gather heather for mattresses. When they didn't come back, I went in search of them."

"By yourself?" Rowan interrupted.

"Nay"—she waved a hand toward Myles. "We tracked Jeanette and Malcolm." She glanced at Duncan, who had once taught her such skills when he was learning them himself. His simple nod of acknowledgment steadied her more than it should have, but not enough. "We found their baskets not far from the shieling, but not them. We went to the shieling and found their tracks again, but from the look of the boot marks in the dirt, soldiers were there, too. We could not find them, nor any sign of them, anywhere after that. We need men to search for them." With each word her voice rose, panic forcing through in spite of her need to hide it.

"Could you tell in what direction the English had gone when they left the shieling?" Nicholas asked Scotia.

"Nay. The grass was well trod from a path in the wood," Myles answered, "but we could not find any trace of the English after just a short way down the path, nor of Jeanette and Malcolm."

Nicholas scowled at the young guard. Scotia knew he had yet to forgive Myles for locking him up in a bothy when it was first revealed that Nicholas was a spy for the English. He had not forgiven Myles, even though it was Uilliam who had put him there; even though it was Uilliam who had then punched him for being a spy.

"Peigi made me bring him along," Scotia said.

"You are sure your sister was not hiding in the wood?" Duncan asked her. "Did you call out for them?"

"I searched," she said, letting her irritation at his doubt lend sharp edges to her words. "I did not call out, in case there were English close enough to hear. I am not daft, you ken?"

"I ken that," Duncan said with a small shake of his head. He turned his attention to Nicholas. "I can start the search from the shieling. Perhaps I can pick up a trail Scotia and Myles did not see."

"By the time you make it there, you'll not be able to see much in the dark," Nicholas said, "and torchlight will only make you a target if there are English still in the area."

Duncan stilled beside Scotia, then looked over at her. "He is right." He drummed his fingers against his thighs. Scotia found the familiar gesture of Duncan's frustration—something she seemed to cause often—oddly calming. "I will head out at false dawn," Duncan said. "'Twill give me enough light to get to the shielings by and I shall be ready to track them once there is enough daylight."

"But they need help now!" Scotia glared at Duncan and Nicholas. They would dally when her sister was in danger?

"There is naught to be done right now. Malcolm is with her, aye?" Nicholas asked.

"He was. There is no guaranteeing he stayed with her. He could be a spy like you, Nicholas, for all we ken." Her words failed to provoke him the way she hoped they would.

"I shall head out early, Scotia," Duncan said, reprimand in his tone, even as the hand he rested on her arm was gentle and reassuring. "'Tis the best we can do. Malcolm will keep her safe. I'm sure of it and of him, even if you are not."

Scotia bit her lip to keep from lashing out at his condescending words. He knew not what it felt like to have his family taken from him one by one. She would see her sister found—for now that was the most important thing. If Malcolm did not keep her safe, his life was forfeit, and this time it would be Scotia, not her father or any other man, who would take justice into her own hands.

CHAPTER TEN

THE PINK AND PURPLE FINGERS OF DAWN WERE VISIBLE HERE and there through the leaves of the trees, but the light had not yet grown strong enough to penetrate the darkness beneath them. Malcolm could not remember the last time he had been so tired, or so determined. He would get Jeanette back to her kin safely, if it took the last ounce of strength and stamina he had.

And he was pretty close to the last of his strength. They both were.

"Are we getting close to the castle, angel?" he asked quietly. He had his good arm wrapped around her waist, supporting her as much as he was able. She was lucky that she had not hurt herself badly when she fell, but even a slight injury grew in pain when not taken care of, and they had not had the time, nor the materials needed, to take care of the scrapes she had sustained.

She did not take her eyes off the ground in front of them as she carefully set her feet, one after the other, on the trail they followed.

"It should be just a little farther. If we had walked along the shore of the loch, we would be there already." Her voice was thick with what he knew must be a potent mix of exhaustion, pain, and hunger. He would give anything to be able to pick her up and carry her back to her home, but his arm would not support her weight. They had debated taking the easier, but more exposed, route once they had found their way within sight of the loch, but both agreed a careful route through the cover of the forest would be wiser, though they would have to be diligent about leaving as little trail behind as possible, which slowed them down even more.

Just then the forest opened up, as if a curtain had been drawn away from a window, and the castle wall loomed ahead of them. The gate was closed, though truly it could not make a difference with part of the curtain wall a pile of rubble and the inhabitants all gone into hiding. They stopped in the cover of the trees and waited.

Jeanette looked around and finally gave a strange *hur-er* sound. Almost immediately they heard the sounds of what must be several men dropping from their watch posts in the trees behind them, but just in case, Malcolm pushed Jeanette behind him and drew his dirk.

"'Tisn't necessary, Malcolm," she said, but her own voice was an almost silent whisper and he knew that she was as on edge as he.

"Jeanette?" A familiar voice came from the shadows.

"Aye, and Malcolm MacKenzie." She stepped from behind Malcolm to stand next to him.

The lanky form of Alastair MacAlpin, Peigi's grandson, stepped into the light. "Why are you here?"

"That is for us to discuss with Nicholas and Rowan," she said, "but we do not ken where the warriors are camped." Two other lads, too old to be weans, but yet too young to be men, came up behind Alastair, their dirks drawn.

"Stand down," Alastair said. He glanced at the lads behind him. "I must take them to the camp. Spread out a bit more so you can watch my area as well as your own." The two nodded, sheathed their dirks, and melted back into the wood.

"How far?" Malcolm asked.

Alastair considered Malcolm, then looked at Jeanette. "Not far. Can you walk some more, mistress?"

Jeanette nodded but Malcolm could see even that was an effort for her. The lass needed sleep, a good meal, and her scrapes and cuts tended, as did he, but they would both have to wait a while longer.

The lad set a steady pace, but not too fast, and Malcolm brought up the rear, determination the only thing keeping him alert. Fortunately, Alastair was true to his word, and it was not long before Malcolm heard the same call Jeanette had used. They walked a few more minutes and came to a stop in the midst of trees and bracken that looked nothing like a camp and everything like the rest of the wood they had been traversing. Alastair gave a shrill whistle and suddenly they were surrounded by the MacAlpin warriors Malcolm had seen at the castle, with their swords drawn.

"Where are Rowan and Nicholas?" Jeanette asked. "We need to speak with them immediately."

"There is no one following them." The voice came from behind Malcolm and though he did not recognize it, he would lay odds it was one of the lads Alastair had sent back to resume their watch. He nodded in appreciation for the caution the clan took.

"Uilliam? I ken you are there," Jeanette said as she turned to look around her. Her voice was stronger than Malcolm expected. "Take us to them." It was not a request, but a command spoken by someone used to having her instructions followed, and it was a side of Jeanette he had not yet seen.

The great black-haired bear of a man he'd met in the castle separated himself from the deep shadows of the forest. "Back to yer posts, lads," he said to the warriors, even as he was glaring at Malcolm, his eyes squinting and his face grim. "Come with me," he said to both of them.

"Rowan! Nicholas!" Uilliam yelled as they came within sight of a less-densely-treed area with a few tents set up in the space between trees. "They are safe!" He held up a hand toward Jeanette and Malcolm as Rowan and Scotia burst out of the largest of the tents set right in the middle of the campsite. Nicholas came running from the far side of the camp and young Myles rose from where he'd been sitting with his back against a tree, not far from Rowan's tent.

"Why are you here?" Scotia demanded even as she swept her sister into a fierce embrace, forcing Malcolm to step out of the way. "You were supposed to return to the caves!"

Rowan hugged both of them.

"Scotia thought you two had been captured by English soldiers," Nicholas said as he joined them.

"We nearly were," Malcolm said. "How did you ken that?" he asked Scotia.

The lass scowled at him as she stood between Jeanette and Rowan, her arms looped around both women's waists as if she needed to touch them, to hang on to them. "When you did not return by midafternoon, Myles and I went in search of you. We could see where you had been harvesting heather—"

Malcolm saw Jeanette's pale cheeks pinken even as he tried to suppress the shot of desire that hit him, in spite of his fatigue, at the mention of their trysting place.

"—Then found your tracks again at the edge of the shieling. 'Twas clear English soldiers had been there and you were nowhere to be found, so I thought . . ." Scotia swallowed hard and blinked fast, pulling her cousin and her sister closer. "I will not lose anyone else," she said, the momentary weakness now replaced by a glittering hardness in her eyes and a determined set to her chin.

"We escaped their notice," Jeanette said, hugging Scotia tight. "In fact, we followed them in the hopes of learning something of use." Her face turned colder than Malcolm had ever thought it could. The lass was as fiercely protective of her clan as he was of his.

"Nicholas," she said, "the bastard Sassenach that Malcolm and I encountered on the ben is acting as scout for them."

"So there are more, as Scotia reported," Uilliam said as he joined the group.

"Six, at least that's how many we saw," Malcolm said. "We cannot say if there are more, for we were forced to break off our trailing them."

Uilliam tugged on his beard and gave Malcolm a harsh look. "Nicholas," he said, "we need to send word to Duncan to return."

Nicholas nodded. "Myles, Alastair: Duncan headed for the shieling to try to pick up their tracks. Retrieve him and his party quickly, but carefully lest the English are about again this day."

"Duncan is looking for us?" Jeanette asked, looking down at Scotia as if she suspected the girl had sent him on an errand.

"He is. His tracking skills are better than anyone else's, including mine and Myles's. I made him promise he would find you."

"What happened to you?" Nicholas asked.

"'Tis a long story, with little good news to come out of it," Jeanette said, with a brief glance at Malcolm. She lifted her skirts just enough to show her scraped-up ankle and shin. "I would have this seen to, and we both need a meal, while we will tell you all that we have learned."

"Come, Cousin. I will see to you. You"—Rowan pointed at Scotia—"fetch what's left of the morning meal to my tent. The rest of you, join us there anon." With that, she took Jeanette from Scotia's embrace and led her to the large tent in the middle of the camp.

"You should not have given in to the lassie's daft notion of following the English," Uilliam snarled at him, his eyes sparking like flints.

Malcolm pushed his hair out of his face and, trying to ignore his fatigue, turned to face the man square on. "It seemed the best thing to do. I did not ken how far we would have to follow them, nor that we would not be entirely successful."

Uilliam's shaggy head lowered and his eyes narrowed to slits. "If they had caught her, hurt her—"

"I would have killed them, or died trying," Malcolm replied, and knew suddenly that he would indeed give his life to keep Jeanette MacAlpin safe.

It wasn't long before they all reassembled in the chief's tent and Malcolm was grateful to find Jeanette sitting on a small bench next to Rowan, an empty porridge bowl balanced on her lap.

"No sign of Duncan yet?" Nicholas asked Uilliam, as Scotia handed Malcolm a bowl of his own.

"Nay, but the man is quick on his feet, he may have gotten farther up the ben than we expected before the lads could catch up to him. I've sent word to Peigi that these three"—he nodded at Jeanette, Scotia, who had taken her seat on the bench, too, and Malcolm—"are safely with us."

Nicholas nodded. "We will start without Duncan, then." He looked from Malcolm to Jeanette and back. "Will you tell us why the two of you spent the night in the wood?"

Malcolm wasn't pleased with the man's tone, but then again, he had managed to return Jeanette to her kin in less-than-perfect health. He would be unhappy should someone else have returned her in a like state. Quickly he explained how they had come to discover the English scouting party, saying only that they had been sheltering from the rain when it interrupted their harvesting of the heather for Peigi's mattress, and leaving out the more personal activities they had enjoyed in between those events.

"We were still following them at a distance when it grew quite dark. We were tired, trying to follow the trail in spite of the darkness. Jeanette tripped on a tree root and the noise drew the attention of the scouting party. We were able to hide in the bracken, thanks mostly to the darkness and Jeanette's stoic nature." He smiled at her and was rewarded with a quiet smile in return.

"We had to wait there while they searched for us," she said, taking up the story. "They had only sent two back to see what the noise was, and they were none too happy about it. I think they must have been as tired and hungry as we were."

"Why is that?" Nicholas asked.

"They were grumbling about spending the whole day traipsing up and down a mountain," Jeanette said. "They said 'twas a waste of time when they'd already found a perfectly suitable location for the men who would soon arrive to wipe out that 'bastard traitor spy and his witch.'"

To Nicholas's credit, Malcolm could see the ire that rose in the man. He was not as cool and detached as he seemed after all.

"Is that all they said?" Nicholas asked.

"Aye," Malcolm answered. "They said nothing else, but they tarried nearby for so long, any lingering twilight had been extinguished and we could not go anywhere—"

"Except to extricate ourselves from the brambles," Jeanette interjected.

"Aye, except for that, until the moon rose, which was hardly an hour before dawn. Once we could see, we made our way slowly to the castle, and then here."

"Kenneth will not like it that you spent a night unchaperoned with his daughter, instead of continuing following the English," Uilliam said, tugging hard on his beard.

"He will not, but we need not tell him, either," Jeanette said. "And it was not as you would imply, Uilliam. We were damp from the earlier rain, cold. We had been traveling almost the entire day without rest or food, and it was too dark to follow anyone. We kept each other warm, nothing more, and when the light came we decided together 'twas best if we found this camp in the hope Duncan would be here. He is far more skilled at tracking than we are. He should be sent to finish what we started."

As if summoned, Duncan slipped through the tent flaps at that moment, joining the gathering just in time to hear his name.

"I am happy to hear you two are safe," he said, smiling at Jeanette and slapping Malcolm hard on the back. "Who am I to track now?" he asked.

"The English," Rowan said, and caught him up quickly with the tale Jeanette and Malcolm had told.

Duncan nodded. "Can you tell me where you lost them?" he asked Jeanette.

"I can take you there," Malcolm said before Jeanette could answer.

Duncan turned his attention to him now. "Are you sure?"

Malcolm wanted sleep more than anything, but that was not to be and it would not be the first time he had forgone it for the safety of those under his protection. He looked at Jeanette, but answered Duncan.

"Aye, but not until I have some answers." The whole way back to the castle this morning, Malcolm had mulled over what they had heard the soldiers say, the murder of Jeanette's mother, the things Nicholas had told him about how he had come to this place, the legend of the Highland Targe that Jeanette had shared with him, and the certainty the MacAlpin clan had, rightly, it would seem, that the English would return to attack them again.

If he was to keep Jeanette safe, and by extension, her clan, he had to know exactly what the enemy was thinking and what the stakes were for success and for failure. Now was the moment when he had some leverage to get these answers and he wasn't about to let it pass.

He wasn't sure what to ask first until the question he most wanted answered slipped from his lips. "Why do they say you are a witch?" he asked Rowan. He wanted to ask if it had aught to do with her being the Guardian of the Targe but he had promised Jeanette not to speak of that knowledge to anyone.

Everyone went deathly silent. Rowan and Jeanette locked eyes on each other. Nicholas would not meet Malcolm's eyes. Only Scotia glared at him.

"He must swear fealty to Rowan before anyone says anything," the younger woman said. Her voice was hard and he thought she would run him through with a sword if he gainsaid her demand.

Quietly, and without prevarication, he held her glare. "That I cannot do, Scotia. My fealty resides with my father and my clan."

"Then he must leave now," she said, not taking her eyes off Malcolm, but clearly speaking to her own chief, Nicholas. "He asks too many questions for an outsider."

"Nay," Jeanette said, breaking away from whatever had passed between herself and Rowan and looking to Malcolm, now. She reached for his hand and he stepped close enough to enfold hers in his. "I have not finished my promise to him, to heal his arm. And even were that finished, we need his knowledge of the English and how they fight."

Scotia started to argue, but Nicholas stopped her with a glance. Malcolm doubted most people could do that as easily as Nicholas could, once the lass set her mind to something.

"Jeanette is right," Nicholas said. "We have need of his knowledge. I know much of the things that drive the English to battle, but not much of battle itself. Malcolm has that experience, and we can benefit from his insight if we are to defend ourselves against this incursion. The more he understands of our situation, the better he can help us." He closed the space between them.

Jeanette squeezed Malcolm's hand tighter, and his heart warmed at her unwavering support.

"You have sworn fealty to your chief and your clan." It was a statement from Nicholas that needed no answer. "You have sworn fealty to your king, Robert the Bruce?"

"Aye. I have served in his army. He is above my father and there is no conflict within my fealty to both of them."

"Good. Your fealty to King Robert seals your lips on matters of import to him, aye?"

"Secrets, strategies, plans. Aye."

"Then your promise to honor your fealty to King Robert will suffice since what we must tell you pertains to the safety of not only our king, but the entire country of Scotland."

Malcolm glanced at Jeanette and found her eyes trained on his. She nodded at him.

"Your promise, Malcolm," she said. "Please."

"Of course," he said, making a point of looking each of the women and Nicholas in the eye, then offering his dirk, hilt first, to Nicholas. "You have my promise that I will keep whatever secrets you tell me. I also promise that while I bide with your clan, I will do everything within my power to help repel the English and keep your clan safe from them."

"Rowan?" Nicholas said. "'Tis up to you if we take Malcolm into our confidence."

"Jeanette?" Rowan took her cousin's hand. "Do you trust him with this?"

"I do," Jeanette said. "I trust him with my life, and the lives of my family. And though I cannot say why, I am certain he was sent here so I could help him, and he us."

Malcolm swallowed around a large lump in his throat. He had the trust of his clan, his men—a niggling idea that maybe that one wasn't as true as it had once been tried to distract him—but never had he received such explicit trust from anyone. He had done little to earn such trust from Jeanette, but he made a vow there and then to be worthy of it, and of her.

"Jeanette, you ken more than any of us about . . . ," Rowan said.

"He already kens that you are Guardian, and that the MacAlpins are said to guard the Highlands." There was grumbling from everyone. "He figured out much of it on his own"—she looked pointedly at Nicholas and Rowan—"as Nicholas did. I but corrected the knowledge he had gleaned. He kens a little of what the Targe is, and what Rowan can do." Quickly she told Malcolm the rest of the lore that he had not figured out about the Highland Targe and its long line of Guardians. "The Guardian is meant to draw upon the power of the Targe in order to safeguard this route into the Highlands from invasion."

Malcolm let the information settle over him. He had heard the tales of such a mythical Targe but to know it was real tested his beliefs.

"Clearly it has not prevented the English from invading so far," he finally said.

"The lore has been lost," Jeanette said. "My mother was able to set protections over the clan, the castle, and use blessings to ensure the fertility of our land and animals. We knew of no need for more than that until Nicholas came amongst us."

"I was sent to steal the Highland Targe." Nicholas took up the story. "Neither the king, nor anyone outside these parts, knew that it was not a true targe. No one knew it required a Guardian." He smiled at his wife.

"I ken Rowan is the Guardian now," Malcolm said. "And Jeanette told me she can move things with naught but her mind."

"Aye," Nicholas said.

"And that is why the king of England wants her dead, why they call her a witch?"

"'Tis."

"Cannot Rowan repel the English with the Targe?"

"I have only just come into my gift recently, and became the Guardian even more recently. I did not have the benefit of previous training for my position, as Jeanette and Scotia did."

"And Jeanette thought she was to be the next Guardian," Malcolm said. It was slowly coming together for him, all the little pieces of information merging to form a picture of an ancient, powerful relic that King Edward would kill to have for his own.

"Aye. After my mum. It might have been Scotia, but . . ."

She didn't finish the sentence. Jeanette and Scotia didn't look at each other, though tension sprang to life between them, as if it bound them together and repelled them at the same time. Malcolm could only guess that the assumption that Scotia would not take her mother's place must be a difficult topic for the sisters, though certainly they were on the same footing now. This explained much of the tension between Rowan and Jeanette, too, and Malcolm began to see the parties in this particular skirmish in a new light.

Jeanette must have been devastated not to follow her mother as Guardian even though she seemed reconciled to it now.

"Why was Rowan chosen then?" he asked, feeling an odd indignation that Jeanette had been passed over in favor of her cousin.

"Her gift. 'Tis strong, defensive. 'Tis what we need, the clan and Scotland, in this time. I have no gift, nor does Scotia. There is no other explanation that I have been able to find or dream up," Jeanette said quietly, as if she were, even now, scouring through her knowledge for a more satisfying answer.

Malcolm resisted the urge to enfold her in his arms and comfort her, for clearly she was unhappy with this situation, though she did her best to move forward and accept it.

And then Jeanette's description of Rowan's gift cut through his emotions and settled in his warrior's mind. Her gift was defensive—though he knew not how powerful, nor how it worked . . . yet. Thanks to Jeanette's odd understanding she'd obtained from the stag, they had escaped discovery yesterday, leaving them in a position of knowledge, of which the English were unaware. His mind began to sort out the things he knew and the things he needed to know.

It was like looking down from the heights over a battlefield— assessing strengths, weaknesses, advantages. And then he remembered the castle bailey and the open space that should have been the curtain wall.

They said the last Lady, the last Guardian, had been able to protect the castle despite the crumbled curtain wall . . .

"What can you do with your gift, Rowan?" he asked.

"So far? I can throw things, bring down stone ledges, topple a tree or two. Mostly I can protect myself, but little more."

He turned his attention from his memory of the castle to the tall, willowy frame of the woman. Fleetingly he thought how much he preferred the soft curves of Jeanette, but he pressed that away lest it distract him from his own particular gift—battle strategy.

"Throw things? Like what? Rocks? A knife?"

Nicholas actually chuckled. "She has thrown a shoe from a window . . . with her mind."

"With her mind." Malcolm shook his head. He had heard the words from Jeanette and now from Nicholas, but he could not imagine how such a thing could be done.

Scotia glared at him, as if she waited for him to question the truth of her cousin's ability. Jeanette smiled, clearly proud of her cousin in spite of the lingering tension between them. Duncan stood with his fists upon his hips, as if daring Malcolm to make light of their Guardian. Nicholas crooked an eyebrow at his wife and she stood, then reached for an ermine sack that Malcolm only now realized always hung at her waist. She did not open it, simply held it in her hand, closed her eyes, and seemed to mutter something under her breath. When she opened her eyes Nicholas held out his hand, Malcolm's dirk laying flat on his palm.

"You'll be wanting to stay on your toes, lad," Nicholas said with a grin.

The next thing Malcolm knew, the dirk was flying out of Nicholas's hand without the man moving any muscles even a wee bit. It flew at Malcolm, just barely missing his head. "Och!" he cried, ducking to the side too late to have it be of any use, but the reflex would not be denied. "God's bones!"

The dirk sliced through the tent, and landed with a thunk that sounded like it had hit a tree.

Rowan grinned. "'Tis not much yet that I can do, but I am getting the hang of it." She released the sack to hang by her side again, and sat back down.

Malcolm was so surprised, he had a hard time forming words. He'd never seen such a thing. "'Tis a formidable weapon if it can be used under duress."

"I have done so," Rowan said, notching her chin up. "I brought down a stone ledge upon the English soldiers who came before in the midst of a battle where I myself had been fighting for my life."

Malcolm added this to his list of assets the MacAlpins could call upon in the coming battle.

"You cannot defend the whole clan, though?"

"Nay, not yet. My aunt could set protections but I have not mastered such a skill."

"How many warriors have you, Nicholas?"

"A score, plus lads, as you have seen this day, who are willing, but not yet well trained."

"Dinna forget the women of the clan," Rowan said. "Even without a gift and the Targe, the women of Dunlairig will defend their homes and their families as fiercely as any man."

Malcolm knew 'twas true of his own clan's womenfolk. He did not doubt 'twas true of the MacAlpin women, as well, though women played a different role in battles. He considered all Jeanette had told him and all he had learned today. He layered upon it the condition of the castle, the English scouting party, and the threat to the "traitor and the witch." He let his gaze linger on Jeanette, still amazed at how much she had come to mean to him in such a brief time, and he made his decision.

"Chief," he addressed Nicholas formally, "do you wish for my help in defending your clan from this English assault?"

Nicholas nodded, moved behind Malcolm, and reached through the rip in the tent, pulling Malcolm's dirk from its landing place. He handed it to Malcolm, hilt first.

Malcolm reached for it with his right hand, only realizing too late that he could not grasp it tightly with that hand. The dirk fell to the ground, its quiet thud loud in the silence of the tent. Malcolm retrieved it from the floor with his left hand, sliding it into its sheath, his humiliation burning in his gut.

Nicholas considered Malcolm for a long time—at least it seemed a long time—before he nodded. "We will take all the help you can give for as long as you can give it. In the meantime," Nicholas said, "we have several immediate problems. Duncan, take Malcolm so he can show you where he and Jeanette lost the trail last night, and find the English party. See if you can learn more about how many there are and what their plans might be. Scotia, you must help Jeanette and Rowan to—"

"We need to return to the caves," Jeanette interrupted. She pushed herself up from the bench. "If you can spare a few guards to return with me and Scotia—"

"I will not go back to the caves," Scotia said, her arms crossed and her chin raised. "I can be of more use here. I can keep watch as well as any of the lads you have doing that task and I will go mad if I have to stay there with all the bairns and weans. I'll not go back."

Jeanette and Rowan exchanged a look that Malcolm could not read, then Rowan looked to Nicholas with a raised eyebrow.

Nicholas considered the lass, and to her credit, Scotia did not fidget or back down, even under the scrutiny of her chief. "You will do as you are told?"

She nodded.

"Without argument?" Rowan added.

"Without argument," Scotia said.

"Very well," Nicholas said. "We can always use more people on watch."

Duncan looked at Malcolm. "We'll away now," he said.

"Do not leave without me, angel," Malcolm said to Jeanette, wondering if he looked as tired as she did. "We can leave for the caves after this business is taken care of. I'll not trust your safety to anyone else."

Jeanette nodded and smiled up at him. "I will wait for you. Find those English soldiers, Malcolm. Find them."

CHAPTER ELEVEN

Two days later, Jeanette sneezed at the dust she was stirring up while sweeping out a tiny cave that would serve well as sleeping quarters for one of the families who were crowded into the main cave with all the rest of the women, children, auld men, and a small contingent of warriors. Jeanette leaned the broom against the wall just inside the cave and stepped out into the waning sunlight.

Malcolm and Duncan had tracked the English to where they had doubled back on Malcolm and Jeanette, but the trail vanished after that. She and Malcolm, along with a few guards, had traveled fast to return to the Glen of Caves and since then she had hardly had a moment to speak to him. He'd been busy training the lads who were big enough to wield anything even vaguely weaponlike, working with the warriors to make sure the passes were watched, and planning ways to protect the clan should the English discover them here. Jeanette had been busy helping the women of the clan clean out the many small caves that riddled the side of the ben, setting up small cookfires, and settling families into the caves as they could. There were far too many of them to continue living on top of each other in the large cave.

Her stomach growled and she yawned. She needed to eat. She needed to sleep. But even more than either of those she needed to get to the chronicles of the Guardians. Ever since that odd moment with the stag in the forest, she had felt there was something ancient at work in her, but she could not remember ever hearing of any Guardian who'd communed with living animals. Animal guides in dreams, yes. 'Twas a common thing for a Guardian to have portentous dreams, but she had not given her dream nearly enough weight, until she'd seen the roebuck in the forest.

She let her gaze settle on Malcolm where he sat near the mouth of the big cave. The day she had seen the stag had been wonderful and difficult. Enlightening and frightening by turns. The time she had spent in Malcolm's company, especially in his embrace, had lifted her spirits and opened her heart to her golden warrior.

She could not help it. She was drawn to the man, thrilling at every small touch, every fleeting glance, every cocky smile and private wink. She always took a bit longer than necessary when tending his arm, taking advantage to feel the heat of his skin against her palms, taking the opportunity to let his scent fill her lungs and linger over her skin. Just thinking about him made her want him just as she had when they trysted near the heather, though 'twas not seemly for a maid to think about a man in such a carnal way.

Suddenly he looked up, catching her eye as if he had felt her gaze upon him. The heat that flared between them took her breath away. Aileas called out that the meal was ready at just that moment. Weans raced between Jeanette and Malcolm, breaking the hold he had on her. And when the clanfolk had settled, Malcolm was nowhere to be seen.

Disappointment was pushed aside quickly when she found him by the fire, getting his food. There was no future for either of them, with the English threatening everything, and his responsibility to his own clan, no matter how much they seemed to crave each other's company, each other's touch, or how many heated looks they exchanged. Nay, there was no future, just an ache that filled her chest. She chided herself for the weakness she allowed the man to create in her.

As everyone waited their turn at the venison, and then settled down around the fire for their meal with the weans, she knew this was her time, finally, to look to the chronicle scrolls. She hurried to the main cave, grabbed a candle, and lit it from the fire that was kept burning just at the mouth of the sheltering rock, then she made her way to the very back of the cave where she had put the scrolls for safekeeping, protected from the damp by their hardened leather tubes. She would find out if what she had experienced with the stag was some sort of gift that ran in the Guardians, for if she was showing signs of a true gift, at least she would have that connection to her mother, and the Guardians that came before her. At least she would have that when Malcolm returned to his own clan and all else had been taken from her.

MALCOLM RETURNED TO THE COOKFIRE WITH HIS NOW EMPTY trencher and refilled it, but not for himself. Jeanette had not joined the clan for the meal. He had hoped she would come and sit beside him, close enough that their hips might touch, and he might be able to lean toward her, whisper in her ear, and feel the heat of her against him. He had thought to tease a laugh from her again, though not in the way he had in the forest overlooking the heather meadow.

His loins reacted to that memory and he had to stop and calm himself. 'Twas a difficult thing to do when the lass had cast him such a look of wanting that he had contemplated dragging her back into that tiny cave she'd been cleaning all afternoon, so he could have her then and there.

He made his way with his laden trencher from the cookfire to the small cave, but it was empty. He looked about, in case he'd missed her, though he doubted he would not have noticed Jeanette's pale hair. She was not amongst the gathering. Instinct had him moving slowly, so as to draw no attention, toward the large cave where their stores were kept and where Jeanette slept. He stopped just inside the gloom, letting his eyes adjust even though 'twas twilight outside. The faint flicker of candlelight shone from the depths of the cavern. He picked his way carefully past the belongings and stores that were amazingly organized and found Jeanette sitting cross-legged on the floor, at least a dozen large scrolls scattered about her. The candle was stuck in a blob of its own melted wax on a large rock she had pulled close enough to illuminate the scroll she was studying.

"Ahem." Malcolm didn't want to startle her.

She glanced up at him, smiled, and motioned for him to sit down. He set the trencher down long enough to move a few of the scrolls, so he could sit close to her, but also so he could look at the scroll that held her attention.

"I brought you food," he said.

"My thanks," she said, not looking up from the scroll and not reaching for the trencher he held up for her to take.

"You need to eat, angel. I have not seen you have more than a morsel since we returned."

She nodded, as if agreeing with him, but she didn't take her eyes from the scroll as she unwound it more, revealing a stunning illustration of fanciful beasts, surrounded by a border of intricate knots.

"I knew it," she said, but he was sure she spoke to herself, not him.

His vanity was momentarily bruised by her lack of attention to him, but then he realized really, it wasn't. She was absorbed in whatever she was reading, her brows drawn down over her clear blue eyes, the left side of her lower lip caught between her teeth. She almost glowed with whatever she was discovering.

Rather than pressing her, he let her focus on the scroll as he awkwardly cut up the meat into bite-sized pieces with his eating knife. He lifted one piece to her mouth and she opened for him, almost as if she didn't realize what she was doing. Slowly she chewed and when she swallowed, he fed her another morsel. The third time he offered her the juicy meat, she looked at him, locking her gaze with his as she opened her mouth, then caught his hand with hers and closed her lips around his fingers, capturing the juice upon her tongue.

Jeanette's breath was unsteady, her lids heavy, and the sigh she gave as he pulled his fingers from her mouth made him swallow hard. Twice.

"You are killing me, angel," he said, knowing his voice revealed exactly how hard he was controlling himself right now. He fed her again and this time, when she closed her eyes and leaned her shoulder against his, he knew he was lost. He would do anything for this woman.

She took the trencher from him then, tugging it from his grasp, and used her own fingers to finish the food.

"Killing is not what I want," she said, but she did not look at him when she said it.

It didn't matter. She wanted him as much as he wanted her and that was enough for the moment.

"What are you reading?" he asked, knowing they needed to think of something besides each other, or risk being found in a very compromising position when the others returned to the cave.

She looked about her. "The chronicles of the Guardians. It is not a complete history of the Guardians, for most surely could not read or write." She lightly touched several scrolls. "These are the oldest."

He added the knowledge of the chronicles to the growing information about the Guardian and the Targe he had collected since he had first met Jeanette, which seemed like months ago but was really only a little over a sennight.

"What are you looking for?" he asked.

She shook her head slowly. "I do not ken exactly." She let her hand trace a beautiful but simple drawing of a stag, her hand not touching the scroll, but hovering just over the lines. "You remember the roe deer at the abandoned cottage?"

"Aye."

"I thought perhaps that might be the manifestation of some gift that runs in the Guardian line."

He took her hand where it had stilled over the drawing and kissed her knuckles. "From what I have been told and have seen myself, there is no doubt that you are of your mother's line."

"I ken that," she said quietly. "I just thought . . . Perhaps . . ."

"Perhaps you were coming into a Guardian gift now?"

She nodded. "'Tis silly. I ken it well. Rowan is Guardian and my only job is to see her trained in the ways of the Guardians, though she does not allow me to do that. I can accept her as Guardian. I have. She did not want it, but she has taken on the responsibilities, chosen her Protector—"

"Her what?" he asked, thinking that sounded like a good role for a husband.

"Her Protector. Nicholas. The Guardian chooses her Protector and he becomes both her husband and the chief of the clan."

"Is that all he gets to do?" He was grinning at her, trying to lighten the mood a little, and he was rewarded for his efforts with a smile.

"He gets to father the next Guardian . . ." And her smile was gone, replaced by a faraway look that he was coming to recognize as Jeanette thinking hard about something.

"Angel?" he prompted her.

"I was just thinking that bearing the next Guardian was another thing that should have fallen to me." She sighed. "'Tis the women of MacAlpin who have always been the Guardian for as long as the chronicle has been kept, until now. I suppose the next Guardian will be of the MacGregor line and I will be only the one to pen the tale." She laid her hand on what looked to be the newest of the scrolls.

Malcolm didn't know what to say so he rubbed his thumb over her knuckles where their clasped hands rested on his knee.

"Did you find nothing about . . . hearing animals?"

She smiled again and it was as if the sun shone down upon the two of them, wrapping them in light and warmth.

"There is some talk of animal guides, but it seems to be a part of other, stronger gifts, which I have shown no sign of."

"Yet," he said.

"I am well past the time my gift, if I were to have one, should have manifested. Scotia, too."

"But didn't Rowan just come into her gift?"

"Aye, but it seems she had it when she was a girl and denied it so long, it ceased to function—until it was needed again."

She leaned against him, once more laying her head upon his shoulder. "I feel so lost, Malcolm. I know not what I am to do with my life anymore. And now Rowan will not let me help her learn the ways of the Guardians just when we need her powers the most."

Malcolm shifted enough to put his arm around her and pull her closer to him, encircling her with his other arm as she put hers around him.

"I have not known you long," Jeanette said, "but I feel . . ."

"I feel the same way," he said, knowing he could not put into words the bond that was building between them anymore than she seemed able. He kissed the top of her head and they sat surrounded by the history of her line in the flickering candlelight until they heard the sounds of fussy bairns being brought into the cave, the first wave of clanfolk settling in for the night.

Jeanette pulled out of his embrace and laid a hand on his cheek. "Thank you for . . ."—even in the faint light he could see her cheeks flush—"for holding me," she finished.

He laid his hand on her cheek, mirroring her soft touch that shot straight through him. "I would do anything for you, angel. Anything."

She rewarded him with another smile, not the bright smile he most wished to see, nor the laughter she had gifted him with in the rainy wood, but it was better than the lost look in her eyes that had torn at him.

"The women and weans are well settled here, are they not?" he asked.

"There is still work to be done clearing out some of the smaller caves so we can spread out a bit, but aye, mostly the work of moving in is done. Why?"

"Tomorrow I need to do a bit more exploring of the glen. I have yet to make it much south of here. Would you come with me? You could say you need to search for herbs for your simples and I could protect you while I do my task, too. Would it raise too many eyebrows?"

"Probably, but I do not care." She gathered up the scrolls and carefully slid them into the hard leather tubes he had seen before. "Peigi will be thrilled if we slip away together."

"That she will," he agreed. "So will I."

CHAPTER TWELVE

THE NEXT MORNING, AS SOON AS EVERYONE HAD BROKEN THEIR fasts and work had been handed out, Jeanette and Malcolm quietly took their leave from the camp with Peigi's full approval, as expected.

Now Jeanette followed Malcolm along a deer trail that tracked along the side of the ben at nearly the same level the main cave was on. Every now and then she'd get a glimpse of the glen below them, spreading out roughly north to south. The pale green of spring's new leaves was maturing, blanketing the entire valley with the deeper green of summer. A hawk wheeled overhead, soaring higher and higher, screeching now and then, until it was little more than a speck in clear sky.

Jeanette let the quiet of the wood sink into her, bringing a calmness to her mind even while her body hummed with expectation. To be alone with Malcolm, even just walking through the wood in silence, was deliciously intimate. She watched him move ahead of her, sureness in every move the man made. He was graceful, really, though she knew that to be an odd way to describe a man. There was no wasted effort on his part, unlike some men who crashed about. She was certain she could be content just watching him for the whole day, and yet her curiosity was getting the better of her.

"Where are we bound?" she asked.

He glanced back at her and grinned, as he so often did. "This trail leads to a narrow pass over the mountain, according to Scotia. She said I must find it, that it would be a good escape route if the clan needed one. I thought, depending on your ankle, we would investigate it. Peigi packed us some food for our midday meal so there's no need to rush."

"She told me we were not to return until dinnertime," Jeanette said.

"Aye, she said the same to me. Do you need to rest, angel?"

"Nay. My ankle is much better and I ken well that it will tighten up if I stop moving for very long. There is something renewing about walking quietly in the wood with no one hunting us, no one chasing us." She smiled at him, amazed that in spite of all the trouble surrounding her clan, she felt almost carefree today. "I think I needed to get away from everything for a while. I think I just needed to set aside my cares for a few hours and remember what it is we are fighting for."

"Aye," he said, looking around them at the massive pines and pale birches that surrounded them. He closed his eyes and took a deep breath. "It smells so good away from the fires and privies."

She laughed and stepped close enough so that he opened his arms to her. She wrapped her arms around his waist and nuzzled her nose into the crook of his neck. "You smell good, too," she said.

"You are tickling me, angel," he said as he managed to capture her lips with his.

Her intention, to simply touch him, changed the instant his lips touched hers. It was as if her skin buzzed and burned all at once. She pressed close to him, moaning when he tightened his arms about her, almost crushing her breasts against the muscled planes of his chest.

How long they stood there, lost in the drugging sensation of the kiss, she didn't know, but they were interrupted by a snort not far away.

A deer stood in the path sideways to them. His rust-colored hide was glossy and he had a small rack of antlers spiking up from his head, one bent at an odd angle. He turned his head in her direction and looked her in the eye, snorted again, and melted into the wood, heading up the ben.

Jeanette and Malcolm stared after him.

"Was that the same deer we saw before?" Malcolm asked. "Did it warn you again?"

She blinked, trying to merge the real deer she had seen twice now, and the deer that had come to her in her dream, into one coherent idea. The same odd barking they had heard at the ruined cottage came from above them, certainly the same deer they had just seen.

"Jeanette? Do we need to take cover?" Malcolm had released her and was scanning the path ahead of and behind them.

She blinked again, still unable to shake the reality from the echo of the dream.

"'Tis the same deer, but I do not think it is a warning this time. He wants us to follow him. I have dreamed this," she said, now looking at Malcolm. "I know where he is taking us."

Without so much as another question Malcolm motioned for her to lead the way.

Unlike her dream, at each turning and branching of the deer trail, Jeanette would glimpse the stag in the distance, as if he waited for her. As soon as she spied him, he'd be off again, disappearing into the forest until another decision about direction was needed.

All the while, Malcolm let her take the lead and set the pace as they followed the stag. The man was remarkably accepting of the things he had encountered since they met at the wellspring. He had accepted that this stag had warned her about the English scouts. And now he had not hesitated to follow her and the stag into the forest. He had accepted that the Highland Targe was not just a story, and that Rowan was the Guardian with something other than the usual abilities of lasses. He had not chided Jeanette for being able to read, nor for looking for answers in the chronicles. He had accepted everything with calm. His trust warmed her in a whole different way than his kisses had.

"Jeanette, have you lost him?" Malcolm's voice was soft, and just behind her, though she had been so lost in her thoughts, she did not know he was there. She had not even realized she had stopped.

"Nay," she said, just as quietly. "Though I ken where we will find him even if I do lose him."

She turned to face him, taking his hands in hers, then looking up into his soft brown-and-green-flecked eyes. He smiled at her, but it was a questioning smile. Jeanette took a deep breath.

"I have seen this before."

"This path? I did not know you had been this way."

"Nay." She shook her head. "I have seen this before, in a dream. The stag, and the entrance to a cave we will find soon."

He lifted one of her hands and laid a gentle kiss upon her knuckles. Heat raced through her, sizzling under her skin in an almost painful yet delicious way.

"You are sure?"

She swallowed. "As sure as I can be of a dream. I do not ken what the importance of this place is where we are led, nor why I am guided there."

"Was I in the dream?"

Jeanette closed her eyes and tried to bring the dream into focus but she did not see Malcolm in any of it.

"Nay," she said.

The stag barked in the distance.

"He is impatient for us to follow," Malcolm said, pushing her a little away from him.

The cool air that flowed between them helped her ground herself in this moment, allowing her to push the dream back into the depths of her mind where it belonged.

"Aye. We have a cave to explore." She tried to make light of it but even she could hear the quaver in her voice.

"Is there danger there, Jeanette?" He gripped her arms now, though one was so much tighter a grip than the other.

"Danger? Nay, I dinna think so."

"Then why do you hesitate?"

"I think . . ." Once more she tried to remember the rest of the dream, searching for a clue as to why she was brought there, but she could not remember anything beyond the deer showing her the dark cleft that led into the mountainside. Her skin prickled at the thought of heading into that passage. "I dinna ken exactly how or why, but I think everything will change in that cave."

"Good change or bad change?" he asked.

The stag barked again, closer now, and more insistent.

"It does not feel bad," she said, not even sure where that sense came from. "But I dinna ken if it is good, either."

"Then we have no choice but to find out for ourselves." He took her hand and pulled her in the direction the stag call had come from.

It was not long before they spied the stag again. The majestic animal snorted at them, as if in disdain that they had tarried when he was in a hurry, but he took off at a slower pace than before, heading straight up the steep slope.

Malcolm followed Jeanette up the steep side of the ben, curiosity and excitement drawing him after her as if they were tethered to each other. He did not understand exactly what was happening, but the lass seemed both sure of herself and tense. Of course, just the idea that they had seen the same stag twice in different places was unusual. And she said she had dreamed about this deer leading them today, which was odd, too. The more he thought about it, the odder it got. She'd dreamed of a

stag with a bent antler, received a warning from him one day—
and he could not deny, no matter how much he'd like to, that the
deer had somehow warned her—then she had seen him again,
the same deer, for the bent antler was unmistakable, doing what
she had dreamed he did . . .

She dreamed it, and then it happened . . .

His mind stuttered and his feet slowed as his thoughts
coalesced into one clear understanding. 'Twasn't a dream she'd
had. 'Twas a vision. She had seen this day, the stag, and the place
that same damned stag was leading them to.

Everything she had shared about her cousin, her clan, and
yet she had not told him what she was. Did she not trust him
with this knowledge? Nay, she trusted him with the secrets of
her clan, so why would she not trust him with this?

"Jeanette!" She was quite a ways ahead of him now and
didn't seem to hear him. He scrambled to catch up to her.
"Jeanette!" He got close enough to tug on her skirt, stopping her
abruptly. She looked back at him from her position just above
him as if he'd awakened her from a deep sleep—or a vision.

She blinked slowly, but didn't say anything.

"Your dream about the stag was no ordinary dream. 'Twas a
vision. You are a seer, angel, are you not?"

"A seer?" She looked away from him but did not resume her
trek up the ben.

"Did you fear what I would do if I knew?" he asked.

"Fear?" She seemed genuinely confused. "Nay." She looked
off into the distance again. "Seer? Do you really think I am a
seer, Malcolm?" The look on her face was hopeful and doubtful,
all at the same time.

Now he was the confused one. "You are, are you not?"

"I do not ken, but I think I might be. 'Tis not uncommon
among Guardians." She stared into the distance again and
Malcolm realized she was not looking at anything, but was lost
in her thoughts, as if she searched deep in her memories as she

had searched in the scrolls last night. "But I am not the Guardian. Rowan is, so why would this manifest now?"

"This has not happened before that dream?" he asked, as puzzled as she was. How could she not know she was a seer?

"A few times when I was a wee lass, but none since then, at least none that I remember." She turned toward him now and sat so that she was looking Malcolm straight in the eye. The stag barked in the distance and she waved a hand in the air as if telling him to wait a moment, though he was not in sight.

"'Twould be a formidable weapon against our enemies, would it not." It wasn't a question, but more like she was thinking out loud.

"Aye, angel, 'twould. Are you certain you have not had more of these dreams since you've been grown?"

She looked off in the distance again, shaking her head slowly. "Dreams fade so fast. But I have always had an uncanny ability to ken where needed herbs are for my healing simples, or what an ill person needs in order to recover, as if the knowledge has been set into my mind when I wasn't paying attention."

"Like in a dream you don't quite remember."

She nodded slowly and only his finger, still under her chin, kept her from gazing away again.

"But this dream you do remember." He did not question her, for 'twas obvious that she did.

She gripped his hand but did not remove it from her chin. "I do—but only to a point."

"Was this conversation part of the dream?"

She closed her eyes this time, then slowly shook her head. "You were not in the dream, at least not that I remember. Let us see what happens and I will know better if I truly had a vision, or if it is only that I have perhaps been here before as a child and do not remember it."

"A test then," he said. "And you will tell me later if you saw this day or if 'tis only an echo of a childhood memory?"

She leaned forward and placed a chaste kiss on his lips, though his blood still heated at the light contact. "I promise." The deer barked again, as if sensing that they were ready to continue.

They only got another glimpse or two of the stag, but the trail was easy to follow, if not easy to climb. As they made their way onto a narrow shelf, there was a final call from the stag.

"He is gone," Jeanette said, and Malcolm could feel that she was right.

"Is this the place?" he asked.

"Aye," she said, wonder in her voice. She reached out and touched the stone face of the mountain, running her finger over what looked to be grooves carved into the rock. "Just as I dreamed it."

He stepped up to get a closer look and found a stylized deer under her fingertips, the right antler bent, just like that of the stag they had followed. A chill ran down his spine. He looked at the ground to see if there were hoofprints there, suddenly not sure if the stag was real or a vision itself, but the shelf was bare stone without even a little dirt to show what had passed by this place.

Jeanette grabbed his hand then and pulled him after her into a dark fissure in the mountainside.

JEANETTE BURST OUT OF THE CONFINING FISSURE, PULLING Malcolm behind her, and into a large sun-filled grotto where the ceiling of what had once been a cave had clearly collapsed long ago. A large pool of crystal-clear water was tucked up against the wall opposite the entrance and took up half the space in the grotto. It was surrounded by jagged rock walls that were covered in ferns and mosses and tiny blooming flowers of blues and yellows that she had not seen anywhere before. The walls were more darkly streaked where water trickled down them from above, splashing just enough to fill the grotto with quiet music, and decorating the plant life with droplets that sparkled in the slanting sunshine. The rest of the floor, from the edge of the pool to the spot where they now stood, was carpeted in thick mosses in more shades of green than she could count.

"'Tis beautiful," Jeanette said, her words like a sigh.

"Aye, 'tis. Do you remember it this way?"

She was quiet as she turned, looking at every part of the grotto before she answered. "I have never been here before, not as a child, nor in my dream, but the entrance . . . the carved deer on the rock next to it . . . those I dreamed about." Jeanette kept her voice even, quiet, though a thrill ran through her unlike anything she had ever experienced before, as if she'd been brought to the brink of discovering a secret treasure. But what was it?

She turned again, taking in the entire grotto. It looked as if it had been hidden here for ages, kept secret from anyone who wasn't led here . . .

Led here. First she'd dreamt of this place, then the stag had literally led her here. But for what purpose?

"Do you see any more carvings like the deer?" she asked Malcolm.

"You look that way," he said, signaling to her right. "I'll look this way. Is there anything specific I should be looking for?"

Jeanette shook her head. "I do not ken, but I have been brought here for a reason and we must discover what it is."

"That we will, angel mine."

The endearment settled her jittery nerves and reminded her that she was not alone in this. Malcolm was here. Malcolm would keep her safe—she knew that, deep in her bones without any help from a vision. He turned away from her and began examining the stone wall surrounding them, and she did the same. Every few feet, at varying heights on the wall, she found carvings of animals done in the same distinctive style. Hares, wolves, an eagle, a serpent, a boar. No more deer.

They called out what they found to each other, for Malcolm found similar animals carved into the walls. When they had both reached the edge of the pool, they walked along it until they met each other.

" 'Tis a magical place," Malcolm said, wonder in his eyes.

"Aye, but I do not ken why I was brought here."

Malcolm reached for her hand, enveloping it in his. "Perhaps we were brought here to understand that your dreams are not just dreams. Perhaps we were brought here to understand that you are a seer."

She looked up and found him staring down at her, wonder and something deeper mingling in his expression as he bent to kiss her.

All thought left her mind as she moved into his arms and lost herself in his kiss. Heat surged through her, as if they stood in the heart of a fire, but it did not hurt. It urged, wrapping around them as if to draw them closer and closer together. Jeanette tilted her head back, baring her neck to Malcolm's lips, building the heat even more. She ran her hands down his back and up again, reveling in the hard muscles that bunched and quivered beneath her touch. But it was not enough. She wanted his golden skin beneath her fingers. She found the pin that held his plaid at his shoulder, and released it, the heavy wool falling behind him. She tugged his tunic free and slid her hands under it, sliding her palms along his back, her breath hitching as his hand cupped her breast and she suddenly needed his palm against her skin, too.

"There are too many clothes between us," she murmured against his lips.

"Aye," was all he said, but he was suddenly busy at the laces of her gown, sliding it off her shoulders and down her arms as soon as they were loosened, the gown puddling at her feet.

When her hands were free of the garment she reached for his belt, letting it fall as her gown had, the rest of his plaid following it to the ground until she was left in her kirtle, and he in his tunic. Suddenly she grew shy.

"Angel?" He tipped her chin up so she had to look at him. "We will stop."

Jeanette swallowed, and let herself see only Malcolm, see only the man she loved. Her breath hitched when she realized 'twas true. She loved him. It had happened so fast, 'twas unseemly, but still, it was true. In the space of ten days she had come to feel more for him than she had ever felt for any man.

Where she had seen only a bleak future for herself when Rowan became Guardian, now she could see happiness, a family of her own, a place for herself in the arms of this strong, honorable man. She was free to choose for herself now, unfettered by the need of the Guardian to choose the clan's chief. She was released from the requirement to bide in Dunlairig, at least once Rowan was trained. For the first time in her life, Jeanette realized, she could do what she wanted without the weight of responsibility that came with being the future Guardian dictating her path.

And she wanted Malcolm for her own.

She shook her head slowly at him. "I do not want to stop, Malcolm. I ken we have not known each other long, and I ken that this is something best kept for the marriage bed, but if there is one thing I have learned these past weeks, it is that life is uncertain and hard and I do not want to depend upon the future for my happiness, for there may not be a future. I am happy with you."

"And I am happy beyond experience with you, Jeanette, angel."

"You did not hesitate in the forest to tryst with me."

"Oh, aye, I did, a lot. But if we continue"—his eyes went dark and the heat that had faded while she pondered her future sprang back to life so fast, it took her breath away—"I will make you mine this day."

She smiled, her heart blossoming at the thought that he wanted her that much. "And I will make you mine."

He pulled her so close, only two thin layers of linen separated her from what she wanted more than anything—this man to be her own.

"Truly?" he whispered as he pressed a light kiss to her lips.

"Truly."

She lifted his tunic once more, breaking the kiss long enough to rid him of it. Stepping back into the circle of his arms, he renewed his exploration of her with his lips as she reveled in the feel of his skin beneath her hands, allowing herself now to explore his back, his arms, skimming lightly over the scar of his remarkably healed wound, his buttocks, then moving her hands between them, running them over his chest. As she skimmed her fingertips over his taut nipples, he groaned and took her mouth with his, letting his tongue play over hers in a dance that sent shafts of desire through her. He swiftly untied the lace of her kirtle and slid it off her, then pulled her hard against him, the evidence of his desire hot between them.

Slowly he lowered her until her back sank into the cool, thick moss carpeting the grotto floor, and he lay over her, nestled in the cradle of her thighs. Instinctively she hooked her legs around his trim waist and pressed against him.

"Not yet, angel," he whispered, his lips against her neck.

Jeanette's heart hammered, and her body hummed with desire and heat. So much heat. And then Malcolm moved down her, trailing sweet kisses over her neck and her breast until he ran his tongue over her almost painfully peaked nipple, drawing a low moan from her such as she'd never heard from herself. She threaded her fingers through his hair, and pulled him closer, closer, until he chuckled and took her into his mouth, pulling hard on her nipple until she writhed beneath him, desperate to reach that peak he'd taken her to before. He moved to the other breast, raising her need even higher. His hand slid over her belly, down between them, until he touched that place between her legs that begged for pressure, for release. He slid a finger into her wetness.

"Aye. There—" Her voice was ragged.

He let out a low growl, as if pleased with what he found, then pulled his hand free.

"Nay, do not stop."

"I have no intention of stopping. Jeanette, sweetheart of mine, open your eyes. I would look into them."

She did, losing herself in the depth of his gaze, the love she saw there, the yearning, and the need that matched her own. She felt a different pressure between her legs, a welcoming pressure, and she followed the demands of her body and let her knees go wide as her hips raised to meet him. Slowly, oh so slowly, he slid into her until she felt a pull, then he retreated.

"You are sure," he said, his teeth gritted together as if he were in pain.

Jeanette took his face in her hands and looked deep into his eyes. "We already belong to each other. I am sure."

He thrust into her, stopping at her quick gasp, holding himself still when all he wanted was to bury himself in the hot wetness of her. After a short moment, she kissed him.

"That is not all there is to it?" she said, a teasing twinkle in her eye that he had not seen before.

"Nay, not nearly." And then he pressed into her, slowly, letting her body become accustomed to him until he could go no deeper, and then she wriggled against him, pressing herself harder to him and he could control himself no longer.

Jeanette's body tightened as he surged into her and retreated, again and again, bringing her closer and closer to that incredible shattering sensation she'd experienced only with this man, bringing her closer, and closer, until he went rigid against her, his back arched, pressing so hard into her she leapt over the precipice, flying with him to heights she had never imagined, both of them shattering, then joining, then shattering again and again and again.

CHAPTER THIRTEEN

Jeanette lay beside Malcolm on the soft moss, slowly coming back to herself as if she had left her body in that moment of union with him and now floated down from dizzying heights. She slowly settled back into herself, the same, but fundamentally different. Gradually, her senses began to gather information from outside her—the trickling and splashing of the water, the lovely green aroma of the moss crushed beneath her, the warm pressure where Malcolm's arm was pressed against hers, their hands clasped as if neither of them could bear to be completely apart from the other after such a wondrous act of joining together.

Cool air settled on her bare skin so she rolled on her side. Malcolm hooked his arm around her and pulled her close against him.

"I did not hurt you badly, did I?" he asked, his voice whisper-soft.

"Nay, hardly at all, and after . . ."—she put her hand on his chest and propped her chin upon it—". . . after, I felt nothing but joy."

"I think you felt a wee bit more than just joy, angel." The teasing glint was back in his eyes and she could not help but laugh.

"Aye, a wee bit more than joy." She stretched up to kiss him when something caught her eye. She stopped and sat up.

"What is it?"

"I am not sure, but I think there is something—" She stood to get a better look and her eyes alit on a large flat stone that sat in the middle of the pool, just below the surface of the water, which was why she had not noticed it before. It was far enough away that she could not step from the shore to the stone.

"Jeanette?" Malcolm rose to stand beside her, looking in the same direction, but he did not seem to see what she did.

She pointed, suddenly sure that was what she was supposed to find.

"Stay here," she said to him as she waded in.

The water was instantly numbing. It was deeper than she had thought, and the stone seemed farther from the shore than she had thought as well. She was quickly up to her waist in the water, but then she scrambled up onto the large stone. Water streamed from her body, disturbing the surface of the stone, which was barely covered by the pool, making it impossible to see the stone itself even while she stood upon it. But she could feel something unusual beneath her feet. She began to trace the grooves she could feel, and quickly determined that they were not natural, but were incised, as were the animal carvings on the grotto walls. She knelt and patiently let the water still as much as it would. Suddenly the carving was revealed: the same three swirling circles within a circle symbol that was incised on the Highland Targe.

She must have gasped or said something, for Malcolm was splashing into the water now.

"Nay, Malcolm! Go back. There is nothing wrong, I was only surprised."

The splashing stopped, but she didn't hear him returning to dry land, either. She looked behind her and found him up to his knees, his expression tense, concerned.

"I am fine," she said. "Go back before your feet turn to icy blocks."

"I shall wait here, lest you need me."

She nodded, realizing just how good a man he was, realizing again that she loved him and she was certain he loved her, too. She would tell him, today, here, in this beautiful place they had discovered together, what her feelings were, but not yet. First she must figure out why this symbol was—

And then she saw a second symbol, just at the edge of the stone, directly in front of her—the symbol her mum had called a mirror, one of the three symbols painted on the inside of the ermine sack that protected the Targe. She ran her finger over it, as she had done with the deer carving, and as she had done with the Targe stone the first time her mother had shown it to her.

She sat back on her heels, closed her eyes, and repeated the prayer of protection and blessing that she had been trying to teach Rowan. Even though Jeanette was not the Guardian, did not have the Targe stone, nor was she trying to use any gift, still she felt it was necessary. Her hands moved through the air in tandem with the words she chanted and a sudden whooshing feeling swept through her as if it rose from the stone itself. Tingling ran under her skin, surging upward through her until she felt the need to raise her arms over her head, hands open to the sky to release it. With that release, a torrent pulsed through her, faster and faster and faster, wrapping her tightly in a maelstrom of images and sensations that enveloped her so completely, she struggled to breathe, struggled to stop them, struggled to hold on to her sanity.

MALCOLM COULD NOT MOVE AS HE WATCHED JEANETTE IN ALL her naked glory as she sat upon the stone, her long pale back to him, saying something to herself as she moved her hands gracefully through the air. It looked to him as if she swirled them in circles, over and over, occasionally throwing them out as if tracing a spike—or the bent antler of their stag guide. This glorious, passionate, smart woman had given herself to him and it had been . . . He did not have words to describe what feelings had rushed through him as they'd coupled.

"Jeanette?" When she did not respond, a spark of worry lit within him. "Angel?" he called again, but she did not seem to hear, and then she rose up onto her knees, her arms stretched over her head. A breeze began to circle in the grotto, lifting Jeanette's pale hair that had come free from its braid sometime while they made love, making it dance about her more and more wildly until, just as suddenly as it had begun, it stopped. Jeanette collapsed back onto her heels, her arms falling limply to her sides. And then she tipped sideways, and fell into the water.

For the longest moment he thought she had done it on purpose, but when she did not stand up he raced toward her, fighting his way through the deeper water, cursing his numb feet, calling her name, louder and louder. When he got to her, he pulled her into his arms, shoved her heavy, wet hair out of her face, and hurried back to the shore. Once there, he laid her on the moss, and checked to make sure she was breathing.

Thank God, she was.

He chafed her freezing hands in his, talking to her all the time, trying to rouse her, warm her. He grabbed her arisaid and his plaid from where they had been abandoned such a short time ago, then pulled her into his lap, pressing her shivering form against his skin, cradling her in his injured arm as he struggled to draw her arisaid around her and his plaid about them both. He tucked her head against him, pressing his cheek to her crown as he tried to rub some warmth into her skin with his good hand and whispered fervent prayers that she would recover quickly from whatever had happened to her.

Slowly, her skin grew less icy against his, but still she did not rouse. Malcolm didn't know when, but the sun had been covered over by thick clouds, leaving the two of them wrapped in the dim coolness of the grotto. He looked toward the narrow fissure and knew he could not carry her out of here, for he had barely fit through himself. If she did not wake soon, they would have to stay the night, and for that they needed shelter, lest it rain, and a fire. But he would not leave her, even for those necessities, until he was sure she was warm.

After what felt like hours, Jeanette finally stopped shivering, though her skin was still icy to the touch. With the clouds thickening and the light dimming, he could wait no longer. He laid her on the soft moss carpet with her arisaid beneath her and his larger plaid carefully wrapped about her, as far away from the water's edge as he could, next to the wall that sloped gently up and inward, giving them at least a little shelter if it rained. She sighed and turned on her side, tucking a hand under her cheek as if she but slept. The vise that had been tightening about his chest loosened slightly as he laid a kiss upon her brow.

"I shall return as soon as I can, angel," he whispered to her, though he doubted she heard him. Quickly, he donned his tunic, securing it with his belt, and slid his dirk into its sheath.

He did not have to go far for ample wood but with the narrow fissure, it took him far too many trips to get enough fuel inside to start a fire. But once it was burning well, he returned to the forest for more deadwood just in case they had to stay the night there, piling it up outside the grotto, where at least it would be easy enough to fetch if they needed more in the night. His stomach grumbled as he laid more wood upon the fire, but he saved the bannocks they had brought with them for Jeanette. It would not be the first time he had spent a day with an empty stomach, though the first he had done so with a heart so heavy.

When he was satisfied the fire would burn for a while, he dropped his belt and dirk nearby, and lay down between Jeanette and the stone wall, snuggling close enough to cradle her back against his chest. Her skin was still cool to the touch, but not icy, as it had been earlier. He prayed his heat, added to that of the fire, would be enough to warm her, enough to hold off a fever. There was little else he could do for her until she awoke. And if she did not awaken soon? He would have to leave her here to get help from someone more able-bodied than himself. He would have to get someone else to rescue his angel when he should be the one to keep her safe. Frustration had him cursing the hand that would not do as he commanded, stopping just short of bashing the offending thing against the stone wall.

He struggled to calm himself but his thoughts kept catching at him, pulling him this way and that. Was this some punishment for their having lain with each other without marriage first? Nay, 'twas not the first time he had done such a thing, though his feelings for this lass— He closed his eyes as he realized that his life would be forever dark if she did not wake up, if she never looked at him again with those summer-sky eyes, if he could not hold her in his arms, if he could not rouse her passion. If he could not simply talk to her, share his meals with her . . . make a family with her.

She belonged to him. She had said it herself, and he belonged to her.

He took a long, shuddering breath as he realized his future had shifted the moment he'd seen her at the healing wellspring. He knew that keeping Jeanette MacAlpin in his life was the thing he wanted most, and once his hand was fully healed, once he was a whole man once more, he would make her his wife. He also knew he could wait no longer to tell her his feelings or to get her promise that she would wed him.

"Jeanette, love? Angel? Please wake up." He rubbed her back between them, hoping just a little more warmth would rouse her. "I have something important to tell you. Do you hear me?"

She slept on, showing no sign of waking, so Malcolm pulled her as close as he could and began to pray.

JEANETTE'S EYES POPPED OPEN AND FOR LONG MOMENTS SHE COULD not remember where she was, nor how she had come to be here.

Nor why her head felt as if someone had taken a hammer to it.

And then it all came rushing back to her—the deer, the grotto, making love with Malcolm.

It was then she realized that she sat in his lap, cradled in his arms. She looked up and found herself face-to-face with the man, his face lined with worry.

"You're awake." His voice was soft, as if he did not wish to startle her. "Are you well?"

She took a long moment, searching inside her for the answer.

"Well enough. I feel a bit like I've been . . ." She couldn't decide how to describe the achy, almost bruised feeling that ran beneath her skin and deep in the middle of her body. "What happened?"

"You were on the rock, then you fell in the water. 'Tis all I know."

"The rock?"

He pointed toward the pool and she remembered walking into it, its icy water numbing her limbs, climbing up onto the stone—then nothing.

"How long?"

"How long have you been sleeping? Half the day but 'twill not be dark for a few hours yet."

"Peigi and the others must be worried for us." She started to rise, but he held her in place, pulling her into a fierce embrace.

"I thought I had lost you when I had only just found you." His voice trembled with his emotions. "Another little while will not make much difference in how much the others worry. You need to eat, and I would make sure you are well enough to travel before we leave this cursed place."

"Cursed?" Something felt wrong about his assessment of the beautiful grotto. She took a deep breath and closed her eyes to calm her racing heart but it only raced faster as she remembered what had toppled her into the water. This was a sacred place. Even more powerful than the wellspring near the castle. But what had happened to give her such certainty? She retraced her actions this day—the stag, finding the grotto, making love with Malcolm. Her entire body flushed at that memory.

"What is it, Jeanette?" His warm hand smoothed over her cheek and cupped the back of her neck. "Open your eyes and look at me. Whatever bedevils you is not real. Look at me."

She opened her eyes to find lines of worry creasing his handsome face. She waited for the twinkle to return to his eyes, but it did not.

"I remember lying in your arms," she said.

"And that causes you worry?"

"Nay. I have no worries, nor regrets, Malcolm." She kissed him, letting the strength of this man envelop her and support her. She took his face in her hands and looked him in the eye. "I love you. I know it has not been long since we met, but in this I am certain: I am yours and you are mine."

"I love you, too," he said, kissing her again. "And I share your certainty." He brushed her tangled hair back from her face. "Will you wed with me, Jeanette?"

"Are we not already?"

He grinned at her then, and she could not help but grin back at him.

"It would seem so. We have declared ourselves, but I think your family would prefer to be present to witness our union. Do you not think so?"

"I do."

"Then we shall wait until we can get your father's blessing. Perhaps I can send word to my kin so they may be here to witness our marriage and share our joy, too."

"Aye, that is the proper way to wed, but I do not want to wait long. I think I shall like sleeping in your arms every night."

"Sleep might not be exactly what you get in my arms."

She snuggled into his embrace where she could feel the low rumble of his teasing laughter reverberate through her body, and gave thanks that such joy had come to her, reminding her that even in this time of such sorrow there was hope for a better future. The moment she thought of the word "future" she remembered what had happened upon the rock.

"Jeanette? What is it? What ails you?"

She scrunched her eyes closed to shut out the images that bombarded her once more, but it did not help, for they had nothing to do with her eyes. Her breaths came fast and hard, as if she were running for her life over rough ground. She tried to push the images away, to stop them, to bottle them up and send them back from whence they came.

"Can you tell me?" Malcolm's voice cut through the onslaught and she reached for it, for him, until she could feel the strength of him surrounding her, protecting her, loving her. His arms pressed her to him. His lips brushed her forehead.

"Visions," was all she could say around the lump that filled her throat and the trembling that overtook her body.

"You are safe with me, Jeanette," he said quietly. "Do not fight them and perhaps they will come more gently. I'll not let anything happen to you." He waited, gently massaging the base of her skull as if he knew that that's where all her tension gripped. Gradually, lulled by his silent ministrations and the need to calm his worry over her, she pushed aside her apprehension and let herself remember.

Visions stormed through her, though this time it was just the memory of them. She took another deep breath and burrowed into his arms. She needed to be grounded in the real as she relived what had occurred. He wrapped his arms around her, one more tightly than the other, and snuggled her against his chest, her head tucked under his chin.

"Tell me, angel. Whatever it was, I'll not let it hurt you again."

She actually chuckled, just a little, at his avowal.

"I swear it."

"I know, Malcolm, but I do not think this is something you can protect me from."

He pulled back just enough to look into her eyes. "I will do everything I can to keep you from harm. Do you doubt me?"

"Nay." Now she reached up and laid her palm against his scratchy cheek, then kissed him lightly and whispered against his lips, "I do not doubt you."

"Then tell me why you do not think I can protect you from whatever happened."

"Because it was all visions—nothing physical—though I feel as if I've been in a battle." She remembered his injury earned in real battle, and amended her words. "A fight. Malcolm, as soon as I finished the prayer of protection—"

"With your hands in the air?"

"Aye. As soon as I finished, 'twas as if a dam broke within me. Visions flowed through me so swiftly, I could not focus on any one of them."

"They hurt you?"

"Not exactly. 'Tis more like they rubbed the inside of my skin raw from passing through so quickly."

He ran a hand down her arm as if he searched for injuries, but he did not look away. "Has this happened before?"

"Like this? Nay. But you said yourself you think I am a seer, and we were led here by the stag for a reason. I think the reason was to release my gift. On the stone, out in the water, there is a symbol I have seen on the Targe stone, and another I have seen painted on the inside of the sack it is carried in. Mum always called it the mirror—a symbol for visions, for seers."

He stilled. "What did you see?"

She shook her head. "I do not ken exactly. The visions all went through me so fast, as if they had been trying to get out for a long time. I cannot separate one from the other enough to understand what I was being shown."

" 'Twas the future?"

She shook her head again. "I cannot say that, either, though I think it likely."

She could see the calculation happening within him as he weighed what she had said.

"'Twould be a powerful weapon against the English if you could see into the future, if we could ken, ahead of time, where they would be, or how many of them gathered to attack Dunlairig—or King Robert."

Jeanette swallowed hard. "I will have to learn how to use it before it will be of any use to anyone."

"Aye."

She pulled herself out of the comfort of his lap and faced the pool, only then realizing that all she had was her arisaid to wrap about her nakedness.

"What are you doing?" Malcolm asked, standing beside her. "You are not going back into that pool, not this day."

"But what if this is the only place the visions will come to me?"

"Then we will return here tomorrow, or the next day." He pushed a bannock into her hand. "Eat, angel, then we must head back to the caves before it gets too dark to do so safely."

She could feel Malcolm watching her as she nibbled on the bannock and considered everything that had happened in this grotto and what could be learned from it. She had given herself to Malcolm, and of all that had passed this day, that was the one thing she understood completely. Yet part of it was not so clear, for it was as if they needed to become lovers, as if she needed his strength, before she could even see the stone in the pool, before she could open up her heart enough for her gift to flow through her as she perched upon the stone. And if the symbols on the stone in the pool were also on the Targe stone and its sack, and she had been led here to discover this, to discover her gift of second sight . . .

Her gift. Impossible. Never in all the studying she had done with the Guardians' records had there been mention of more than one Guardian at a time. Never. The power shifted from one Guardian to the next. It was never shared. Did that mean Rowan was no longer Guardian? That Nicholas would no longer be the Protector and chief? Would her gift work better with the Targe stone, as Rowan's did? And was that rush of visions that almost burned up through her feet and out through her body really the power of the Targe claiming her as a Guardian, or simply the next stage of the second sight coming upon her?

And if it was the Targe choosing her . . .

She dared not look at Malcolm. If she was Guardian, then she was once more tied to Dunlairig, to her clan, and he was destined to be chief of his. Tears filled her eyes at the implications. He was hers but she could not let him abandon his destiny just because hers had once more changed. She would have to tell him.

But not until she was sure.

"We must get back to the caves," she said, still not looking at him, for she did not want him to see the sadness that swamped her at the mere thought of being parted from him. "I must tell Rowan of this place and what has happened here immediately."

"We cannot keep it our secret?" he said, wrapping his arm around her waist and tucking her against him as they gazed over the pool in the dim light.

She leaned back into his embrace. "Some, aye, some is just for us, but the rest—I cannot keep that secret. I would if I could." She laid her head against his shoulder and stared at the darker spot in the pool where the stone lay hidden just beneath the icy water. "I would if I could."

CHAPTER FOURTEEN

ONCE MALCOLM AND JEANETTE HAD MADE THEIR WAY DOWN the steepest part of the trail from the grotto, the rain that had threatened all afternoon poured down upon them in cold, heavy sheets. Malcolm looked for shelter as he walked behind her, following close enough so he could reach out and steady her when she stumbled. And she was stumbling more and more. But he saw nothing more than trees to shelter under, and the rain was hard enough that even the thick canopy of leaves did not stop it.

They had no choice but to get back to the caves as quickly as they could. When the trail widened, Malcolm drew even with Jeanette and took her icy hand. She did not need to be drenched in icy water twice in one day without ever properly warming up in between. Worry lodged in his gut and knotted in his throat. She had been so glassy-eyed just before they left the grotto and he had not been able to decide if it was unshed tears or the onset of fever. The temperature of her skin said 'twas not fever, but then if it was tears, he did not understand why. She had been so happy until she'd seen that stone, so passionate and alive in his arms. And he had been alive in hers, something he had not felt in longer than he could remember.

Was she afraid of the visions? Had she seen something that disturbed her that she had not shared with him?

Jeanette stumbled, then slipped on a muddy patch, Malcolm's hold on her hand the only thing keeping her upright.

"We can slow down, love," he said, pulling her close enough to wrap his arm around her, simultaneously pulling her nearer and holding her up more firmly, though she did not slow her pace. The need to protect her, to take care of her, was so fierce it shook him.

"Nay." She wiped the rain from her face but did not look at him. "The rain is getting harder. If we slow down, the entire trail may be impassable. We need to get back to the caves and then I need to go to Rowan at first light."

"If the rain has stopped and the trail is passable."

"Even if those conditions still exist." She trudged on, almost dragging him with her.

He could not help but admire her determination even as he struggled not to tell her what she could and could not do. He needed her to be safe, to be well, but he also understood the importance to her clan of what she had discovered today. The question was how to honor her need to share the news of her gift with her cousin, and to keep Jeanette safely at the caves until he was sure she was not falling ill from so many drenchings. He could go himself at first light, though he did not know these bens well, and had no idea where the camp of warriors was now, since they moved it every day.

There were plenty of lads at the caves now who were old enough to be well acquainted with the bens and trails in this area. Perhaps he could ask Peigi which one of them he could send to fetch Rowan and Nicholas. At worst he would send his messenger near the castle, as he and Jeanette had done, to find someone who could take him to the camp. He wished Jeanette's da, Kenneth, would return from his trip to gather their allies. He had a question for the man that he needed to have answered before he sent for his family to attend his wedding to Jeanette. As much as Jeanette needed to get word to Rowan as fast as possible, he felt the same about speaking to Kenneth so that he could claim Jeanette openly as his, and she could claim him as hers, in front of all her kin.

A chill that had nothing to do with the torrential rain ate inward to settle in his bones as he recalled Jeanette's glassy eyes. Had she seen something that would keep them apart?

Nay, he would not let that happen, no matter what she had seen. He sped their pace as the trail leveled off and he knew they were now very close to the cave site. He needed to get Jeanette settled and dry, and then he would speak with Peigi.

Moments later they were at the edge of the clearing around the caves and for a moment he feared something had happened, for the place looked as if it had been abandoned abruptly, but then he saw a movement at the mouth of the large cave—Aileas, one of Peigi's sisters, waved them in out of the rain.

"We were worried for you two," she said as they stepped out of the downpour and into the dank but relatively dry cave. "Peigi! They are here!"

Peigi came from the back of the cave at a much brisker pace than he'd expect from a woman her age. She had toweling over her arm and was leaving a trail of commands for dry clothes, hot food, and blankets in her wake.

"Ye tarried too long," she said, shaking her head at the two of them, and it was only then that Malcolm realized he still held Jeanette close against him like the lovers they were. "I hope 'twas worth it." And with that remark she patted his cheek as if he were indeed a laddie. She barely suppressed a grin while she extricated a now shivering Jeanette from his hold and guided her to sit near the fire at the mouth of the cave, just out of reach of the rain.

"You are a troublemaker, Peigi," Jeanette said.

"Aye, that I am." She handed each of them one of the lengths of toweling, but she was looking at Jeanette, who looked even paler than usual, her beautiful blue eyes gone big in her face. "Let us get you both out of those wet clothes," Peigi said, "afore you catch your deaths." But she was no longer laughing and teasing as she helped Jeanette get her sopping arisaid off. "Turn your backs, lads," she commanded as she unlaced Jeanette's gown. "Betty, where's a dry kirtle, and we need a plaid or two. She's cold right through to her bones if I'm any judge."

Jeanette smiled a little and nodded her head. "Right through to my bones."

Malcolm turned around, though there was no need for it after this day, but he did anyway, dropping his own dripping plaid to the ground and doing his best to dry his hair. When he was allowed to turn back, Jeanette was sitting near the fire once more, swaddled in a dark plaid with thin yellow and red stripes running through it, her hair spread over her back, while Peigi combed the tangles out of it as if Jeanette were a wee lass. A feeling he was not familiar with warmed him and he decided it was gratitude. He was grateful that Peigi was taking care of his angel when he did not yet have that right. He let the homey image of the two women sink into him, and then he took that opportunity to find his own belongings and change into a dry tunic. He snagged the plaid he'd been sleeping on and wrapped it around him.

"Peigi bade me gather your wet things and hang them to dry," said a woman he'd seen now and again about the camp.

"I thank you, mistress . . ."

"I am Helen," she said, picking up the wet tunic he had dropped to the ground. "Thank you for getting Jeanette safely back." She shook out the tunic. "There has been so much heartache for this clan of late, I don't know what we would do if something happened to any of the lassies."

"The lassies?"

She smiled. "Aye, that is what we call them, though they are all grown women now, or almost grown. Jeanette, Scotia, and Rowan. The lassies. The three of them have always held the hearts of the clan as if they belonged to all of us."

He started to say Jeanette was his now, but he stopped, wondering if his own clan felt the same about him and his sisters.

Wondering what this clan would do when he took her to live in the MacKenzie stronghold, when he took her to be his wife. Wondering how Kenneth would react when he asked for his daughter's hand and took her from the clan.

Helen laid a hand softly on his forearm. "Dinna fash yourself. She will be fine as soon as she gets warm. Jeanette is much stronger than she looks, as are all three of the lassies." She looked about the ground then. "Where is your plaid?"

He motioned back toward the mouth of the cave, where he had left it in a pile.

Helen nodded. "I'll just get these things drying then."

Malcolm followed her back to the fire, only to find Jeanette sound asleep, leaning against the hard stone wall of the cave.

"We should get her to her bed," he said quietly to Peigi, who sat next to her.

"Not now. She sleeps soundly and I expect that is just what the lass needs." She picked up a wooden bowl that sat almost in the embers of the fire and handed it to him, along with several bannocks. "Eat. I expect that is what *you* need."

Malcolm's stomach rumbled, answering her better than words could. He lowered himself to sit next to Peigi, enjoying the warmth of the fire and the oat-thickened stew. When the bowl was empty, and the bannocks gone, Peigi looked about her, then leaned toward him.

"Are you not going to tell me what happened this day?" There was no teasing in her tone, indeed, she was more serious than he had ever seen her. "Bedding a lad and getting drenched in the rain does not make a lass that pale, or that worried looking."

Malcolm did not think 'twas possible, but the woman made him blush.

"You did bed her, aye?" she asked, a hint of teasing lightening her voice now.

"'Tis none of your business, Peigi."

"True enough, but an auld woman gets little attention from

the lads anymore"—she elbowed him in the ribs—"so I have to live that part of my life through others now."

"I have never met a woman like you before, Peigi."

"Nor one like Jeanette, I wager."

"Never one like Jeanette." He looked over at his angel where she slept awkwardly against the wall. He moved to sit near her, his back to the wall, his legs stretched out in front of him, his feet almost in the fire, then he carefully lowered her from the wall to pillow her head on his leg so her neck would not afflict her when she woke. He smoothed her rapidly drying hair back from her cheek, noted the warmth of her skin now, and watched her simply breathe for long moments. A calmness warmed him from the inside out. A rightness settled into him.

"What else happened, Malcolm?" Peigi said, just loud enough for him to hear but not loud enough for her voice to carry beyond them.

"'Tis not my place to say, but we need to send someone to fetch Rowan, for Jeanette needs to speak with her and she will insist upon traveling to the warriors' camp at first light tomorrow if we do not fetch her cousin."

"And Nicholas, the chief, will need to come."

"—And Nicholas, of course."

Peigi nodded but said nothing.

"Have you had any word of when Jeanette's da will return?"

"Nay. You wish to ask Kenneth for his daughter's hand?" Now she slanted him a look that dared him to say otherwise.

"I do."

"Does she wish to wed you, too?"

He sighed and smiled, remembering when they had claimed each other as their own in the grotto. "She does."

Peigi let out a cackling laugh and slapped her thighs. "I kent it! I kent you were the one for her and she for you. You will treat her well, lad."

"I will, Peigi, of course I will." He looked down at the sleeping lass. "I love her."

"As do we all," she said, then added with a sly grin, "Well, perhaps we do not love her exactly as you do." With a wink she was off to send a lad to fetch Rowan and Nicholas.

JEANETTE FOLLOWED THE DEER WITH THE BENT ANTLER through familiar wood, past the heather bank where she and Malcolm had trysted, past the shielings, and on down the ben toward Dunlairig Castle. She tried to look about her, for she could not remember how she came to be in the wood, nor even what time of day it was, but everything around her—except the deer and the trees immediately around him—were oddly grey. A thick fog separated her from her surroundings, leaving her with an odd floating sensation, as if she rested in the loch, or among the clouds.

Time had no meaning to her so she knew not how long she followed the deer. When he turned, she followed, understanding that he was taking her somewhere, as he had taken her and Malcolm to the grotto. Warmth infused her entire body at the thought of Malcolm and the memory of what they had shared there.

The stag stopped, looked back at her, and gave that odd bark of the roe deer, as if to chastise her for letting her mind wander from whatever his mission was. She heard shouts in the distance and, at the same moment, the deer took off with a giant bound into the thick forest. He took great leaps through the wood, moving so swiftly and so effortlessly that Jeanette could not keep up, but neither could she make her voice work, though she tried to call out to him to wait for her.

The shouts grew louder now, and the unmistakable sound of swords sliding free of their scabbards sliced through the air, sending unseen birds flapping and squawking from their perches all around her. She ran until she saw the stag, standing still just within the wood at the edge of a small clearing.

In the open area stood a dozen English men-at-arms in a circle, their backs to each other, swords drawn and a look of fear and anger on their faces. Two large, freshly toppled trees, judging by the vibrant green of their leaves, hemmed them in on two sides.

Across the clearing, Rowan stood just within the shelter of the trees, her coppery hair glinting in the shifting sunlight filtering through the leafy canopy. The white ermine sack that held the Highland Targe was clutched in her upraised hands and Jeanette could see her cousin's lips moving, though she could not hear her voice. A crackling came from Jeanette's right, like a thousand ropes snapping, one after the other, and then she watched as a massive pine tree tipped toward the clearing, gathering speed as its roots separated from the ground around them and its branches pulled free of its neighbors. With a boom that almost knocked Jeanette from her feet, it landed across the other downed trees, closing a tight triangle about the English.

Before the last tree had even settled, the English soldiers began streaming over the downed tree nearest Jeanette, scrambling away from the clearing shouting, "Witch! She's a witch!"

Jeanette froze, not knowing where to go to avoid being overrun by the English when one of them passed right through her.

Jeanette woke with a start and a gasp, her heart pounding. She swallowed and tried to remember how she'd gotten from that clearing to . . .

She was in the main cave, the night's fire gone cold in front of her and the day fully dawned outside. She pushed herself upright trying to meld what she had seen—the English soldier passing through her without knocking her over, nor any pain—with her waking up here in the cave.

She remembered coming back to the caves in the rain, and Peigi helping her dry her hair . . . and then nothing until she'd followed the deer again.

A vision. And if it was true, then Rowan was still the Guardian, for she had called upon the power of the stone to guide her gift and fell those trees. Which meant Jeanette, with her new-found gift of second sight, was what? Another Guardian? Was it really possible that there were two Guardians at the same time?

She stood and shook out her skirt, then headed to the back of the cave where the Guardians' chronicles were safely hidden. She hadn't gotten more than a few steps when she heard her name called, and a hand landed lightly on her shoulder.

"You're awake at last, ye slugabed," Malcolm said, turning her to face him. The smile that lit his eyes dimmed as he looked at her. "What is amiss, angel?"

"Another vision. The roebuck again." She stepped into the comfort of his arms and laid her head on his chest where the quiet, even thumping of his heart calmed her. "I saw Rowan and at least a dozen English soldiers in the forest."

She could feel Malcolm holding his breath.

"She will be fine, at least she was when I woke up. It seems she has learned to protect herself and her people without my help after all."

"She was alone?"

Jeanette thought about it for long moments, running through everything she remembered, until at last she said, "I do not think so, but I saw only her and the soldiers. One of the soldiers ran right through me, Malcolm, as if I were a ghost watching them."

"'Twas a vision. Perhaps they could not see you, though you saw them."

"It did seem they could not. What does it mean? Do you think Rowan, and whoever was with her, really did meet up with the English in the forest?"

"The roebuck has not steered us wrong yet, so it would seem he is trustworthy, which means aye, I do think so, or they will, if you are seeing the future."

Jeanette pushed back so she could look up at Malcolm. "We must go to her, tell her what I've seen. We might even be able to stop her from venturing into the forest and meeting up with those soldiers if it has not happened yet."

"Nay, we do not need to go to her. She should be on her way here by now with Nicholas at the very least. Peigi sent a lad off as soon as the rain stopped last night, to fetch them here. If what you saw was her on her way, then 'tis too late to stop the meeting, and if 'tis in the future, then there is naught to gain by traipsing into the forest where we may run into the same Sassenachs."

"You sent for her?"

"Aye, I did not wish for you to make the trek after yesterday. Besides, she'll want to see the grotto where you came into your gift."

She considered all he said and could do naught but agree.

"Are you hungry?" he asked, tipping her chin up so she was looking at him.

She had to think about it. "Nay, not really," she said at last. "I want to look at the chronicles again, to see if there is any mention of multiple, simultaneous Guardians, or at the very least to see if there is more I can learn from those who held the gift of second sight."

"'Tis a good place to start. Perhaps you shall find something about how to call the visions to you so you do not have to wait for dreams."

"Aye, or roebuck in the forest."

He kissed her on the forehead. "By Peigi's estimation, the lad should have made the other camp before sunup. Rowan and the others could be here as early as midday, if they left immediately."

"And aren't slowed down—or harmed—by the English I saw."

"Did you see Rowan hurt?"

She shook her head. "Nay. In fact, the English ran away from her. They called her witch."

"What did she do to them?"

"Dropped trees all around them with naught but her wishes and the Targe stone."

"Remind me not to get on Rowan's bad side."

"Aye, 'twould be good for all of us to remember that."

"You do not truly fear your cousin, do you?"

"Nay. She has ever had a level head."

"Good. Now, get you to your scrolls. I will fetch you at least a bannock or two to break your fast."

"I'm not hungry."

"But you'll eat. You'll need your strength if yesterday is anything to go by, angel."

She smiled at him, warmed all the way through by his easy endearment and his care of her. She would not dwell on how they must part if she really were a Guardian, not until she had to.

MALCOLM BROUGHT THE BANNOCKS AND A CUP OF COOL WATER to her at the back of the cave, but then left her to the chronicles on her own. He returned what seemed like hours later with a bowl of porridge and another cup of water.

"Have you learned anything?" he asked as he put the bowl and cup down next to her.

She rolled her shoulders, trying to loosen the ever-tightening muscles there and in her back. With each scroll she despaired a little more of discovering anything useful. She rubbed the heel of her hand against a sore spot on her chest, just over her heart. She could not decide if 'twas good that there was nothing here to prove she was a second Guardian, or if 'twas a terrible gap in the chronicles.

"You need to eat, then perhaps get out of this dank cave for a bit," Malcolm said. "It might help you to see things more clearly."

"Do you make a jest, my Malcolm?"

At her endearment his eyes went soft and his breath grew shallow. He reached out and ran a finger softly from her forehead, down the side of her face, to the point of her chin, leaving a trail of sparks in its wake. "I did not make it on purpose, but if it made you claim me for yours again, I will endeavor to do so on purpose in the future."

She pulled his hand to her and placed a kiss in the middle of his palm.

He knelt beside her and pulled her palm to his lips. "I can think of no one but you, Jeanette," he said against her sensitive skin.

She regretted that she could not say the same, at least not in the same way. For her it was not the pleasure they could find together, or even the strength of their feelings for each other that she dwelt upon, but rather the pain she was sure to deal him if her suspicions, that she was a second Guardian, were true. She could not ask this man to give up his destiny for her.

Unless . . . If she could look into the future on purpose, divine his future, perhaps she could discover if she was in it . . . or not. Did she really want to know? Aye, if it meant she could lighten the blow she feared was inevitable, she did, most fervently, want to know.

She kissed him, relishing the feel of his lips on hers, the heat of his fingers threaded into her hair at the nape of her neck, the need and desire that burned between them. How could she ever give him up now that she had found him?

The despair that threatened her made her lay her fingers over his lips before she lost herself completely in his arms again. She knew she must try to discover what their future held for them, good or bad.

After Jeanette finished her porridge, Malcolm led her out of the cave. He knew Peigi watched as he all but carried Jeanette across the narrow clearing in front of the cave and into the wood. He had no idea where he was taking her, but he knew this sudden onset of second sight troubled her and he would do whatever he could to lessen her worries. Learning how to use it was the only thing he could think of at the moment. It was a place to start.

"Where are we going?" Jeanette trailed behind him, tugged along by their clasped hands.

"I do not ken," he said without stopping. "Not far from the caves, for Rowan should arrive soon. Either the roebuck will show us or we'll figure it out ourselves."

"Malcolm?" She tugged on his hand but he did not slow his trek through the trees. "Malcolm, stop."

At her calm but determined words he did, turning to face her but not releasing her hand.

"There is a burn that runs just over this way," she said, pointing to her left. "The chronicles mention that water is one of the things a seer can use to call visions. If the grotto, or the stone in the pool, were what triggered my visions yesterday, a simple burn might not work, but it is at least worth a try."

"'Tis a good thought. Lead the way."

Before too long they could hear the burn and shortly after they found the fast-running water where it rushed headlong over rocks and tree roots for the bottom of the glen.

"Now what?" Malcolm asked.

Jeanette went still and her eyes lost focus and Malcolm knew now that she was searching her memories and all the things she'd read or heard that might pertain to her current need.

"Seers use still water to scry in, or mirrors, or crystals, or sometimes nothing at all." Her words were dreamy, as if she wasn't completely aware she said them, but then her eyes focused on him again. "I should have brought a bowl with me to collect the water."

"You have a cup in your arisaid, do you not?" he asked, remembering how she had used it that first day to pour water over his wound. It was healed now, he suddenly realized, and so quickly after months of pain and festering. At least it was healed on the outside, bless the saints. His hand still refused to grip well enough to hold his claymore, but even that was getting better day by day.

"Aye." She pulled the cup from the fold in her arisaid where she always carried it. She dipped it so full of the crystal-clear mountain water, it almost overflowed. She set it on a flat rock near the burn, then scooped more water into her cupped hands and let it trickle into the cup until the water bulged at the rim, but did not spill over.

"What can I do?" Malcolm asked.

"Come, sit beside me. I know not what will happen, if anything." Her hands were trembling despite her best efforts to still them.

Malcolm took them into his own and caught her gaze. "I'll not let anything bad happen to you, Jeanette, I promise. I will protect you, keep you safe, no matter what. I vow it."

His words echoed the oath of a Guardian's Protector so closely, they stole her breath. It was the second time they had made oaths that should bind them together, yet they could not. Not until she knew for sure if she was a Guardian or not, for she would not hold him to oaths given without understanding exactly what they would mean for him.

"I know you will," she said when she could breathe again. "For now, just watch over me."

He nodded and she took a deep, steadying breath, as her mother had taught her to do. She made the prayer of protection, gliding her hands through the air in tandem with the words she spoke but did not understand, even though she did not have the Targe stone, nor did she call upon its power. Still, she called upon some power, so protections seemed wise. Malcolm would watch over her, but the protections were for more than just the human sort of trouble. Calling upon any power could awaken other magics . . .

She closed her eyes and went back to that awful day when her mother had been killed. Rowan had called upon the power of the Targe to bring the rain and to hold up the burning hall so Nicholas, Scotia, and wee Ian could escape. She had not known the prayer of protection, and wouldn't have taken the time to say it anyway. Had Rowan brought other magics into the world? Is that why Jeanette's gift had awakened at last? And if it had happened for Jeanette, would it do so for Scotia, or others? And what did that mean Jeanette's gift was? Was it from the Targe or just a rogue magic that had been unleashed by Rowan?

Jeanette rubbed the heel of her hand against her chest and slowly opened her eyes to ground herself in the present. The past was done and could not be changed. She had enough to worry about now without letting anger muddy her mind. Once more, she called upon her training to calm herself, pulling fresh air deep into her lungs, over and over again, until the steady rhythm of the air moving in and out calmed her body and her mind. Working on instinct, for she had found precious little in the chronicles about how to call a vision on purpose, she lowered her gaze to the cup of water, noticing how it mirrored the trees and specks of blue sky above her. She let her gaze move deeper, past the reflection. At first she saw only the darkness of the wooden cup, but slowly what she saw began to swirl, as if a whirl-pool were gathering, moving faster and faster, sucking her down into its depths. Jeanette resisted the sensation. Her stomach roiled and her head pounded, but when she realized she could not pull herself free, she quit fighting it and let herself be swept up into the current.

Images pressed against her, almost as rapidly as had happened in the grotto yesterday, but this time Jeanette let them fly by until Scotia's scowling face came into view. Jeanette reached for that one—perhaps with her hand, or perhaps only in her mind, she didn't know—and pulled it from the flow so she could examine it.

Anger, outrage, and fear assailed Jeanette as she tried to understand what the vision held. In it, Scotia sat at the base of an ancient standing stone, tied there, her emotions rolling over Jeanette again and again until she had no choice but to wrench herself from the vision, flinging it away like a leaf into the storm of visions that still rushed past her.

CHAPTER FIFTEEN

MALCOLM COULD SEE NOTHING CHANGE IN JEANETTE EXCEPT for the pace of her breath, but then she cried out and he grabbed her fist. "Jeanette? Jeanette, can you hear me? Come back, angel. 'Tis only a vision you see. There is no harm for you here, Jeanette." The last he said more firmly. If she did not awaken from her visions, he would knock over the cup of water but he did not know what that would do to her, so he pried open her fist and wove her fingers with his, clasping her hand and repeating her name once, twice, thrice, and at last her lashes fluttered and her fingers bit into his hand.

"She is in trouble." Her voice shook.

"Who?"

"Scotia. I saw her. I felt her emotions. She is angry . . . and frightened."

"Was Duncan with her?" The man had watched over her for so long, he was like Scotia's shadow, seldom far from her side, and always pulling her out of trouble.

"I do not ken. I could not see anything but her."

"You could not tell who had taken her or where she was?"

She got that faraway look in her eyes, then excitement lit up within her, quickly chased away by worry and a furrowed brow. "She's at a clearing down Glen Lairig from the castle. There is a standing stone in the middle of it."

"Hellfire."

"Aye, and damnation. We must get back to the caves. We must send someone to rescue her quickly. Her tongue is sharpest when she's afraid and that is not a good thing when you are held by an enemy."

"The English scouts?"

She hesitated, her eyes going soft again. "I cannot tell, but I think so." She pressed the heels of her hands to her eyes. "But I do not ken why I think so."

"Are you sure this has already happened?"

Her hands fell back to her lap as she shook her head and narrowed her eyes. "Nay. Curse it all. What good are visions if I cannot tell if they are in the past, the present, or the future?"

Malcolm gazed up at the sky, a crystal-blue sky just visible here and there through the trees. "It is getting on to midday. Perhaps Rowan will know where Scotia is. Perhaps she'll even travel here with Rowan, so you can warn her." Malcolm looked down at the still overfilled cup, then back at Jeanette. "It would seem you can call upon the second sight when you wish." Pride in her accomplishment filled him. "Is there something we need to do with the cup?"

"I do not ken . . . I hate that."

"Hate what? The cup?"

"Nay, not understanding what it is I need to do. Not understanding this gift that I suddenly have. I do not like feeling stupid."

Malcolm rose and used their still clasped hands to pull her up, too. "You are not stupid. Do not ever say that. Look what you just did with little guidance. Perhaps you are blazing a trail the Guardians have not trod before *because* you can figure it out without guidance."

In her way, she considered his words carefully. "Perhaps, but I still do not like it." He laughed and she smiled up at him. "We must get back. I do not know how far into the future I have seen, if indeed it is the future, and I would keep Scotia from being captured by those southern vermin." She picked up the cup and carefully walked back to the burn, where she returned it to the flow with a few muttered words that he could not make out.

"Do you think it works that way?" he asked as he followed her back toward the caves. "Do you believe you are shown a possible future that can be changed?"

" 'Tis another thing I do not ken, but I cannot sit idly by and wait for Scotia to be captured. If I can see something of the future, is it not so that I may act on that information?"

" 'Tis an excellent question, but now I am the one who does not ken the answer."

"At least I have company in my confusion." She paused long enough for him to draw even with her, then she hooked her arm around him and they continued side by side.

"Always, angel. Always."

THEY MADE THEIR WAY QUICKLY BACK TO THE CAVES. THE FIRST thing Jeanette saw was Rowan's coppery hair, with Nicholas next to her. Duncan stood nearby, speaking with Peigi. While Duncan had not been proclaimed Nicholas's champion yet, he acted in that capacity, just as Uilliam had been Kenneth's champion, which was probably why he had come with them.

"You are safe!" Jeanette rushed to Rowan and hugged her hard, only then realizing that despite what she had told Malcolm, she was very worried for her cousin. "Is Scotia with you?"

"We are safe," Nicholas said from his wife's side. "And Scotia is not with us. She refused to return to the caves."

" 'Tis a good thing, too." Rowan's hands trembled as she grasped Jeanette's hands. "We were nearly caught by English soldiers not an hour past. I stopped them, Jeanette." There was a quiver in her voice, but a look of wonder lit up her face. "I used the Targe and I—"

"Dropped trees around them," Jeanette said, knowing now that she had dreamt of the future, for her dream had come to her before the event had taken place.

"How did you ken that?" Rowan asked.

"Aye, how did you?" Nicholas echoed.

Jeanette looked at Malcolm and his nod warmed her. "I had a dream early this morn. I saw Rowan, with the Targe stone raised, facing twelve English soldiers who stood in a small clearing, swords drawn. I saw you toppling trees around them until they fled," she said, still holding her cousin's hands tightly in her own.

"You saw?" Nicholas asked, his eyes wide. "Like a vision?"

Jeanette nodded as she looked about to see who might be close enough to hear, and found Duncan staring at her. Peigi pushed him toward the two couples, then shooed the weans away and set them to chores that would keep them busy for some time to come. Bless her.

"You dreamt it . . . saw it . . . exactly as it happened," Rowan said, her eyes as wide as her husband's. "A dream? Like when you were little?"

Duncan shifted on his feet but said nothing, though his attention was rapt.

"Aye, like when I was little, but just now I tried to call the visions while awake."

"And?" Rowan prodded as she leaned a little closer to Jeanette.

"And I did." There was a collective intake of breath with that answer. She looked at Nicholas and Duncan. "Scotia is in trouble, or will be soon. I do not ken how far into the future I am seeing, or if 'tis even the future."

"That one has been out of trouble for too long," Duncan muttered. "'Twas inevitable."

"Are you sure you are seeing something real, Jeanette?" Nicholas asked. "Something that will indeed happen?"

"Aye. I have reason to believe I am seeing things that will happen, or that might already have happened. This time the English take her."

"You saw this?" Duncan asked before anyone else could react to her revelation. He did not wait for her to answer. "I must get back to the warriors' camp. I shall drag her back if I have to. She will stay here until we can rid ourselves of the English once and for all."

Nicholas grabbed Duncan's arm and held him in place.

"Is there aught else you can tell us?" Nicholas asked Jeanette.

"They take her to the Story Stone." She looked at Malcolm. "That is what we call the ancient standing stone I saw." She looked back to Nicholas. "I could not see if anyone was with her there."

"I found an abandoned English camp near that stone," Duncan said, tension clear in the sharp planes of his face and the tight control of his voice. "They must be returning there."

"Go, Duncan," Nicholas said. "Get to her and keep her within arm's reach at all times until you return here. We cannot let the English have her. We cannot let them get a hostage. Watch yourself, too. I would not have them capture either of you."

Duncan nodded, then sprinted out of the clearing and up the ben.

"I pray he will arrive in time to keep her safe," Rowan said, her eyes still fixed on the path Duncan had taken.

"As do I," Jeanette said. "Perhaps, when I have learned better how this ability—"

"Gift," Rowan and Malcolm said simultaneously.

"—Perhaps it is a gift," Jeanette allowed, "but I do not ken that yet. I hope that when I understand it better, I will begin to know what is the future, what is not, and if what I see is carved in stone or if it can be changed. I pray it can be changed, else Scotia will indeed meet the English."

Rowan and Nicholas started peppering her with questions about the visions: when they had started, what she could see. Jeanette spoke of the grotto, of how they had found it, and of what had happened to her there when she knelt upon the stone in the pool. Malcolm filled in details she could not, and of course neither of them spoke of the intimacy that had passed between them.

"Can you direct the visions to what you want to see?" Nicholas asked, excitement speeding his words.

"I do not ken. Not yet at least. I only just this morning tried to call the visions to me while awake."

"And that worked, aye?" Nicholas asked. "That is when you saw Scotia?"

She nodded, then swallowed hard. Her next request was likely to cause much consternation with her cousin.

"Rowan, I would like to see if the Targe stone will help me with this gift."

"Why do you think it will?" Rowan asked, much more calmly than Jeanette had expected. No Guardian in the records had ever shared the Targe with another until the Guardianship was passed along. Jeanette had never seen her mother even allow another to touch it while it was in her care—not even Jeanette, at least not until her mum had taken so ill. Even then, Jeanette had only handled it in its sack, never the stone itself.

"The stone I found in the grotto, the one in the pool, it had the same symbol as the Targe stone, three swirling circles within a circle, but it also had one of the symbols that are painted inside the sack." She paused, letting that sink in. "It had the symbol Mum called the mirror, and 'twas when I found it that the visions erupted within me."

Rowan pulled the sack from her belt without a word and spread it wide, draping it over her palm, where she cradled the fist-sized grey stone in the middle of it, covering the swirling circles in the middle of the sack with the stone itself, which had the same symbol carved into its surface. Three other symbols were spaced around the outer part of the sack that hung from her hand and there, clearly, was painted the same mirror symbol Jeanette had seen in the grotto.

Malcolm stepped close, examining the stone that had both protected them and brought them all this recent trouble.

"It is smaller than I had imagined," he said. He pointed at the symbol on the stone and looked at Jeanette. "This is the one on the grotto stone?"

"In the middle, aye, but this is the other symbol." She lifted an edge of the sack and laid it over her own palm, showing him the mirror.

"And you thought of the water this morning because it is like a mirror?"

"I did, and it was. I did not try to direct the gift this morning, but I was prepared for it and was able to look closer at the vision of Scotia, for it caught my attention as it tried to rush by me."

Rowan was quiet and Jeanette gave her time to consider all she'd been told. At length she asked the question Jeanette had been waiting for.

"Is there anything in the chronicles that says there can be more than one Guardian?"

"I have searched, but found naught."

Rowan nodded, the stone still held in her palm, the four of them standing close enough to shield it from those curious enough to shirk their duties. Protecting it was more habit than need here in the heart of the MacAlpin clan.

"Perhaps my gift is not enough to protect us from the English king," Rowan said quietly. "Let us find out if you are a Guardian, too, as you were always destined to be."

Scotia had been happy to stay behind at the warriors' camp when Rowan, Nicholas, and the annoying Duncan, along with a handful of warriors for keeping the Guardian and the chief safe, had left before dawn. She had no use for the women's camp, for women hiding in caves, trembling in fear of their enemies. And now, at last, she was free of the ever-watchful eyes of Duncan and Rowan. Uilliam had no doubt been left with orders to keep a tight rein on her, but it would be easy enough to slip by him as he had his hands full overseeing the watches.

She'd not be managed any longer.

Triumph and anger mixed with the deep slash of festering grief within her, heating her blood like a fever, making her more determined than ever to do what she had sworn to do: avenge her mother's death.

Sure, the man who had murdered her mum had died by Kenneth's hand in front of all the castlefolk, but she had found little satisfaction in that. She wanted the English to fear the people of Clan MacAlpin. She wanted the English to fear her. She had lived in fear of them for far too long. Today she would end that once and for all. Today she would prove to everyone that she was not some wee lass that had to be managed and protected. She wasn't a wee lass anymore. She thought about how she'd spent her days, flirting with the lads and manipulating everyone she knew to do her bidding . . . except Duncan. He was the one person who never fell for her charms. He was the one who always had the sour face when looking at her, as if he could approve of nothing she did. As if she needed his approval. Hah.

Today she would show him and all the rest of her clan just exactly who she was, and wouldn't they all be surprised when it was Scotia who brought the English to their knees, quaking in fear.

She slipped into the tent she shared with several women who did the cooking and washing for the warriors. Once inside, she donned the tunic and trews she had "borrowed" from one of the kitchen lads before she left the castle, then dug in the sack that contained everything important to her, including her mother's eating knife and the dirk, long and mortally sharp, that had been used to kill her. That bastard spy's dagger would do more damage this day. She secured the weapons in the belt she had buckled about her waist to keep the trews up.

Now the question was simply, Where would she start looking for the English? Duncan, the ass, continued to claim he had not found them, only their abandoned camp near the Story Stone, though he had let slip that it appeared there were only a handful of English in the glen so far. The Story Stone was west of the castle, not far from the loch, while she was south and east of her home now, huddled in a glenlike fold of the mountain. She peeked out of the tent and waited until she could exit it without being seen. Quietly, she slipped around the side of her tent and headed into the thick wood in which the warriors' camp had been set up. She passed a place where someone had been chopping wood. A small ax lay on the ground, left behind by its owner. She picked it up and slid the smooth wooden handle through her belt without stopping. It was no battle ax, but then she could not wield a heavy battle ax. She could hear Duncan's derisive retort in her head: "You cannot wield any weapon. You are just a scrawny lass."

"Not anymore," she said aloud from between clenched teeth, and banished Duncan's voice from her head.

Indeed, since before they had left the castle, Scotia had been working hard to make herself stronger, running up and down the ben, hefting stones ever bigger, ever heavier, until at night her fingers would be bloodied and her extremities and back would ache. She had not been able to do any of that since they had been driven out of the castle. She cursed Duncan again, even though she knew he was not responsible for that decision. She hadn't been able to train, but she had watched the warriors training since she'd come to the warriors' camp, memorizing their moves and the tips they gave each other, so she could move as lethally as they did when her chance arose.

Just then the trees opened up, allowing her a view of her home. She stopped, her breath caught in her throat. She missed her home. She missed her mother. She missed how safe she had felt there, and how simply she'd viewed her world and her place in it. She knew how naïve she had been. She had never been safe there. No one had. Wall or no wall. Guardian or no Guardian. If her mum had not been able to keep them safe, Rowan had not a hope of doing so.

And while the rest of them seemed content to wait for the English to arrive in force, she was done waiting. She was taking the fight to them, even if she had to do it alone.

MALCOLM AND JEANETTE LED ROWAN AND NICHOLAS TO THE burn where Jeanette had seen Scotia in trouble this morning. They needed privacy for the next experiment and the grotto was much farther away than the burn. This place had worked for Jeanette's scrying once, so it seemed likely, if she could use the Targe stone, it should work here again.

When they arrived, Rowan and Jeanette stood near the water. The men held back far enough to be out of the way, though Malcolm positioned himself close enough to Jeanette to catch her if she collapsed, as she had in the grotto.

Rowan handed the sack to her cousin, then joined the men. Jeanette placed the sack on the ground, loosening the ties until the circular piece of ermine pelt lay flat, the stone in its center, as Rowan had held it, and with the three symbols, now visible, painted around the edge. Jeanette knelt next to it and began to chant and move her arms in the air.

Malcolm recognized the graceful arcs and swishes of her hands in the air from yesterday and this morning, when she had whispered whatever she was now chanting. It warmed him, in an unaccustomed way, to know that he was trusted with this secret of Clan MacAlpin, that he stood shoulder to shoulder with these people who had lost much more than he had in the fight against the English, though they had never gone to war. They fought their own sort of battle for their home and their country.

Jeanette lifted the stone into her hands, raising it up as if she were offering it to God. They all waited, expectation thick in the air, but Malcolm knew it wasn't working. She wasn't seeing anything.

After a long time, she lowered her hands to her lap. "Nothing." But she didn't look at those gathered there, she narrowed her eyes and studied the open sack as if she'd never seen it before. No one moved. They clearly knew that look as well as Malcolm was coming to know it. She was working through the problem, sorting through all she knew and adding what she had just learned to it, before she came up with—

"Rowan," she said quietly without lifting her gaze from the sack. "Will you help me?"

Rowan quickly joined her cousin, kneeling opposite her, the sack between them.

"How?" she asked.

Jeanette was quiet again, then nodded, as if she was satisfied with whatever she had decided. "Take the stone." She laid it in Rowan's outstretched hands, then Rowan turned the sack until the mirror symbol sat in front of Jeanette, and an inverted V with three wavy lines beneath it lay in front of Rowan. A third symbol that looked like an arrow broken in two places, so it formed the shape of a Z, lay closest to the men. Jeanette laid her own hands over the stone.

"Draw forth the power of the Targe, Rowan. Send it through the stone. Send it through me."

"Send it through you?"

"Aye. 'Twas your use of the Targe without the protections that brought my gift forth, I am sure of it. Perhaps you will open the power of the Targe for me."

"I dinna ken how to send it through you."

"Clearly you have learned how to send your gift through the Targe in order to focus it where you need it to go, as I saw when you toppled the trees in a perfect triangle around those soldiers. Just send the power of the stone, the power that you direct with your gift, to me instead of a tree."

Rowan shook her head. "I do not want to hurt you, Cousin."

"And you will not."

"You cannot be sure."

"I trust you," Jeanette said, and Malcolm could see Rowan's breath catch but she nodded slowly and locked her gaze on Jeanette's.

His angel didn't chant and move her hands this time. The two women sat quietly, tension cascading off of them enough to fill the wood. Birds abandoned the trees nearby and even the little telltale sounds of small animals moving through the forest ceased.

Malcolm couldn't stand it any longer.

"Jeanette." He kept his voice soft, quiet, trying not to startle her. "Think of the water in the cup, the water in the pool covering the stone. 'Tis the water that brought you the waking visions."

She took a long, deep breath and nodded slightly. She kept one hand on the stone where Rowan still held it between them, and reached out with the other, letting her fingertips dip into the edge of the burn. A sudden wind whipped through the wood, scattering leaves and dropping bits of trees in its path. Jeanette threw her head back. Both women's hair lifted and danced about them in the wind. Gooseflesh rode Malcolm's skin. He took a step toward them and was stopped with an iron grip upon his arm.

"Nay," Nicholas said. "Do not stop them. The wind is a sign that Rowan's gift is active. She will not hurt Jeanette with it, but she will hurt you if you try to interfere. As will I."

Malcolm itched to go to Jeanette with the same white-hot urgency that had propelled him into his last battle. In his mind Nicholas became Cameron, Malcolm's cousin and best friend, who had also bade him not to act upon his instincts. Cameron, it turned out, had been right, he now realized. His men had been battle weary, injured, ill, but Malcolm had seen nothing but a chance to beat back the English and their Scottish allies. Cameron had seen more clearly than Malcolm that it was not time to engage in battle again. Nicholas understood his wife's gift, and likely the Targe, far better than Malcolm could and he counseled patience. He shrugged off Nicholas's grip but did not retreat from his position halfway between the chief and the women. Neither did he move to Jeanette's side, though the need to do so was fierce. His angel learned from what did not work for her. He could do the same, learning from his mistake that had almost cost him his sword arm, but that had also brought him to this clan and Jeanette.

Just when he thought he could hold his position no longer, Jeanette yanked her hand off the stone. Rowan slumped and the wind immediately died; leaves fluttered to the ground in the sudden still and quiet.

"Now," Nicholas said, striding to his wife.

Malcolm was kneeling by Jeanette instantly. "Angel? Are you well?" He brushed her silky hair away from where it tangled over her face, searching for any sign of injury. He was rewarded with a smile full of wonder, her blue eyes alight with what he knew was a look of understanding, of knowledge gained.

"What did you see?" he asked.

The light in her eyes went out like a storm cloud covering the sun. "They will be here soon, too soon," she said. "Nicholas, the English are drawing near. I saw a soldier on a horse, leading I know not how many men. He had dark hair with a lock of pure white."

Nicholas narrowed his eyes. "He rides a honey-colored horse, aye?" he asked Jeanette.

"He does. There were three red stars upon his surcoat, too. You ken who this man is?"

Nicholas took a deep breath and pushed his fingers through his hair. "I do. He is Lord Sherwood. I have met him several times during my service with King Edward. He is a very able commander of men. Sly, good with tactics. King Edward relies on him for advice in battle." He shook his head. "He is a formidable foe. Did you see more?"

"I could not tell where they were, except that it looked like they were moving toward the coast—I could smell the salt air. I could hear the sound of men marching but I could not see them clearly enough to tell how many there were. I cannot tell exactly when I saw them, but 'twas still summer to be sure. The purple and yellow Heel Cups were in full bloom, so I cannot be seeing far into the future, for they will start blooming very soon now."

Nicholas nodded. "It is as we thought, but good to have verification that they will be upon us soon. Did you seek out that vision or did it just come to you?"

"Both. Three times the visions have come through me in a stream, all jumbled together, but I am learning how to grab a specific one long enough to look at it. I can't see much—there always seems to be a fog around all but something or someone specific. I searched the stream for something of the English this time, once I figured out how to call the visions to me through the stone."

She leaned against Malcolm then, and he pulled her close.

"Thank you for reminding me of the water," she said. "I was so intent upon the Targe that I forgot what I had learned only this morning."

"You have learned a lot," Rowan said, a smile on her tired face. "You learned how to use the Targe much faster than I did."

Nicholas looked down at his wife where she stood leaning against him. "She used the Targe?"

"Aye, my love. It would seem we have two Guardians to fight the English," Rowan said with a broad smile.

Malcolm felt Jeanette stiffen against him. "What is it, angel?"

"It is the destiny I always expected," she said, looking at everyone standing in a circle about her, "but not the one I want now."

CHAPTER SIXTEEN

"Why, angel? 'Tis what you have prepared for your whole life," Malcolm said. Jeanette could not make herself look up at him lest she cry. She was about to break his heart and it was breaking hers first.

"Is it because of Malcolm?" Rowan asked.

"I need to speak to him alone," Jeanette said. "He does not ken what this means, Rowan."

"What is it I do not ken?" he asked, his voice rough now. "What have you not told me, Jeanette?"

"We will return to the caves," Rowan said, pulling Nicholas by the hand, back the way they'd come. "Do not be too long, my cousin. We must decide how best to use two Guardians."

Jeanette nodded, waiting as long as she could before she had to tell Malcolm the truth of her new status, but he was impatient.

"What is it you have to tell me?" His voice was gruff but she could not tell if it was from anger or concern.

She turned to face him. "I love you, you ken that, aye?"

"I do, and you ken I feel the same?"

She nodded, swallowing hard against the lump that rose in her throat. "I cannot marry you, Malcolm."

"Because you are now a Guardian?"

"Aye."

"But Rowan is a Guardian and she is wed to Nicholas. We are no different. You said you were mine, and I was yours." He took her hands in his iron grip as if he knew he was losing her. "In the old way, we are married already."

"But you did not know, *we* did not know, that I would be a Guardian of the Targe. I am no longer simply a member of the clan, free to make my own choices."

"There is another you must wed now?"

"Nay, never. There will never be anyone but you in my heart. You are my heart, but I will not hold you to vows given without understanding what you would have to give up."

"I give up nothing to marry with you, Jeanette, my angel. I only gain."

"Nay. To marry me now, you would have to give up everything you want for your life. You would have to give up your birthright, your destiny."

"But you are my destiny. Can you not feel that?" She could hear the confusion and the knife edge of anger in his voice now and see it in the tense lines around his mouth. "You dinna want to be my wife now that you are a Guardian? Is that it?"

"Oh, Malcolm." She reached up to touch his beloved face but he flinched away from her, anger now clear in the sharpness of his glare. "I want nothing more than to be your wife, to live by your side for the rest of our years. I want to have your bairns, and watch them grow up strong and wise, like their father. That is what I want above all else. But I will not have my wishes at the expense of yours."

"I do not understand, Jeanette. What are you not saying?"

She stood as tall as she could, girding herself against the pain she was inflicting on both of them. 'Twas best to just say it straight out, 'twas kindest, though she longed for one more kiss, one more precious moment between them. But that was a selfish desire. She would have to satisfy her aching heart with what they had already shared. What she must say to him now would end everything between them. It must.

"As a Guardian, whomever I marry must forsake his own clan, his own home, and bide with me at Dunlairig. He must swear allegiance to the MacAlpins and forswear all other allegiances. As

Guardian I cannot leave this land, for now I am truly a guardian of it, holding it safe for all the generations that have come before me, and all who will come after. I cannot even offer you the traditional role of the Guardian's Protector, for the Protector is also the chief, and I will not ask Nicholas to step down from that post. The Targe chose Rowan first for a reason, most likely because her gift is a powerful weapon. Her chosen Protector is chief."

She waited for him to say something but when the silence grew too heavy to bear, she said, "You see I have nothing to offer you that mitigates the loss of your birthright. You were born to be the chief of the MacKenzies. You cannot be the chief of the MacAlpins. If you marry me, you must renounce your family. You will simply be a warrior of the MacAlpin clan and I will not let you do that."

"You will not let me? What if I wish to give up my birthright?"

A flicker of hope sparked in her heart, but was quickly extinguished. "You would come to hate me, I fear. Malcolm"—and this time she did not let him flinch away as she took his beloved face between her palms—"I love you with all my heart, but I cannot let you throw away your own destiny simply because mine has changed. If I were not a Guardian, I would be free to wed you and live amongst your people. I would be free to be your Lady at Blackmuir Castle and I would gladly make that choice, though I would miss my family. I do not have that choice."

"And you would make my choice for me?"

She reached up on her toes and kissed him lightly. "I do not wish to hurt you more than I already have. Your arm is healed. Your hand is getting stronger every day. Soon you will be ready to resume your place in King Robert's army, and then you will become the chief of your clan. It is what you have wanted all along."

"But now I want you, too." He took her lips in a bruising kiss that spoke of the love and loss that battled in both of them. "I want you, too," he said, resting his forehead against hers.

"But you can't have both. Neither of us can. Not now. I am sorry." She kissed him on the cheek, and felt a tear trickle down her own. "I do love you," she said, turning away quickly before the single tear turned into a torrent.

MALCOLM WATCHED HIS FUTURE WALK AWAY FROM HIM, TOO stunned to follow. He shook his head and rubbed the back of his neck. The pain of his battle wound had been easier to bear than this. Why had she not told him sooner? He had known Nicholas had changed sides to wed Rowan, but he had not understood that the man had no choice. That Rowan had no choice. And now Jeanette would take all choice away from him. He fisted his hands, the right one now almost closing completely, and, for the first time, found himself wishing Jeanette was not such a gifted healer, that his arm would never fully heal. If he could never wield a claymore again, he would not be worthy of taking his father's place as the chief, and he could stay here, with her. He could be her husband, her protector, even if he was not the chief.

But his arm *was* healed. His hand did grow stronger every day.

There must be a way. Malcolm had never given up a battle, and he would not give up this one, either. Jeanette would be his. 'Twas only a matter of figuring out how.

Figuring out how . . .

His hand was not fully functioning yet, so he had time before he must decide his fate. Perhaps there was some compromise that could be found, some way to allow them to be together without giving up their duties to their clans.

Malcolm had to laugh at himself with that thought. Compromise. 'Twas what his father had been trying to teach him all along, and all it had taken to teach him the value of it was for him to fall in love. He hurried back to the caves. Jeanette might believe there was no way they could be together now, but he'd not give her up without a fight.

JEANETTE QUICKLY PACKED HER FEW THINGS IN A LEATHER travel sack as the events of the day preoccupied her: the joy of that moment when the power of the Targe surged through her, the visions coming fast but somehow under her control this time, and the despair that swept all the joy away when Rowan confirmed what Jeanette already knew—she was a Guardian of the Highland Targe and her future was no longer hers to decide. Did any of the visions contain happiness or was her gift only the bringer of pain?

She swiped an errant tear from her lashes. She had no time to wallow in self-pity. She had become what she had always wanted, though not in the conventional way. As a Guardian of the Highland Targe, she would be able to help her clan in far more important ways than seeing them settled in the caves. She should be elated, as she had always imagined she would be. But never had she seen Malcolm in her daydreams.

And she knew she would not see him much more. As soon as he could wield his claymore again, he would be gone. If she could go back to the stream and change what had transpired there . . . if he had not reminded her of the water's role in her visions . . . would she?

She knew the answer. She would not. This was her birthright and she could not give it up, any more than she could ask him to give up his.

"Enough," she said out loud, needing to hear it. She stuffed the last kirtle into the sack, then looked around to see what else she needed to take with her to the warriors' camp. She was a Guardian now. She must participate in the plans to fight back the English, and if what she saw in her vision came true, if Scotia was held hostage by their enemies, what then? She prayed Duncan had returned to the camp fast enough to prevent that, but even so, Scotia was headstrong and often did not listen, especially not to Duncan. "Enough," she said again. There were only so many things she could worry about and at this moment, packing to leave the caves needed her full attention. She headed toward the mouth of the cave, grabbing an empty waterskin as she passed a small pile of them.

Water. It seemed she needed water to call the visions to her. She grabbed three more waterskins and called for a lad as she stepped into the dappled sunlight outside the cave. Quickly she told him what she needed, and sent him off at a run.

Rowan looked at her oddly.

Jeanette shrugged. "If I need water for the visions, 'twill do me no good to be without a ready supply."

"Do you think 'tis that water specifically?"

"I do not think so. It did not look like the water in the grotto spilled out of there. 'Tis possible there is something about the water in this glen, but it does not seem likely to me. Water, mirrors, some crystal stones—those are the tools used for scrying."

"You have learned this from the chronicles?"

"Aye, but little else of use. There is no mention of there ever having been more than one Guardian at a time. Nor any mention of more than one Protector, either."

"Malcolm did not like what you told him."

"He did not. Is it that obvious?"

"He is like a bear with a thorn in his paw, growling at everyone about everything."

Jeanette closed her eyes, pushing the grief she held over hurting him, and over her own loss, as far down as possible into the blackness where all her other grief lived, but still it clogged her throat and lay like a stone in her belly. The lad sprinted back into the clearing just then, skidding to a halt in front of Jeanette and handing her the four heavy, wet bags without a word.

"We should go," she said to Rowan.

The hike to the warriors' camp went swiftly and silently. Nicholas had instructed the six warriors who had been keeping watch at the pass into the Glen of Caves to surround them as they traveled, but to keep out of sight of the group, making it easier to surprise any English soldiers they might run across. Then he set a fast pace that Rowan and Jeanette had trouble keeping up with. Malcolm walked just behind them, his claymore drawn for the first time since Jeanette had known him. The men were all positioned to protect Rowan, but then Jeanette remembered that now she, too, was a Guardian. It was both women they protected.

After a couple of hours they reached the camp, which was little more than a large cooking fire, out now in order to limit the opportunity for them to be found by its scent or smoke. There were scattered piles of belongings here and there amongst the trees, and a few tents. But no people. Jeanette knew there had been scouts watching their approach, for she had heard the owl call they all used as a signal as they drew near the camp.

"Where is everyone?" Jeanette asked.

Nicholas let out a shrill call like that of a hawk and Denis, the old gatekeeper, stepped from behind the trunk of a huge pine tree.

"What's happened?" Nicholas asked as the rest of his party came to a stop behind him. Their six warrior escorts fanned out to keep watch around them all.

Denis limped forward. "Duncan arrived with the warning for Scotia but she was not here. We do not ken if she left on her own, or was somehow taken from our midst without any of us knowing."

Jeanette's breath caught in her throat.

"Duncan found her tracks, and only hers, leaving her tent and heading into the wood that way." Denis pointed in the direction of the castle. "Uilliam went with Duncan to track her and took about half the men who were here with him."

Jeanette did a quick figuring and decided that was probably seven or eight men.

"He told me to stay here and await your return. He sent the women deeper into the wood with a couple of the older lads, and set the rest to watching for you in case this was some sort of ploy by the English to set up a trap here and capture Rowan upon her return."

"So far that does not appear to be the situation," Nicholas said. "Though we definitely need to see to the safety of the Guardians."

Denis looked from Nicholas to Rowan and back, his eyes full of questions that he did not ask. Nicholas pointed at one of the warrior escorts. "Go and join the watchers in the wood. Tell them to spread out around this camp so they may warn us upon anyone's approach, friend or foe. The rest of you"—he indicated the five warriors left standing with them—"spread out and keep watch just beyond the camp, in case someone slips by the watchers."

"Should we not abandon this camp, Nicholas?" Jeanette asked.

"Aye, we will."

"But . . ." Rowan's brows were drawn down, and she held the ermine sack in her hand, stroking the soft fur with her thumb. "What if . . ." Nicholas, Jeanette, and Malcolm waited for her to finish but she didn't.

Jeanette wondered if this was what she looked like when she was lost in thought. Her curiosity got the better of her. "What if what, Rowan?" she said, more sharply than she'd intended, earning her a scowl from Nicholas.

Rowan looked up at her. "What if we could set a barrier around this camp? Like Auntie Elspet did when the curtain wall fell?"

"Can you do that?" Jeanette asked. "'Tis a variation of the blessing I was teaching you."

"You were trying to teach me. I have not mastered that yet." She rolled her eyes. "I have not even practiced it. But *you* ken it already and now you are a Guardian."

Jeanette was startled by the idea, and a little ashamed that she had not thought of this herself. Her ideas about the Guardian and what she could or couldn't, should or shouldn't do, were so strong, she had not considered that she might now take up some of the things her mother did for the clan that Rowan and her unusual gift could not, at least not yet.

"Perhaps this is *why* I've been made a Guardian," Jeanette said, now lost in her own thoughts as she considered whether she could do it or not. "Someone must know the prayers and rituals, or perhaps it is only something the line of MacAlpin can do?"

Rowan nodded. "Perhaps that is why the ways of the Guardian, the traditional ways of the Guardian, are so hard for me. We have always made a good partnership, Cousin. Now we shall see if that remains true for us as Guardians. What do you need to create the barrier?'

Jeanette let her travel sack slide off her shoulder. Malcolm grabbed it before it hit the ground and laid it at the base of a nearby tree, leaving his own there, as well as the four water skins he had insisted on carrying himself.

"I shall need the Targe stone. I do not ken if I will need any of the water, but it could not hurt."

Before she could even ask, Malcolm was filling the wooden cup she pulled from its carrying place in her arisaid. "My thanks," she said. He nodded, his face now a scowl that was so at odds with her grinning golden warrior, he seemed a stranger to her. Sadness wrapped around her. She already missed him and he wasn't even gone yet. What would she do when he did leave? Would she be required to choose another as her champion?

"Jeanette?" She was grateful that Rowan drew her attention back to the task at hand. Jeanette took the ermine sack from her cousin, loosened the thong that cinched it closed, and set the wide-open bag on the ground with the stone centered on the sack. Although she couldn't explain why, she felt compelled to turn the sack until the mirror symbol was closest to her. She noted that once more Rowan stood where the inverted V symbol lined up, leaving that third symbol, the broken arrow, without anyone near it. Once more the question of exactly what the symbol meant drifted through her thoughts, but she set that aside to be pondered later.

"I was not able to draw the Targe's power on my own this morning," Jeanette said, now setting the cup of water between her and the sack, though she knew not how she would perform the blessing properly if she needed to touch the water at the same time. "But I'd like to try now. If I shake my head, I want you to draw it and focus it through me as you did at the burn." She turned to tell Malcolm to stand near to catch her if necessary, but he was already there.

"I am ready," he said.

"As am I," Rowan said.

Jeanette performed the basic blessing first, letting herself sink into the ritual of unknown words and graceful hand motions, but she felt nothing unusual, nothing powerful as she had when Rowan had focused the Targe through her this morning. She knelt and gazed into the water as she repeated the blessing. Again, nothing happened. She placed the fingers of her left hand so they just touched the rim of the cup. Nothing. She stood, shook her head, and prepared to start the blessing yet again.

As Rowan lifted the stone in her hands, holding it between them, a surge of pure joy and light rushed into Jeanette, through her, swirling up and over her, around her. She began the blessing and euphoria swept her up. When she moved on to the barrier ritual her mother had used to protect the castle, it was as if she could see the power as she released the words from her mouth, one by one, moving them through the air with the motions of her hands, until she could see the words she did not understand and the power of the Targe weaving together like an ethereal basket of light turned upside down, arching over the entire camp.

Even when the protection was in place, she did not wish to stop the flow of the Targe that was energizing her, pushing all thought, all sorrow, away, while joy flowed from it, through her and out. Her heart was at peace, finally, here doing what she was born to do, being what she was born to be, a Guardian of the Targe.

Just as suddenly as the flow of power had begun, it stopped, dropping her abruptly out of her euphoria and back into the world. Malcolm was shaking her, shouting her name, but she did not understand why he seemed so agitated.

And then his words sank into her, slowly taking recognizable form. "You are hurting Rowan! You must stop!"

"What? Hurting Rowan?" She blinked and looked about for her cousin, only to find Nicholas crouched over her crumpled form, as if she had collapsed right where she stood. "What did I do?!" She pulled free of Malcolm's grip and dropped beside Rowan. "What did I do?" she asked Nicholas.

"I do not ken. As soon as she joined you, she went rigid, gritting her teeth, her eyes clenched as if she were in pain, but she held firm for a long time."

"Long time? It was but a moment," Jeanette said, looking back at Malcolm to confirm her statement. It was then she noticed how much the shadows had lengthened. "How long?" she whispered.

"An hour? Maybe more." Malcolm offered his hand, lifting her to her feet.

She looked about at the clearing but could no longer see the barrier she had built. "Is she all right?" she asked Nicholas.

"She breathes," he said, brushing her hair back from her face. "Rowan, love, wake up. I need you to wake up now."

Jeanette knelt beside her cousin again and opened her healer's bag, rummaging through it for the pungent salve she used to stop wounds from festering. She removed the leather cover and waved the small pot under Rowan's nose. Rowan almost knocked it out of Jeanette's hand while trying to swat it away.

"What are you doing to me?" she asked, her eyes flying open and pinning Jeanette in place. "What did you do to me?"

"I do not ken, Cousin. I am sorry I caused you pain. Can you tell me what happened, what you felt?"

Rowan sat up with Nicholas's help and blinked, as if trying to clear her vision.

"Jeanette, you built a barrier. I could see it but I could neither move, nor speak. It was as if you were pulling all the power of the Targe from me, taking it before I could even offer it to you."

"It hurt you?"

"Aye, it was as if I was caught in a maelstrom, thrown around like a leaf in a gale. I tried not to let you take it, but I could not hold it back. You are very strong, Jeanette."

"And dangerous." A sudden, terrible thought came to her. "I did not take it from you permanently, did I? You are still a Guardian, are you not?"

There was silence all around her as her companions slowly realized the import of what she asked.

"Where's the Targe stone?" Rowan asked, her voice tight.

"Here, love." Nicholas grabbed it from where it lay nearby.

Malcolm picked up the sack from where it had been spread on the ground and handed it to Rowan. She laid the sack over her lap, and then settled the stone in her hands, resting them on the sack. She closed her eyes. Jeanette, Malcolm, and Nicholas waited in silence.

A breeze suddenly wafted around them, lifting strands of Jeanette's hair to tickle her face. Rowan dropped the stone onto the sack and the breeze stopped as quickly as it had started.

"I am still a Guardian," Rowan said. "But the barrier is gone."

CHAPTER SEVENTEEN

SCOTIA MOVED AS QUICKLY AS SHE COULD THROUGH THE FOREST, keeping an eye out around her and trying to be as quiet as possible. She knew the English soldiers could be anywhere, and despite her intention to do grave harm to them one way or another, she wanted to be the one to surprise them, not the other way around. Before too long she reached the familiar path that led from the back of Dunlairig Castle, up the ben to the wellspring, but she didn't take it. Instead, she crossed it and picked her way down the ben from the cover of the trees. The sudden longing to see her home again hit her and she hurried her pace.

"Scotia!"

She stopped and looked around. The raspy call came from nearby but she couldn't tell exactly where.

"Who is there?" she called back, trying to keep her voice from carrying too far.

"Wheesht! Up here."

She looked up and found Myles perched in a tree nearby, watching her. She cursed under her breath, turned away from him, and continued down the ben.

The thump of him landing on the ground behind her told her he would be following her any minute. Busybody.

"Scotia, wait!" he hissed at her, but she kept walking until he caught up enough to grab her arm and spin her around so she would look at him—look up at him. When had he gotten taller than her? She remembered teasing him unmercifully, not too many years ago, about how she could look down upon his head from her greater height, just as he'd teased her unmercifully when her teeth had started falling out years before that. At one time they had even been friends, playing together along the edge of the loch on peaceful summer days. But that was in the past. There was no peace to be had now.

"Why should I wait for you?" she demanded.

"Where are you going?"

She crossed her arms and studied him for a long moment. "'Tis none of your business where I am bound," she said.

He mirrored her pose. "But it is, Scotia. I was told to watch for anyone coming or going from the castle and that includes you. Are you alone?"

Her ire rose at the tone he used. "Do you see anyone here with me?"

"I do not."

"Then get back up in your perch and I'll be on my way."

"You ken I cannot do that, aye? There are others watching. If I let you go on unescorted, they will see and there shall be hell to pay when your father or the chief find out." He held out a hand to her. "Come, let me escort you back to the camp. We might even make it back before anyone finds you are gone."

"I will not return to the camp like some sort of prisoner." She cocked her head and examined him as if he were a bug. "I think I see why the chief does not like you. You are quick to escort people where they do not wish to go."

"I am only doing my duty, Scotia."

"Duty? You watch and wait and do nothing. Is that your duty? It is not mine." She whirled and continued down the ben.

"Wait!" Myles's voice was low but commanding and that just made her angrier. She was so tired of everyone telling her what to do, where to go, how to behave, while they did nothing to find the English who had them cowering in the wood like frightened rabbits. They did nothing. She was not going to do nothing any longer.

"Scotia, damn it, stop!"

Scotia sped her feet, but Myles was able to catch up with her with little trouble and once more grabbed her arm, only this time he did not let go, but instead pulled her back up the ben.

"You cannot go that way," he said, anger clear in his voice now. "I shall not let you."

"Let me!" Scotia yanked her arm from his hand. "Let me? I did not ask for your permission, Myles."

"Aye, she did not ask for your permission, boy."

Three English soldiers stepped from behind trees, swords drawn, surrounding them. Scotia's anger spiked, even as her heart sank. She was supposed to be the one to surprise the English, not the other way around. She heard Myles pull out his dirk as he tried to push her behind him. She was so mad at him, at the English, at herself for not being more aware, that she could not even speak.

"Put your back to mine," Myles said, and she saw the merit in such a position as she pulled her own dagger and the ax for good measure.

"She isn't the one," one of the English soldiers said, a man missing most of his front teeth.

"Are you sure?" another soldier asked.

The first one glared at the other. "I do not think I will ever forget an auburn-haired witch who dropped a wall of stone on top of my detachment."

"You were there?" Scotia asked, the question popping out of her mouth before she realized she spoke aloud.

"Aye, I was there," the man responded, his words clipped and his eyes glittering. With a smack of the side of his sword against one of her hands and then the other, he had the ax falling to the ground and her dagger flying up in the air. He deftly caught the knife and examined the hilt while he gathered the ax and slid it into his own belt.

"'Twas Archibald's dagger," he said to the other two. "How did you come by this?" he asked Scotia.

"That Sassenach used it to kill my mum."

Myles groaned and she realized that if this man discerned who her mother was, he might also figure out her other relations.

"It was very kind of the two of you to let us know you were here," the third soldier said.

"You could not find us without a bit of help, aye?" Scotia said, a sneer in her voice.

"Wheesht!" Myles cast her a glance hot with irritation.

"Who is this girl?" the third soldier demanded of the one with missing teeth.

"No one," Myles said.

"I am no girl, to be sure," she said at the same time.

The third soldier stepped closer and rested the tip of his sword at the base of Scotia's neck. When she tried to back up, Myles did not move.

"Who are you . . . wench?" the third one asked again, pressing the point just hard enough to prick her skin.

"I am . . . I am . . ."

"Wheesht!" Myles turned his head to hiss at her. "Do not answer their questions." At the same moment, the soldier holding her dagger made a move that she could only see out of the side of her eye, and Myles collapsed behind her with a scream.

"Myles!" Scotia tried to turn around but the sword at her throat was joined by one at her back. When she tried to look down, the sword tip lifted to her chin and forced it upward until she could do naught but stare into the muddy eyes of the English soldier.

"Tell me now. Who. Are. You?"

"Do not!" Myles said, and Scotia could hear a movement by the other soldier as she heard another grunt of pain from Myles.

"Stop! I will tell you who I am if you promise not to hurt him anymore."

The soldier in front of her considered her request for a moment before replying, "You have my promise."

She hesitated, unsure if what she was about to do was the best thing for her or for Myles, but she did not seem to have any choice if she was to stop them from doing further harm to him.

"I am Scotia MacAlpin, daughter of Kenneth."

"That would make her cousin to the witch," one of the other soldiers said. It sounded like the one with missing teeth.

She saw the one in front of her nod slightly, then heard Myles grunt one more time. Quickly, the smell of blood filled the air.

"Myles? Myles!" There was only a gurgling sound and then nothing. "You promised!" she screeched at the soldier still holding her chin up with his sword.

"And I did not break my promise, Scotia of MacAlpin. I promised that *I* would not harm your companion and *I* did not."

Rage boiled up within her, roiling through her veins. "I should have expected as much from a Sassenach. What did you do to him? Let me see him!"

The sword at her chin was lowered just enough to let her look down and to the side. Myles was looking straight up at the sky, his eyes unblinking. His right leg looked odd and was covered in blood, as was his neck. Her knees trembled and her breath caught in her chest. The rage that had boiled a moment ago turned to ice, heavy and cold. The dagger that had killed her mum stuck out of his gut, buried to the hilt.

Her stomach threatened to empty itself but she would not give these men the satisfaction of seeing her weakness. She swallowed hard, and forced herself to look at everything they had done to Myles, to remember it, to remember her part in his death, though she did not understand why they had killed him.

Sorrow swamped her then as the reality that Myles was dead hit her, as her part in their being found hit her. This death was on her. She was the cause of it. Myles had not deserved such an end.

She added his death to the tally she kept in the dark place where her heart used to be. She vowed in that moment that she would see Myles avenged, just as she would see her mother's murder avenged upon these men.

If she lived.

DUNCAN SCANNED THE PLANTS AHEAD OF HIM, PICKING OUT the telltale signs of Scotia's passage in a broken leaf here, a scuffed-up piece of moss there, and every now and again, an actual footprint. He needed to teach her how to move through the wood more carefully so she could not be trailed so easily, though to be fair, perhaps the difficult woman listened to his lessons sometimes after all, for he doubted many would find her as easy to follow as he did. Still, if she was going to continue to get herself into trouble, she needed some real skills to minimize the risk she brought to others. Her trail might be hard to follow, but it wasn't impossible, and it could easily lead the English, wherever the bastards were, back to their camp.

"We shall have to move the camp when we get back," he said quietly to Uilliam, who trailed behind him.

A grunt was all he got. It was all he'd gotten from Uilliam since they'd left the camp to find the wayward Scotia, and experience told him Scotia would not like the greeting she would get from the man when they caught up with her. Uilliam might not be her father, but he was her father's best friend.

Duncan stopped and studied the ground. "Someone joined her here." He looked around and could not find a direction the footprints might have come from. Uilliam was looking up and pulling on his black bushy beard.

"Whoever it was, was up in the tree," he said. He looked in the direction where they both knew the castle lay. "That high up," he said as he pointed at a large branch that would have been an easy place for a man to sit. "I expect you could see the castle from there. But was it one of our men, or an English soldier lying in wait for one of us to wander by?"

"And did he join her, or follow her as we are doing?"

Uilliam grunted again. Duncan swallowed the worry that seemed his ever-present companion where Scotia was concerned. For as long as he could remember, he had watched over her, rescuing her from trouble again and again, though she had not ever asked him to. She had been such a sweet lass when she was little, winning his heart with charming smiles and a ready laugh. When had she changed? He could not say, but he missed the enchanting lass she had once been, and he despaired of ever seeing her again, even if they succeeded in rescuing the angry, grief-filled, vengeful young woman she had become.

He studied the footprints but the ground was hard and he could not tell much. He motioned for Uilliam to follow him as he continued to track Scotia and whomever she had encountered. It was the only way they would get their answers.

Not much farther down the ben, Duncan spied a body lying in an opening between the trees. The body was a bloody mess with a dagger sticking out of his gut. Duncan stopped abruptly, drawing his claymore, and readying himself for an attack.

"Myles," he whispered as Uilliam caught up with him, his own sword drawn. " 'Twas Myles who joined her."

Duncan pointed ahead of him. Myles had been a good man, young, aye, but loyal, brave. He would have been someone's champion eventually, Duncan was sure of it. And the man was a good fighter. If someone did that to Myles, it was because he'd been protecting Scotia and wasn't able to fight the way he could. And if someone did that to Myles, what would that person do to Scotia? A muscle twitched in his jaw and his mind tried to follow that question with every atrocity he had ever seen or heard about. He clamped down on the horrible possibilities and examined the area around the body. If anyone harmed her in any way, they would answer to Duncan's blade.

When he and Uilliam were satisfied that this was not a trap, they moved closer to the body.

"There were two . . . no, three, soldiers here, and so was Scotia," he said.

"Aye, 'tis where they got this dagger," Uilliam said, drawing the weapon from the body and examining the hilt. "'Tis the one taken from the spy who killed Elspet. Nicholas had it after Kenneth killed the bastard. Scotia asked for it and he could not think of a reason not to let her have it. Are you sure Myles was killed by the English? That lassie has never struck me as dangerous, but she's changed since Elspet died."

Duncan looked at all the marks on the ground, the faint impression of feet standing heel to heel, a defensive stance. Where Myles had fallen, it was clear one set of those prints were his. The other prints were too small to be a man's. He let go of a breath he hadn't been aware of holding. "'Twas not Scotia's doing," he said, pointing to the evidence. "Myles had her at his back, as he had been taught. I've no doubt she drew that dagger to protect herself." He shook his head, imagining Scotia, dark eyes narrowed as she said something to their attackers that would only rile their anger. He only hoped that was not the reason why Myles had been killed.

Uilliam hunkered down next to Myles and closed the guard's eyes. "He was a good lad." He sighed. "Is the lassie alive, do you think?"

Duncan looked around and found no sign that she had left the area on her own feet, but he refused to draw any conclusions from that.

"I cannot say." He expanded the area he had inspected. "It looks as if they must have carried her out of here, though it does not look as if she made it easy for them." He looked about some more, hoping, praying that he'd not find her in the same state in which they'd found Myles. He would never forgive himself if she came to the same end, even if it was her own folly that brought her there. "There is no trail of blood from here, but that only means she wasn't bleeding when they took her."

MALCOLM OPENED AND CLOSED HIS RIGHT HAND, IGNORING the pain that ran up his arm, amazed that it was finally strong enough to hold his claymore securely, though it had not been easy to carry it in his hands during the trek from caves to camp. He had been happy to sheathe it when they reached their destination. Jeanette had noticed, but said nothing. What was there to say except that the time had more than come for him to take his leave of the MacAlpins, just as he'd always said he would.

Before he had fallen in love with Jeanette.

He looked over at his angel as she talked quietly with Rowan and Nicholas. Jeanette had been magnificent as she channeled the power of the stone. Malcolm had felt her joy as she took up the task, the duty, she had been trained for all her life. It was not unlike the way he had always imagined he would feel when he became chief of his clan: strong, sure, and doing what he was meant to do.

The way he felt in battle. The way he felt with Jeanette.

Doubt tried to pry its way into his thoughts but he would not allow it. Jeanette had her duty, and it was so clear that being a Guardian was what she was meant to do. He would never ask her to give that up.

Just as she had not asked him to renounce his duty.

He hated that he could not see a way for them to be together, and the mere thought of leaving her left him twisted up with fury and agitation. He glared at his hand as he clenched it so tightly that pain sliced up his arm to his shoulder, but he didn't care. It was time he returned to his place in the king's army, to his duty as the heir to his father's position as chief of MacKenzie.

He understood all too clearly why Jeanette had not been happy when she'd come into her destiny as a Guardian.

MALCOLM'S FEW BELONGINGS WERE PACKED IN A TRAVEL SACK. His claymore was strapped to his back. Now would be the easiest time to leave. Jeanette and Rowan, with Nicholas's support, needed to figure out how to work together to protect the clan, but there was naught Malcolm could do to help that along. The chief, with Uilliam's support and counsel, and Kenneth's when he returned with reinforcements, would find a way to rid themselves of the English—those who were already in their glen and those who were coming. Rowan and Jeanette were powerful and if Jeanette had created a barrier already, then she could do it again to protect the castle. Rowan would help her find a way to help stabilize it and the clan could return to their home.

He could try to convince King Robert to send men to help the MacAlpins repel the English, though he could not decide if he would prefer to join such a contingent or prefer not to return. He feared if he did return, he might not be able to leave again.

He feared if he waited longer, he might not be able to leave at all, though honor required that he fulfill his vow to the king and his duty to his clan.

And yet he would not leave Jeanette when her sister was missing and English soldiers roamed these bens, hunting for Nicholas and Rowan.

He watched as Jeanette handed Rowan the cup of water, as Nicholas helped his wife to steady it while she drank. The bond between Nicholas and Rowan was strong. Their love for each other was clear in the little touches, the way they looked into each other's eyes as they spoke, the gentle smile on Nicholas's face when Rowan insisted on standing.

An ache set up in Malcolm's chest. He wanted those things with Jeanette, but that was not to be and the sooner they went their separate ways, the easier it would be for both of them to move on, to do their duties to their clans.

"Jeanette," he said quietly when Nicholas folded Rowan into his arms and Jeanette turned away from them. Her eyes were full of worry. Her lower lip was caught between her teeth. He wanted to comfort her, take her cares from her, but he could not. "I need to speak with you."

She looked him in the eye and swallowed and he had the sense she knew what he was about to say. He took her hand and led her away from Rowan and Nicholas, but still within sight of them. There were men watching the perimeter of the camp, but he did not want Jeanette out of the reach of Rowan and the Targe should anything happen.

When he stopped, he pulled her into his embrace, rested his cheek against her soft, flaxen hair, and inhaled, pulling the sweet scent of her deep inside him. They stood there for long moments. Never had words been so hard to find.

"You are going," she said, saving him from saying it.

"Not until we find Scotia and discover exactly what the English threat is. But aye, as soon as those are accomplished, I will leave. 'Tis time."

"Your hand and arm still need time to return to full strength. Another fortnight, maybe more."

He wished with all his heart he could justify lingering here, but he knew it would only hurt both of them more when the time came and he had to leave anyway. "The healing is done. It is up to me now to make them strong again." He pulled her away and looked into her eyes. "You have your duty and 'tis very clear you will be brilliant at it. I have my duty, too."

"Will you go home?"

"I need to send word to my father that I am not dead. I need to make sure he kens that, but I must return to the king's army. I gave my vow I would fight in his army against the English for the freedom of Scotland."

Her lips formed a tight line and she blinked quickly. "I understand." She pressed her palm to his chest but did not meet his gaze. "We both have a duty we cannot shirk."

"If there were any way to stay with you, I would, angel. You ken that, aye?"

She looked up at him. Her clear blue eyes held sadness so deep, he could lose himself in it, and it pained him that he was the cause of yet more grief in her life. "I understand," she said. "I have not discovered a way for us to be together, either."

"I will go as soon as possible, angel. I do not want to bring you any more pain than I already have." He bent to kiss her when a commotion from the far side of the campsite caught their attention.

Jeanette whirled in his arms and raced across the camp. "Scotia?"

Malcolm quickly followed her back toward Rowan and Nicholas just as Uilliam burst out of the trees, a bloodied body in his arms.

"Nay!" Rowan and Jeanette said simultaneously. Malcolm grabbed Jeanette's arm to keep her by him as Uilliam slowed and approached them. Nicholas did the same with Rowan.

"'Tis not Scotia," Uilliam said as he came to a stop. "'Tis Myles, slaughtered like an animal by those bastard English with this." He nodded to the dagger that lay now upon Myles's chest.

"Scotia claimed that dagger. You did not find my sister?" Jeanette asked.

"Nay. Duncan believes she was taken by the English. He has continued tracking them. Please, God, he finds them this time."

"Duncan is alone? He did not take the other watchers from the castle?" Nicholas asked.

"Duncan did not want to take the time. He is beside himself with worry for what may befall the lass." He looked down at Myles but they all knew death was just one thing that might befall Scotia. "The lad blames himself for not getting back to camp in time to stop her."

"He cannot blame himself for that," Jeanette said. "He did not ken she was in trouble until I saw it. If anyone is to blame, 'tis Scotia. She understands how dangerous these times are." She rubbed the heel of her hand against her chest in a gesture Malcolm now knew meant she was trying to stop the emotions flooding through her. "She understands." She looked to Rowan, who nodded at her.

"Let us not hobble ourselves with blame," Rowan said quietly as she reached for Jeanette's hand and squeezed it. "Right now we need to get her back, and Duncan, before he does something equally as rash. He has always considered her his responsibility to protect, ever since they were both weans, though it is beyond my understanding why."

Malcolm watched as Jeanette reclaimed her calm and nodded at her cousin. "Well," she said, looking from Malcolm to Nicholas and back. "How are we going to do that?"

"We need to join Duncan as quickly as possible, with every man we have," Nicholas said.

"We will need to take them all out," Malcolm added. "We cannot leave a single English soldier standing any longer."

"I was hoping Kenneth would return with reinforcements before we had to engage them," Nicholas said, "but we can wait no longer."

"Aye," Uilliam said. "I do not like that Duncan is alone. I would wrap this body, first. I do not want to leave him exposed to the birds and beasts of the forest. I could not look his mum in the eye ever again if I did."

Jeanette grabbed a plaid someone had folded carefully and placed by a nearby tree. Rowan helped her spread it on the ground and Uilliam laid Myles's body on it.

"Do you have any idea how many English there are?" Rowan asked as she and Jeanette quickly wrapped the body in the grey and brown plaid.

"Duncan says there were three there today." Uilliam pulled on his black beard as he watched the women at their sad task.

"We saw six near the shieling a few days ago," Malcolm said.

"And we saw at least a dozen just this morning when I dropped the trees around them." Rowan tucked an end of the plaid tightly into a fold, then stood. "Was that all of them, or are there more?"

Malcolm knew one never had a sure count of the enemy when entering into battle, but he also knew the better the count, the better the plan of attack.

"Angel, you saw this," he said to Jeanette. "Did you have any sense of how many English were holding Scotia?"

Jeanette looked up at him from where she crouched as she tucked the last end of the plaid about Myles's body, then her attention turned inward and she closed her eyes. "I remember her at the Story Stone—she was tied there at the base of it. She did not look hurt . . . but I could not see who was with her." She opened her eyes. "I'm sorry. My gift is not as useful as Rowan's when it comes to battle." She rose. "Duncan kens I saw her at the Story Stone. Will he go there, or follow the tracks?"

Malcolm knew what he would do. "I would follow the tracks in the hopes of catching them before they could join the rest of their company. I think Duncan will, too."

"Aye," Uilliam agreed. "'Tis what I would do, too, and I trained the lad."

"Which means we could head directly for the Story Stone," Nicholas said. "If we get there before Scotia and her captors, we can backtrack and ambush them."

Malcolm stared at the dagger that now lay on the ground next to Jeanette. "It could be a trap," Malcolm said. "They would not have left that knife behind unless they knew it would mean something to someone specific."

Nicholas looked at him. "I agree, but we have to go. Perhaps they think to hold her hostage in exchange for me. I expect there is a large reward offered for my head by King Edward."

"But they will also want me," Rowan said, then she lifted the ermine sack, "and this. They do not know about Jeanette yet, thank the saints."

Nicholas gave the shrill whistle that sounded like a hawk, and warriors began to join them from their posts in the wood.

"We won't let them have any of us, love. We'll get her back."

"How?" Jeanette asked.

"We shall have to make a plan when we get there, once we know exactly what we are up against. Duncan will be able to tell us more if he can prevent himself from rushing to Scotia's aid long enough for us to get there."

"I've trained him better than that. He will ken what we need to know by the time we get there, I have no doubt."

Denis stepped forward from the gathered warriors. "'Tis Myles?" he asked, pointing to the wrapped body. "I heard his name. I will be of no use in battle so I will stay and bury the lad." He looked at Nicholas and Malcolm, the echo of the warrior he must have once been etched on his face, brought to life again by his clenched jaw and snapping eyes. "Bring our lassies back," he said, "all three of them."

Nicholas and Malcolm nodded.

"Uilliam, fetch the men still watching the castle and bring them with you to the Story Stone," Nicholas said. "Find us when you get there."

Jeanette gave Uilliam's arm a squeeze as he passed her on his way into the trees, then she grabbed the dagger that had been left in the dirt, the dagger that had killed her mother and Myles. "I do not have a scabbard for this," she said to Malcolm. "Will you carry it? I suspect Scotia will want it back when we free her."

"You would put yourself in danger by going into battle, too?" he asked, not really surprised that she would go with the rest of them, but wishing there was somewhere safe she could stay.

"I will. I am a Guardian now. It is my duty to protect the clan, though I have not a gift that will be of much use in battle."

He saw several men stop and look at Jeanette with surprise painted on their faces, but Malcolm scowled at them, daring them to interrupt, and they wisely kept their questions to themselves.

"And Scotia is my sister. I'll not sit by while yet another of my family is threatened by the damned English." She lifted her chin. "Would you?"

"Of course not. We will get Scotia safely back amongst her kin," he said, "and do everything we can to dispatch those who took her." And then he would leave his heart behind with his angel.

CHAPTER EIGHTEEN

Jeanette was already weary from their day of traveling, first from the caves to the MacAlpins' camp, and now an hour's fast walk east across the ben, well past the path where she and Malcolm had first fought the gap-toothed English scout together. Now she, Rowan, and all the warriors they could gather, including Malcolm and Nicholas, headed uphill until they came to the edge of the forest where it opened onto a high mountain meadow. It was nearing sunset when they stopped, just in the cover of the trees, but there was enough light to easily see the ancient Story Stone where it stood near the center of the broad open area atop a hillock. The stone was twice the height of the tallest warrior, and in the dim light they could see a figure bound to it and surrounded by twelve English soldiers.

"I did not see the soldiers in my visions," Jeanette whispered to Malcolm and Nicholas. How could she trust what she saw in the visions if something so important was kept from her?

A quick search turned up Duncan, keeping watch over Scotia from the thick branches of an ancient Scots pine tree.

"Have you had any contact with them?" Nicholas asked Duncan as he joined them on the ground.

"Nay. Scotia was already bound to the stone when I finally tracked them here. I think they must have knocked her out to bring her here, for she was silent and still, her head hanging for the longest time. She is awake now and goads them every now and then." He shook his head slowly. "Daft lassie," he said quietly. With a sigh, he continued, "They have been standing in that circle around her since I arrived here."

"So the dagger *was* a message," Rowan said.

"Aye," Duncan replied.

"My kinsmen will never give you Nicholas and Rowan for me!" Scotia's shrill voice, loud even from a distance, startled them all.

Duncan raced for the forest's edge with Nicholas, Rowan, Jeanette, and Malcolm on his heels.

"She is taunting them again," Duncan whispered.

"Aye, and giving us information." Nicholas smiled, though his eyes did not. "Do you think she kens we are here?" he asked Duncan.

"I cannot say. 'Tis not the first time she has shouted at them since I have arrived."

"What else has she said?" Malcolm asked.

"She said, 'There are only five warriors left of my kin but they are strong and will rip out your hearts.'"

"Bloodthirsty wench." Nicholas shook his head. "I doubt they believe her, about our numbers or their hearts, but perhaps she plants doubts in their minds about how many we really are."

They carefully slipped back to where their warriors were gathered in the thicker trees away from the edge of the meadow, arriving just as Uilliam and three more warriors joined the gathering, bringing their total to thirteen, plus Jeanette and Rowan.

Nicholas and Uilliam quickly sent men out to keep watch over the meadow and Scotia, then turned their attention to a plan of attack.

"How many English have you seen?" Nicholas asked Duncan.

"Just the twelve that are surrounding the stone. If we attack after dark, we will be able to surprise them."

"The moon will not rise until late tonight," Malcolm said. "We will have no light once the sun sets. We either go soon, or wait for the moonrise."

Jeanette looked at Rowan. "What can we do, Cousin?"

"We?" Uilliam was looking at her like she had sprouted wings.

"Jeanette is also a Guardian now," Malcolm said, taking her hand in his. There was pride in his voice that warmed her.

"Is this true, Rowan?" Uilliam asked.

"Of course 'tis true," Jeanette said, relishing the spurt of irritation that Uilliam's doubt sparked in her, letting it damp down the fear and worry that filled her, if only for a moment.

Uilliam looked from her to Rowan, to Nicholas, and back to Jeanette. "My apologies, Jeanette. 'Tis only that I have never heard such a thing was possible. When? How?" He shook his head. "Nay, that will keep for later. What is your gift?" he asked. "That is the important question."

"Visions . . . and I can build a barrier, like Mum did, with Rowan's help"—though it brought pain to Rowan, but she did not say that—"but I cannot hold it yet."

Uilliam was pulling at his beard, a sure sign that he was deep in thought, pondering this news.

"Can you see the outcome of the coming battle?" Duncan said.

Gooseflesh danced over Jeanette's skin. Did she want to see the outcome? What if it went against them? Did she want to see her loved ones die before they actually did? If she saw the outcome, could she do something to change it? So far, what she had seen in her visions had come to pass exactly as she had seen them, but did it have to be that way?

"Angel?" Malcolm squeezed her hand and she realized she held his right hand. His injured arm was pressed against hers and the squeeze of his hand was only a little weaker than if she held his strong one. It was then she understood that there really had been healing power at the wellspring, for an injury such as his should have taken much longer to heal. "Jeanette? Can you?"

She looked up at him, confused for a moment about his

question, until she retraced her thoughts. "I can try to see the outcome, but I cannot promise anything."

Malcolm slipped a waterskin from his shoulder and filled the cup she set on the ground, until it nearly overflowed. Jeanette knelt before it. Rowan knelt next to her, holding the Targe, wrapped in its sack, in her hand. She took Jeanette's hand in her other one.

"Let's see if this makes it easier for you to find the vision you seek," she said.

"I do not want to hurt you again," Jeanette whispered.

"We do not know that you will. You did not hurt me by the burn this morning and the visions came easier to you, did they not? Let me sit with you and we'll see what happens."

Jeanette looked up to find Nicholas and Malcolm standing close by. She nodded, more to herself than to the others, and leaned forward to peer into the water, letting her gaze sink past the surface of the cup once more. An odd sensation trickled into her hand from Rowan's, up her arm, and suddenly she was in the flood of images. She searched for some vision, anything, that included Scotia, the Story Stone, the English soldiers, her own kin. She reached out, trying to see each vision, but nothing caught her attention. Finally she relaxed and let the visions swirl around her, hoping something useful would find her.

The stag. She almost missed it but was able to reach out and hold the vision still long enough to watch the stag with the bent antler leading her through the wood, cutting an arc around . . . the meadow with the Story Stone. She thought she gasped but could not tell if it was part of the vision or in truth. She followed the stag, as she'd done before in a dream, until he came to stand in a fast-flowing burn. She waited for him to continue but he just stood in the water, staring at her, until she understood: She was to stand in the burn. "Why?" she tried to ask him, but the vision had gone and she was once more kneeling by the cup, Rowan's hand still gripped in hers.

"It is done," she said quietly.

"Did you see the battle?" Duncan asked before she had gotten her bearings again. "Did you see us freeing Scotia?"

"Nay." She looked up at the men gathered around her and Rowan. "I am sorry but I saw nothing of the coming battle, nor of Scotia," Jeanette said, feeling as if she had failed in her first attempt to help her clan.

"It was like a dream," Rowan said quietly beside her. She cocked her head and squinted her eyes as if she was trying to see the vision again. "We followed a stag with a bent antler. What did that mean?" Rowan asked her.

"You saw it, too?" Jeanette's heart began to hammer.

"You saw the stag again?" Malcolm asked.

"Again?" Rowan, Nicholas, and Duncan all asked at the same time.

"Aye," Jeanette said, closing her eyes in an effort to remember every detail of the vision.

"What else did you see, angel?" Malcolm crouched in front of her.

"He stopped at the edge of a burn, pawed at a stone, then looked at me," Rowan said when Jeanette did not immediately speak. "It was as if he wanted me to stay out of the burn." She looked over at Jeanette. "And then he walked in and looked at you, Cousin. And then the vision stopped. What did it mean, Jeanette?"

Jeanette ran through the vision again in her head. She had not noticed that Rowan was with her, or that the stag had hesitated at the edge of the burn. But clearly that part was meant for Rowan.

"I have seen that stag before, in dreams and in the forest. He leads me, warns me. I think you and I have work to do at that burn, but I do not ken what. Do you?"

Now Rowan turned thoughtful.

"I cannot topple trees upon them," she said. "They have clearly chosen a spot that limits that. I cannot even topple the Story Stone upon them, for that would harm Scotia. There are not stones large enough to do any damage to them in the field."

"It would seem they are well versed in your abilities, love," Nicholas said, helping Rowan to rise to her feet. Jeanette poured the water out and stood, putting her cup away.

Rowan walked over to where a warrior's targe leaned against a nearby tree. The round shield, with a spike protruding from the center of it, was both protection and weapon.

"If only we could create a shield, as the ancient Guardians could," she said. "But I do not ken where we could place it that would help."

Jeanette looked at the targe that held Rowan's attention. She cocked her head.

"'Tis not unlike the barrier I created today," Jeanette said quietly, deep in thought. "If I could create another one and hold it—without hurting you—could you move it?"

Rowan's eyebrows went up and Jeanette could see her cousin considering what Jeanette proposed. "I think it would work, though the wind that comes with my gift will likely throw up anything it can, so the barrier would be visible, in a way, to the English."

Nicholas was nodding. "What about Scotia? If it is harmful enough to drive the English before it, will it not harm her, too?"

"Not if they drive the barrier toward us," Malcolm said. He looked at Jeanette. "You could drive the English away from Scotia and toward us. The stone would give her some shelter if the barrier came from the far side of the meadow."

Jeanette chewed on her lip. "In the vision, the stag took us to a burn that way"—she pointed to her left—"but around the meadow. Does anyone remember if that burn runs anywhere close to the meadow across from where we are now?"

"Aye, it hugs the far side but you would likely be in view of the English from there," Uilliam said.

"If we position ourselves as much as we can directly across from here, Scotia should be sheltered by the stone. We may not be able to move the barrier over the stone anyway. For that matter, I may not be able to hold it long enough to do us any good at all, or Rowan may not be able to move it."

"If this works, if you two can do what you plan, we shall need to have most of our warriors here, with three"—Malcolm looked at the few men around them—"two ready to free Scotia once the English are driven or drawn away. I will go with Rowan and Jeanette to keep them safe while they do their work."

"I will go, too," Nicholas said. "As the Guardian's Protector, Rowan's safety"—he looked surprised—"and I suppose Jeanette's now, too, are my first duty." He gave Malcolm a sidewise look.

Jeanette caught Nicholas's eye and barely shook her head, willing him not to say what she knew he was thinking, what she wished for but could not have: that Malcolm would be her Protector.

"Uilliam," Nicholas continued, "you should engage the English, hold their attention while we circle around. They do not ken that I am chief, so use that to our favor. Make them think you are the one, the new chief, that you are willing to entertain turning me over, but not Rowan. They would not believe you would turn over Rowan. Our warriors will hold here until the English are clear of Scotia and the stone, then attack. Duncan, take someone with you and position yourself to the north. Be ready to free her. If we can, Malcolm and I will join you there, but do not count on it, aye? Does anyone have a better plan?"

Duncan, Malcolm, and Uilliam looked at each other and back to Nicholas, but none had anything better to offer.

Jeanette's palms were sweaty and her heart sped. Her sister's life, and the lives of those who sought to free her, rested on the skill of two Guardians new to their gifts.

THE LIGHT WAS FAILING FAST AS MALCOLM, JEANETTE, ROWAN, and Nicholas rushed as quietly as they could around the meadow to position themselves across from where the MacAlpin warriors waited. They had not gone far before Malcolm heard Uilliam shouting for the English to hand over Scotia or pay the price. They moved rapidly, but not so fast that he and Nicholas couldn't keep an eye out lest there were any English lurking in the wood. Duncan had done some searching before they arrived and had seen no one.

They continued to hear shouting but Malcolm did not spare his attention to listen to exactly what was being said. Before long they found the burn. Jeanette splashed into it and looked around.

"Nay, this is not the right place." She climbed out of the water and began to run along its bank, lifting her skirts high enough to keep herself from tripping. Malcolm stayed as close as he could, scanning the wood around them for danger. Rowan was right behind him with Nicholas on her heels.

Soon the trees began to thin around them and just as he was about to call out to Jeanette to stop, she skidded to a halt and stepped back in the water.

"This will do. I would rather be out there"—she pointed to where the burn broke out of the wood and into the open meadow—"but we do not want to warn them what we are about."

"I doubt much that they could have any idea what we are about, angel, even if they did see us. They do not know about you."

She grinned at him and he did not know how he would live without her when this was over.

Rowan stood on the bank of the burn, the Targe sack open over her hands, the stone settled on top of it in her palms. Jeanette took a breath, then shook her head and took off her brogues, tossing the sopping shoes up onto the bank. She touched the stone, then began the ritual he had seen earlier this day. Her hands flew through the air. Strange words flowed from her mouth.

"Is it working?" he asked quietly, hoping Rowan could tell.

"Aye." Rowan's voice was almost flat, as if she was deep in concentration.

"Are you in pain, love?" Nicholas asked.

"A little."

Jeanette stilled. "I do not want to hurt you, Rowan."

"We must free Scotia. If it means a bit of pain for me, I will manage it. We cannot lose her." The fierce words were at odds with the worry in her eyes.

"Can you place the stone on the ground?" Jeanette asked. "Let me try to create the barrier on my own."

"But—"

"I promise I will ask for your help, as I did this morn, if I need it, but I think I understand better now what I need to do."

"Promise?"

"I do."

Just as Rowan reluctantly settled the stone on its opened sack on the ground, the sound of a branch cracking rang through the wood around them. Nicholas and Malcolm looked at each other.

"I shall see what company we have. Nicholas, keep them safe!" And Malcolm melted into the trees.

Jeanette felt the stirrings of panic but refused to let it take her over. Too many people were counting on her ability to use the Targe, to build a barrier, as her mother had done before her. She squatted down in the burn. The feel of her wet skirts pulled by the current was oddly soothing, reminding her of the power of water. She remembered standing on the stone in the grotto, the icy water lapping at her feet, and the power that surged through her with the visions. She had the Targe stone. She had water. And she was a Guardian.

She began the ritual again, this time keeping her eyes on the Targe but her mind on the water. She imagined herself pulling the power of the water into her, through her, and directed it to the Targe. Suddenly power was whooshing through her, tingling under her skin in its rush to the stone. The sounds of swords clashing broke her concentration. She looked around but could not see who was fighting.

"Malcolm?"

"He is doing his part," Rowan said. "We must do ours. Do you need my help?"

Jeanette looked her cousin in the eye. "Nay. I was almost there. Let me build the barrier and then you will need to use the Targe with me to push it away from us. I cannot promise it will not hurt."

"Hurry!" Nicholas said.

Jeanette was able to find the power almost immediately, as if it had been awaiting her returned attention. It flowed through her, to the Targe, and then, as she repeated the chant and made the motions, she could see the barrier taking form but it was too small. She pulled the energy through her as hard and as fast as she could, but it grew no larger than the size of a cottage.

"I have it, but it is not as big as I had hoped," she said to Rowan, though her attention was fixed on the barrier now, her hands flying through the air, reweaving it where it began to unravel. "I do not know how long I can hold it," she said through gritted teeth. "Move it now if you can!"

Rowan scooped up the Targe and raised it up in her hands. Wind whipped around them, almost knocking Jeanette over, but she refused to lose the focus needed to keep the barrier from disintegrating. Jeanette flipped her hands then, as if she was turning a basket over, balancing it on its edge, then continued with her constant repetition of the words and hand signs that kept the barrier intact.

"Now, Rowan!" Jeanette said, her teeth gritted together as if she held a great weight.

Out of the corner of her eye she saw Rowan push her hands, still holding the Targe, away from her chest. The trees that stood between the burn and the open meadow bent under the force of the wind and the barrier.

"It is working!" Nicholas shouted.

Malcolm's whoop joined Nicholas's shout, signaling his return, but Jeanette dared not look to see if he remained uninjured. She kept her focus on the barrier, her hands moving swiftly through the air, the chant continuously flowing from her lips. In her mind she could see the barrier was now beyond the trees and moving across the meadow.

"Malcolm," Nicholas said, "follow the shield and see how far it has traveled. I will keep watch here."

MALCOLM RACED OUT INTO THE OPEN, NOT FAR FROM WHERE they stood, and the sight before him left him speechless.

"Malcolm!" Jeanette's voice was tight and worried.

"It is still working!" he shouted back, no longer worried about being heard or seen. Where he was there was a gentle breeze, but over the meadow, almost to the hillock, a storm raged. Leaves, dirt, gravel, and anything else in the path of the protective barrier had been scraped up and hurled into the air. He could hear the growl of the wind and was grateful he was not caught in it. "You are at the stone now!" he shouted back as he jogged farther out into the meadow. "The stone stands!" He jogged a bit farther. "Keep it going! I have to get closer," he yelled back at them, then ran full out as far as he thought he could go and still be heard.

"Drop it now! Drop it now!" he yelled as he could just make out the MacAlpin warriors surging out of the forest and clashing with the English soldiers who were running for their lives in front of the barrier. The sound of all the debris dropping when the wind stopped was like a heavy rain. He lifted his claymore and ran to the stone to free Scotia. He made it to the hillock just as he heard the first clash of swords. He skidded around the side of what he now saw was an almost square monolith, praying that Scotia was alive, unharmed, and still there.

The same gap-toothed soldier Jeanette had felled the day Malcolm met her had an arm around Scotia, holding her close against his chest, a dagger to her throat.

Malcolm cursed. "Let her go. You have lost. Release her now."

"As long as I have her, I have not lost." Gaptooth sneered at him. "I see you got my message."

Malcolm saw Duncan streak out of the wood behind Gaptooth, instantly recognizing Duncan's dark brown hair and determination. Another warrior was not far behind. Malcolm needed to keep the soldier occupied to give Duncan and the other man time to join him.

"We did. What would you trade her for?" Malcolm asked, waving his claymore around, holding it comfortably in both hands, to keep the soldier's attention right where he wanted it.

"You know what I want—the traitor spy and his witch, along with that stone she always carries with her."

"Ah, Nicholas and his lady wife." He pretended to think about it, still waving his sword about just enough for the soldier to continue to watch Malcolm and his weapon. "I do not think that will happen."

"Then the girl dies."

Duncan was almost there.

"I think not. If the girl dies"—he moved just a little to turn the man toward the stone slightly, and he saw Scotia move her hands along the man's arm where she gripped it, toward where his dagger arm crossed over it—"you will follow her immediately."

The fool took a step back, only then discovering that Duncan stood behind him, his sword tip now against the man's spine.

"I'll slice her neck open." Sweat popped out on the man's brow and trickled down the side of his face.

"You will release her, or I shall slice through your spine," Duncan said. The other warrior stood a few steps away, wisely leaving Duncan and Malcolm room to work.

Scotia stared at Malcolm as if she was trying to tell him something.

"Duncan," she said, her voice breathless and weak, though the glint in her eye claimed otherwise. "If I die, promise me you will slice this man in quarters and feed him to the carrion birds."

Malcolm saw her take a deep breath as if preparing herself, and then, with a shout, she pushed the soldier's dagger arm away with all her might. Malcolm swung his claymore, slicing the man's now outstretched hand, and the dagger it still gripped, from his arm. Gaptooth screamed. Scotia dropped to the ground like a deadweight the second the soldier's grip loosened on her, then scrambled behind Malcolm as Duncan ran the man through. Gaptooth dropped where he stood, facedown, his blood pumping slowly from where his hand used to be, and blossoming from the center of his back where Duncan had severed his spine.

Malcolm pulled Scotia to her feet and only then did he notice that there was a shallow slice that oozed blood from just below her left ear, almost to her chin. A hair's breadth deeper and she would be lying on the ground losing her lifeblood. She had scratches on her face and hands, probably from the debris flung into the air by Rowan's gift, and there was a place on the side of her head where her black hair looked matted.

"Are you well?" he asked her, but her eyes were trained on the man who had held her.

Duncan stared at Scotia, his eyes full of relief and anger, his mouth working as if he tried to speak but could not form the words he needed to say.

The shouts and clangs of sword on sword, which Malcolm had not noticed while his attention was focused on freeing Scotia, suddenly drew his eye to the open area near where the Scots had hidden in the wood and the men still fighting hard there. His heartbeat doubled as it always did at the prospect of battling the English.

"Duncan, take her to Jeanette and Rowan." He pointed to where he had left the two Guardians with Nicholas. "That cut on her neck needs tending. If Nicholas will leave the lasses in the care of the two of you"—he nodded at the other warrior still standing a few paces away—"tell him I await his company in battle!"

With that, Malcolm wheeled toward the fighting, the battle cry of the MacKenzies bursting from his lips, as it had in so many battles before, and his claymore held at the ready.

CHAPTER NINETEEN

It was dark when Jeanette, Rowan, Scotia, Duncan, and the other clan warrior ventured out of the shelter of the wood, but a bright half-moon had finally risen and cast enough light for them to make their way across the meadow and head back toward the battleground. As they reached the hillock in the middle of the meadow, Duncan signaled for them to stop as he crept up the wind-scraped mound to peer over it. He quickly returned to them.

"Let us go around the hillock," he said.

Jeanette started to ask him why but he just shook his head, his mouth set in a grim line, and she stopped. She forgot about her question as they neared where the battle had been joined. Even in the dark she could see bodies scattered about where they'd fallen. She quickly scanned those closest to her to see if any were known to her amongst the dead, if any of them had golden hair.

"These are all English soldiers," Duncan said as if he, too, had been searching for their kinsmen.

Nicholas walked out of the darkness of the forest nearest them, his face and clothes spattered with what must be blood, though Jeanette could not make out the color in the moonlight. Rowan ran to him.

"Are you hurt?" she asked before she closed the distance between them.

"Nay, love." His smile looked tired, but genuine. "None of the blood is mine, thanks to Uilliam's tutelage these past weeks and Malcolm's presence at my back this day." He kissed his wife, then looked at Scotia. "It is good to see you alive. I hear we have Malcolm and Duncan to thank for that."

Scotia had been silent since Duncan had brought her to them near the stream and she continued that now by replying with a slow nod.

"Where is Malcolm?" Jeanette asked.

Nicholas looked around. "He must be digging graves with some of the others."

"We are not leaving them here to rot?" Duncan asked, indignation thick in his voice.

"Nay. Malcolm made the point that leaving them here to be found would give anyone looking for us information about how many we must be and at least an inkling of our tactics, though I do not think anyone would believe what really happened here." Nicholas looked down at Rowan, then over at Jeanette. "You two make a formidable weapon. I am very glad I am on your side in this business."

Scotia looked quickly from her cousin to her sister and back, her eyes filled with questions, but rather than ask them, she gave a quick, curt shake of her head, as if she'd answered them herself. She crossed her arms and looked at her feet.

"You should have seen the fear in the eyes of these men as they fled into our trap." Uilliam waved a hand toward the dead as he joined them. "I confess, I had my own worries if you could not stop your barrier before it overran us as well."

"We would not do that to the ones we love," Rowan said. "It was impressive, aye?"

"Aye. There will be tales told around the fires for many nights to come."

Shadows seemed to separate themselves from the darkness of the forest, MacAlpins come to drag bodies into the wood.

"I need to speak to Malcolm." Jeanette left her family and headed into the forest. She needed to see if he, too, was unharmed, and then she needed to ask him to stay. The terror that had over-taken her, when he did not return with Scotia and Duncan, had filled her mind with horrible possibilities. Her mouth had gone dry at the thought that he had been harmed, or killed, and she had not been able to sit still. Even if he lived, the idea of watch-ing him leave her to return to a life of battles, where she would never know if he were alive or dead, was almost more than she could bear.

She reached for calm now that she knew he was alive, but she could not find it, not until she had seen him for herself. Not until she convinced him to stay.

As soon as she stepped into the wood she realized that she would not be able to see where she was going, for the leaves blocked almost all of the wan light cast by the moon.

Frustration and fatigue hit her all at once. "Malcolm?" she called out. "Malcolm?"

She heard footsteps at about the same moment she saw a small, flickering light.

"Angel?"

"I am here, but I have no light." And suddenly he was in front of her. A candle in one hand, the other cupped around the flame to keep it from blowing out. He dropped the candle, extin-guishing it as it fell, and swept her into his arms.

"You were magnificent," he said, taking her face in his big hands. "You and Rowan, both."

He kissed her then, quick and hard, crushing her against his chest as his tongue danced with hers. Desire kindled low in her stomach and she wanted to lose herself with him again, to love him, and have him love her, as they had loved each other in the grotto. And she knew he had been as worried about her as she was about him.

"Do not go," she whispered against his lips between kisses. "I ken it is selfish of me. I ken that there is more than you and I at stake. But I do not want you to go."

He kissed her again, softer this time, lingering as he kissed the corner of her mouth, then sliding the tip of his tongue along the line between her lips as if inviting her to open them to him, which she did, though she couldn't help but notice that he had not replied to her entreaty.

At last he held her close and rested his head against hers. "I would stay if I could, angel. I would have you come with me if you could, but neither of us can forsake our duties. And we would not like ourselves much if we did."

Her throat clogged with grief and she struggled to draw in breath as she hugged him tightly to her.

"'Tis the hardest thing I have ever done, angel mine," he whispered to her, his voice gruff as if his throat, too, were clogged with grief and heartbreak. "But I still cannot see another way."

She knew he was right, but the grief—more grief—fought against reason and for a moment she tried to think of ways to manipulate him to stay with her, but only for a moment. That was not her way. She closed her eyes against the tears that begged for release and she listened to his heartbeat one last time before she stepped back. He grabbed her hands and they stood there looking at each other, though it was so dark, she could hardly make out his beloved features.

"When will you leave?" Her voice shook and she swallowed back her heartbreak lest she fall apart in front of him. She struggled to think of his grin, his twinkling eyes, the feel of his skin beneath her hands, the wonder of joining with him in the grotto, and the way he always made her feel safe when he was near.

"At first light." He ran a finger down her cheek and she could not help but close her eyes and lean into his touch. "I do not ken where King Robert's army fights now, so it may take me some time to find them."

"Will you ever return here?" she asked, not sure if she really wanted to hear his answer.

"I do not ken. Angel, you are the seer." She could hear a smile in his voice. "Perhaps you should see what the future holds for us."

She shook her head. "I do not want to."

"Nay?"

"I fear I will not like what I see, that it will destroy my fervent hope to see you again one day." She stepped back into his embrace, hugging him tightly to her one last time as the tears she had fought streamed down her face.

SEVEN LONG DAYS LATER, MALCOLM APPROACHED THE CAMP OF King Robert's army late in the afternoon. It had not been easy to learn where the king was, though he had heard of the great Battle of Loudoun Hill and the routing of the English army. King Edward of England was no doubt livid that the king of Scotland had remained free once again.

"Who goes there?" a sentry shouted at him. The shout was meant as much for Malcolm as to warn the other sentries, and anyone else close enough to hear, that there was possible trouble.

"'Tis Malcolm MacKenzie of Blackmuir," he replied.

There was silence as he continued to approach the sentry.

"Malcolm? Step closer."

When he was close enough to make out the sentry's shaggy red hair and short stature, Malcolm smiled at the familiar face.

"We thought you dead!" the man said, slapping Malcolm on the back.

"I thought so myself, a time or two, but I am alive, and so it seems, are you, Gregor."

"Where have you been?" the man asked, his excitement quieting.

"That is something I must speak to the king about. He is here, is he not?"

"Aye, you can see his tent just there." He pointed toward the center of the encampment where a tent larger than the others flew a pennant of red and yellow. "Come and find me tonight. I would hear this tale of yours."

Malcolm smiled but promised nothing. He could not tell the secrets of Clan MacAlpin to anyone but the king, and even in that he would be careful what he told and what he did not. 'Twas bad enough that one king wanted the Highland Targe and its Guardians. He'd not tempt King Robert with the full story of what Rowan and his angel could do.

A familiar pang of remorse hit him, turning his mood dark, as it had been every day since he'd left Jeanette. If he could find a way to discharge his duty to the king and to his clan, he would surely do it, but even after a sennight of battling the problem, he could not see a solution for himself, though he hoped he had found one for the MacAlpins.

He waited outside King Robert's tent for some time before he was finally summoned inside.

"It is good to see you alive, Malcolm," the king said, motioning for Malcolm to take a seat on the stool across the table from him. He pushed a stack of maps aside. "We have missed your sword in our battles since last I saw you. It was Dalrigh, was it not?"

"Aye, sire, it was. I was sorely wounded there and it has taken me a long time to recover."

He then began the story of the MacAlpins and King Edward's desire to obtain a relic they had. He did not say anything of the Guardians, nor did he say anything about the true power of the stone, though he did relate the lore of it.

"They have fought back the English twice now, but have paid dearly for it. They have had to abandon their home and take to caves until they can be sure the English are no longer after their relic, or until they can repair their castle enough to return there. They need help, my lord."

"And you expect me to send men to their aid?"

"Not expect, but I do ask. There is reliable information that Edward has sent a contingent of men against them, led by Lord Sherwood, and they're due to arrive in Glen Lairig anytime now." He hoped the king would not ask where that reliable information came from, for he was certain the man would not believe it came from a vision.

The king grew thoughtful. "We had reports of ships leaving Ayr, with Sherwood and forty men aboard today. But we could not learn where they were bound." He cast Malcolm a calculating look. "If the relic is just a stone, why do they not give it over to the English and be rid of them?"

Ire burned in Malcolm's bones but he tried to keep his tongue civil. "Some say the Stone of Scone that you would have been crowned upon, if Edward had not stolen it, is just a relic. Should we not worry about retrieving it from English hands?"

The king steepled his fingers against his mouth, his head barely nodding. "You owe this clan something in exchange for their care of you, aye?"

"I do, but this is more important than what I owe them. King Edward hopes to crush the spirit of the Highlanders by taking this relic and crushing the clan that protects it, but I think he underestimates the spirit of the Highlanders."

King Robert narrowed his eyes as he considered what Malcolm had told him.

"Do these Highlanders not have allies they can call upon?" he asked at last.

"The former chief has been dispatched to rally them, but he had been gone at least a fortnight, with no word, when I left the clan." He carefully considered his next words. "Sire"—he rubbed his right hand with his left, as Jeanette had taught him to do to loosen up tight muscles, a thought only now occurring to him— "since it is the English they fight, would you consider sending me back there as fulfillment of my service to you?"

"You would go back to fight with them even if I send no one with you?"

"I would." Malcolm leaned forward, rested his elbows on his knees, and looked straight into the king's eyes in the hopes that Robert could see that every word he spoke was sincere. "They are good people fighting for Scotland, every bit as much as this army does. They are loyal to you and your cause. They have done nothing to merit these repeated attacks by an avaricious king, except that they protect something he covets, something that has been in their keeping for generations, something he knows nothing about except that it is revered in the Highlands as a protector of the place and its people. He does not even know if the lore is true, yet he harries this clan with spies and scouts, and soon, by the sound of it, a full detachment of soldiers. They are a small clan. I do not know if they can stand against those numbers on their own. I do not ken if one more warrior will turn the tide, but I would try."

Robert leaned back in his chair and propped his feet on the table. He laced his fingers across his midsection and once more considered Malcolm.

"And the lore is true, aye? Would you be so adamant about this clan if it was not? Would you ask me to send men with you if you did not worry about what would happen should Edward get his hands upon the relic?"

Malcolm did not let his gaze waver. "That is not for me to say, my lord. But this I can tell you. The chief of the MacAlpins of Dunlairig, Nicholas, was once a spy for Edward. He kens well what Edward is capable of and he fears for the well-being of his people. You have seen firsthand what the English king is capable of when his will is thwarted. Do you think this small clan will stand against his forces for long?"

King Robert said nothing.

"If they fall, sire, there will be nothing to stop the English from swarming across the Highlands. If they break through, they will strive to close a noose about the Lowlands. There will be nothing to stop King Edward from taking the thing he covets most . . . your throne."

King Robert sighed and rubbed the back of his neck. "I do not have men to spare, Malcolm."

Malcolm closed his eyes and did his best to quell the anger and fear that threatened to overtake his reason. Without help, he doubted the MacAlpins would survive to see summer's end, Jeanette would not survive. It was bad enough that he had left her there. He did not think he could live with her death upon his conscience. "But sire—"

King Robert held a hand up to stop Malcolm before he could make further entreaties. "You do make a compelling argument, though," the king said. "I will release you from your duty here to return to this clan."

Malcolm nodded, grateful that at least he could return to Dunlairig and to Jeanette, at least until he had to return to his home. Time, if they survived the coming English attack, might show them a solution to their inevitable separation.

"I thank you, sire."

"Do you give up so easily, Malcolm MacKenzie? I never knew you to accept less than you demanded, even of me."

Hope sprung up in Malcolm. "I have learned of late that my old ways were not always the best. Perhaps I learned that lesson too well?"

The king laughed. "Perhaps you have, but even so, you have convinced me that I must do what I can for these MacAlpins. I cannot spare many for your cause, but if you can convince your kinsmen to follow you into battle again, you have my leave to take them with you."

IT TOOK MALCOLM A WHILE TO FIND WHERE THE MACKENZIES of Blackmuir were in the camp of over six hundred men, but finally, as the sun was settling on the horizon and the shadows were long and cool, he discovered his kin. A kettle hung over a fire and the scent of a savory stew hung over the seven MacKenzie men sitting near it.

"Malcolm?" Jock, a distant cousin and the eldest of the seven, saw him first. He was on his feet and striding toward Malcolm, gripping him in a bone-crushing bear hug before Malcolm could say anything. "You are alive!" Jock had him by the shoulders now, shaking him hard in his excitement. "Look, lads! 'Tis Malcolm himself!"

The others were on their feet, but there was something reserved about them. Perhaps it was just in comparison to Jock's strong welcome, but Malcolm noticed looks passing between the men, and they did not look so happy to see him.

"Are you hungry, lad?" Jock asked, scooping some of the stew into a wooden bowl, handing it to Malcolm with a horn spoon, and motioning for him to sit on the small keg Jock had been using, without waiting for an answer.

"I am. My thanks." He looked about and accounted for all the men who had been with him on the day he had been injured, except for one. "Where is Cameron?"

Another odd look passed from man to man and Malcolm could not help but assume the worst.

"He is dead?" he asked.

"Nay," Jock said, but he was no longer excited and the smile that had split his face a moment ago was now replaced by a frown and the man did not look him in the eye. None of them did.

"Then where is he?" Malcolm prodded. "Is he maimed?"

"Nay," Jock said again. "He was called back to Blackmuir just a few days ago."

"Do not make me drag it out of you, Jock." Malcolm set his still full bowl on the ground next to him and began rubbing his right hand again. The action reminded him of Jeanette, both when she massaged it for him and when she chided him for needing her to do what he could do himself. He almost smiled at the memory but kept his mind on the task at hand. He needed to convince his kin to return to Dunlairig with him, to take their part of the battle for Scotland's independence away from here.

Jock was looking at his kin, as if hoping someone else would tell Malcolm what he wanted to know.

"I'll not bite your head off for the truth, lads," Malcolm said. "Is Cameron well?"

"He is well," Jock said, as if that answer was easy enough to give. "He is gone back to Blackmuir because your da . . ." The man rubbed a big hand along the back of his neck and sighed. He looked Malcolm in the eye once more. "We looked for you as best we could after the battle at Dalrigh last summer, but the English and those damned MacDougalls crawled over that battlefield for days and we could not get close enough to even claim our dead. When your da heard the news that you were likely dead, he named Cameron his successor as chief." He paused and sighed again. "Your da died a fortnight ago. Cameron went home because he is now chief of the MacKenzies of Blackmuir."

Malcolm knew all of them were tense from the hard lines of their mouths, the bouncing foot of Turval, and Hector chewing his fingernails, as he always did before a battle. They were waiting for him to react, to explode, to deny the news, but in truth, he did not know what to feel.

His father was dead. As much as they had disagreed, he had never really believed his father would die. And yet, he had. An ache opened up in his chest, like someone had scooped out his innards and left him hollow, empty.

"How did he die?" he asked quietly.

"Fever," Jock said.

"Fever," Malcolm repeated, trying to understand this news. "Are my sisters well?"

"Aye. The message told us many had the fever but only a few died. Your sisters were amongst those that survived."

"And Cameron has taken my place as the new chief." The words had not sunk in until he said them himself. Cameron was chief. Not Malcolm. Cameron.

"We all thought you dead," Aiden, Cameron's younger brother, finally said. Jock took the opportunity to drain a cup of what was probably ale.

"Can I have some of that?" Malcolm asked Jock.

"Aye, but I think a wee dram of whiskey would be better for you, lad."

Malcolm agreed, though he might need more than one wee dram this night. No one spoke until they all had whiskey in their hands.

"To my da," Malcolm said, raising his drink in the air, then draining it. The others echoed his words and his actions.

Malcolm looked about him and realized that, with the exception of Cameron, these were all of the men who had fought with him last summer, all that had been left alive of the twenty MacKenzies that had joined the king's army that spring. After almost twelve months of Cameron's leadership, these seven were still alive. Did he keep them at the rear of the battles, or was he simply better at keeping their men alive than Malcolm was?

"Tell me about Cameron," he said. "Will he make a good chief?"

For the next several hours Malcolm's kin regaled him with tales of battles, hard weather, meager rations, and their recent victory at Loudoun Hill. In every tale, Cameron had proved to be a good leader of his men. In every tale, Cameron had proved to be a better leader of his men than Malcolm had been. It was hard to hear, but slowly Malcolm came to understand that these men trusted Cameron as they had not trusted him. He came to understand that his headlong rush into battle in search of glory made him a good warrior, but not the kind of leader these men needed.

And then he realized he was no longer that foolish man. His last battle with them had been the end of that foolish man. They had followed Cameron's instructions, not his, because Cameron knew it was a fool's battle. He had argued with Malcolm that they should retreat and live to fight another day, a better day when they were not already exhausted by the rout at Methven and the rapid march westward. But Malcolm had been too focused on proving himself to be the best warrior for his clan, while missing the point that he needed to prove himself the best leader for his clan. It was a lesson his father had tried to teach him again and again but Malcolm, in his arrogance, thought his father daft, and thought Cameron weak-minded for agreeing with Malcolm's father. But on that day at Dalrigh his men had followed the better leader, not the arrogant warrior, and it had likely cost him the use of his arm for most of a year. And yet he was not angry.

This surprised Malcolm. He was not angry with them anymore. He himself had followed Nicholas's instructions in the recent battle, though he knew the man was not the warrior Malcolm was. But Nicholas was a good leader, soliciting opinions and advice when needed, while still making his own decisions, using each person's strengths to the best advantage for the clan. It was easy to follow him because Malcolm trusted him, everyone trusted him, and so they all did their part in Nicholas's plan. Just as these men had followed Cameron.

"You were right to follow Cameron that day," he said when the tales tapered off into silence. "If you had followed me, some of you, maybe all, would have died on that battlefield. I almost did. Cameron, in his wisdom, has managed to keep you all alive while fighting the good fight for King Robert and Scotland." He looked at each one of them carefully now, weighing the stories they had told against the evidence of new scars, and a quiet strength that had not been there before, etched on their faces, along with the clear surprise at his words. "Will you follow him as chief?"

They each nodded.

"We swore our allegiance to him before he left here," Aiden spoke again.

Malcolm nodded. "It was the right thing to do."

"But you always wanted to be chief," Aiden said. "Do you accept so easily that you will not follow your da in that position?"

"Easily? Nay, not easily. In truth, I did not want it anymore, but I would not have admitted that to anyone if it were not already done." Only now was it sinking in, what it meant for Cameron to be chief of the MacKenzies, and that hollow place inside him began to fill with warmth and hope.

"You must have taken a hard hit on the head, Malcolm," Jock said as he poked at the fire and threw another piece of wood on it.

Malcolm smiled at the man. "Nay, it was my arm that took the hit." And his heart. He pulled his sleeve up and showed them the injury on his arm that had finally healed into a long pink scar. "It took me a long time to realize it was my own pride and arrogance that caused my injury. If I had listened to Cameron that day, I would have been with you all for this last year. But if I had been with you, then . . ." He wasn't ready to talk about Jeanette just yet, not until he had things settled with these lads.

"Will you rejoin us now, Malcolm?" Dugald, the youngest of his cousins, asked.

"Nay. I have come, with the king's blessing, to ask if you will come with me to fight on another front." Before anyone could interrupt him, he put up a hand to stay their voices. "I understand you do not trust me to lead you." Here there were denials, but he could tell their hearts were not in them. "Know that I am not the leader in this fight, but a simple warrior looking for reinforcements."

"Who would we be fighting?"

"The English are mounting an attack against the MacAlpins of Dunlairig. They are a small clan who are said to protect the southern route into the Highlands along the Great Glen. Have you heard the tale of the Highland Targe?"

"Aye," Gillean said. His hair was almost as pale as Jeanette's and the lad had filled out in the year since Malcolm had seen him last. "My granny used to tell me that one. It was a shield big enough to block invaders, but I did not believe the tale, even when I was a wean."

"King Edward believes it and seeks to take the Targe from them before he marches into the Highlands."

"Why would he march into the Highlands?" Jock asked. "'Twould be daft to take an invasion force into that country if you did not ken the way through it."

"I think he's likely planning to make his way east, not north, in the hopes of circling the Scottish forces."

"Did you tell Robert of this?"

"I did, and he agreed 'twas a likely plan. We believe there are twoscore English soldiers heading to Dunlairig. The MacAlpins have twenty fighting men—well, ten and nine without me—and their former chief has gone to rally their allies, but it is uncertain if he can do so. Even if he does, we cannot ken how many men will heed his call to arms. You seven could change the odds for the MacAlpins and for Scotland.

"Nicholas of Dunlairig is now the chief there and he is an able leader both in and out of battle. I trust him with my life, and I trust him with the lives of those I claim as mine," he said, thinking not only of his cousins but how he had left Jeanette's welfare in Nicholas's hands. "I ken I ask much of you and that your loyalty lies elsewhere now. I ask only that you consider what I have said. With you, or without you, I return to Dunlairig at first light."

CHAPTER TWENTY

"Have you seen Scotia this morning?" Jeanette asked Duncan as she came out of the large cave and blinked in the bright sunshine of midmorning.

He stopped sharpening his dirk and looked up at her. "Aye, she's down in the glen. Uilliam is with her."

"He had better keep a sharp eye on her. I do not trust her to stay where she is told."

"He will. He does not trust her any more than the rest of us do."

Jeanette sat next to him on the tree trunk that served as a bench near the fire, carefully not looking at the place where she had first slept in Malcolm's arms. The ache that had taken residence in her heart since he left eleven days ago seemed to grow bigger every time she thought of him. It grew harder and harder to keep up the pretense that she didn't care that he had left. She thought it would grow easier but she was so wrong.

"Has she yet told you why she left the camp?" Jeanette asked to get her mind away from difficult feelings. She had questioned her sister several times over the last ten days but the stubborn lass would not tell her.

"Nay. I think she is embarrassed," Duncan said. "She will not look me in the eye, nor even rise to my teasing."

"She saw much that day that haunts her dreams, too."

"It was a bloody day for all of us."

"I fear it will not be the last." She sighed and looked about to see what task needed tending, but there were so many people living in the Glen of Caves now that most jobs were handily taken care of, leaving Jeanette with too much time on her hands. She had taken to poring over the chronicles for hours at a time, until her back ached and her eyes were gritty with fatigue, as she had been doing since well before dawn today.

"Do you think he will come back?" Duncan asked as he once more took up the sharpening of his blade.

Her heart leapt at the idea, but she ruthlessly killed the hope that Duncan's words encouraged. "Nay. He will fight with King Robert and when his duty is fulfilled there he will return to his home in the north." She took a deep breath and tried to swallow the pain that strangled her heart tighter and tighter each day. She rose and decided to find Rowan so they could practice using the Targe stone, as they had done every spare moment since the battle. "He will be chief of his clan," she said. "It is as much his duty as being a Guardian is mine."

She could feel Duncan's eyes on her, could feel the pity he and everyone else seemed to feel for her. She needed to get away by herself, compose herself, a task that seemed almost impossible, but she was determined to go on as if her heart wasn't broken, as if her life was exactly as she wished it to be, though there was little about her life that was as she wished it. She made herself walk toward the thicker trees that circled the main cave and she had just stepped onto a path when she heard a horn sound from up the ben in the direction of the pass. One blast—friend. Duncan's last question leapt to her mind but she immediately chided herself for her wishful thinking. It was probably just the scouts who kept watch for the English soldiers, whom she dreamed about nightly, returning to the glen.

She walked a little farther into the wood, then stepped off the path and went to a large boulder that made a perfect seat. She had taken to coming here often when it all got too much for her. This was a place where no one looked on her with pity and no one asked questions she didn't want to answer. This was a place where she didn't have to think, didn't have to feel. This was a place where she could just be. Maybe, if she tried very hard, she could find that calm center she had had before she met Malcolm, before her mother died, before she became a Guardian, before her entire life had turned upside down and left her heart in tatters.

It was not long before she heard a commotion. Whoever had entered the glen must have made it down to the caves fast. And then she heard her name called. Someone must be hurt. She took a deep breath and settled her face into what she hoped was a serene smile, before she rose from her stone seat and headed back the way she came.

"I am here," she said as she stepped into the open in front of the cave. "Who is hurt?"

A group of seven men she did not know looked at her, then stepped aside.

Malcolm stood amongst them with the same grin he'd worn the day they met.

Jeanette couldn't move. She couldn't speak. Her mind kept telling her it wasn't him, it wasn't him. But her eyes proved otherwise.

"You . . ." She put her hand over her mouth and tears started to stream from her eyes. "You came back," she managed to get out as her heart burst free of its chains. "You came back."

Malcolm's grin faded to a smile as he closed the distance between them. "Do not cry, angel mine." He took her face in his hands and kissed her gently, as if she was fragile. He wiped her tears away with his thumbs, then pulled her into a fierce hug. "I came back to you. Are you still mine, Jeanette?" he whispered in her ear.

She smiled through her tears. "Always. Are you still mine?" she whispered in his ear, nuzzling it with her nose.

"Always and forever."

Two days later Jeanette donned a beautiful blue gown the women of the clan had found for her wedding day.

"It is the very color of your eyes," Rowan said as she laced it closed for her cousin. "'Tis a good thing you shall have Malcolm's help undressing, though, with the laces in the back!"

Jeanette felt her skin go hot, partly from embarrassment that Rowan should speak of such things, and partly from the memory of the things she and Malcolm had shared in the grotto before and would do again this very day.

"I think that was the idea when the women chose this for me."

"Aye, I'm quite sure Peigi had a hand in the choosing. You ken she takes full credit for this marriage, do you not?"

"I doubt it not." The two of them laughed quietly together.

Scotia sat nearby, solemnly watching. "I will arrange your hair for you, sister, if you will let me. It should have been Mum's privilege but . . ."

Rowan patted Jeanette on the shoulder to let her know the lacing was finished.

"I would like that," Jeanette said. Scotia rose, giving her seat on a small barrel to her sister. "I think Mum would be happy today, do you not?" Jeanette asked her.

"I think she would be sad to miss this day," Scotia said quietly as she began to run a comb through Jeanette's long flaxen hair, "but happy that you have found Malcolm."

"'Tis a good thing Uncle Kenneth likes Malcolm," Rowan said as she watched Scotia's work. "I was not sure, when he first arrived yesterday, if that would be true."

Jeanette smiled, remembering the sight of her blustering father as he burst into the cavesite yesterday afternoon with

Uilliam and Duncan, who had found him already on his way back to Dunlairig, on his heels. Kenneth had been ready to run Malcolm through with his sword. Uilliam, bless him, had calmed Kenneth down enough to give Malcolm a chance to convince her father he was an honorable man who was in love with Jeanette. After several hours of the men conversing by themselves, she watched as Malcolm formally asked for her hand in marriage and her father agreed, giving his blessing to both of them.

Scotia settled a wreath of flowers and greenery on Jeanette's head, weaving thin braids of her hair about it like ribbons.

"Have you heard aught of whether Da was able to convince any of the other clans to send help?" Scotia asked.

"Nicholas said there were a few chiefs who pledged men," Rowan said, "but most were unwilling to leave themselves vulnerable in case the English turned their attention upon their clans."

"And they call us their allies?" Scotia's voice was a low growl. "Let us see what happens when they need our help."

"Wheesht, sister," Jeanette said. "Today is a day of happiness and celebration. Tomorrow will be soon enough to consider our options."

"I think it is time," Rowan said.

Scotia tucked one last braid around the wreath, then motioned for Jeanette to stand.

"You make a beautiful bride, Cousin," Rowan said quietly, and Scotia nodded.

It seemed only moments later that she stood outside the main cave, Malcolm by her side, with her clan and his kinsmen gathered about them as they made their vows, just as they had done the day in the grotto, only this time it was witnessed and they were declared married by her own father.

Somehow, Peigi and her sisters had organized a feast, complete with delicious venison stew and honey cakes.

Rowan came to sit next to Jeanette and leaned close enough to whisper to her. "I have prepared a small cave not too far away for you and Malcolm," she said, smiling at her cousin. "I wish I had a feather bed for you on your wedding night."

Jeanette laughed and hugged Rowan. "I have Malcolm now. I do not need a feather bed."

Malcolm saw them laughing and came over to them. "Are you ready, angel?" he asked, holding a hand out to help her up.

"Aye, my golden warrior." She could not keep from smiling at this man, her husband, the keeper of her heart.

"Where are you going?" Rowan asked, drawing the attention of everyone nearby.

Jeanette looked down, suddenly sure that everyone could see the anticipation that coursed through her, even though she knew that what they were about was expected on a wedding night.

"We are going someplace special—" Malcolm laughed when Duncan, Jock, Nicholas, and Kenneth all started to complain. "It is not far away, and it is within this glen. I can guarantee that should it come to anything, Jeanette can keep me very safe." Everyone laughed, though his kinsmen looked at each other as if they didn't entirely understand why that was funny. Malcolm thought it best they keep the real strength of the two Guardians secret for a while longer and Nicholas had agreed.

Jeanette leaned close to Rowan and kissed her on the cheek. "We are going to the grotto," she said for Rowan's ears alone. "Tomorrow we will take advantage of the cave you have prepared."

Rowan grinned. "I imagine you will."

Peigi arrived with a basket full of food and a wineskin Malcolm had brought back with him for just this occasion.

"How did you ken we would need that?" Jeanette asked.

Peigi gave a loud cackle. "A golden birdie told me." She patted Malcolm on the cheek, then Jeanette. "Do not hurry back!"

ACKNOWLEDGMENTS

MANY THANKS, AS ALWAYS, TO MY DEAR FRIENDS AND SISTERS-of-my-heart Pamela Palmer and Anne Shaw Moran. I don't know what I would do without you two to keep me steady, grounded, and focused. Your friendship makes me a better person. Your critiques make me a better writer. I'm so glad we are journeying through this life together!

An equal number of thanks go to my daily writing friends Phyllis Hall Haislip and Kathy Huffman. Thanks to you two, I have gotten really good at writing every single day. I hope I have had the same effect on you!

And a big thanks and hug for my nephew, Dr. Wesley Watkins, for helping me understand Malcolm's injury. All errors are my own.

And last, but definitely not least, the team at Montlake Romance has my great thanks for being so terrific to work with!

ABOUT THE AUTHOR

Michael Taylor, 2012

LAURIN WITTIG WAS INDOCTRINATED INTO HER SCOTTISH heritage at birth when her parents chose her oddly spelled name from a plethora of Scottish family names. At ten, Laurin attended her first MacGregor clan gathering with her grandparents, and her first ceilidh ("kay-lee"), a Scottish party, where she danced to the bagpipes with the hereditary chieftain of the clan. At eleven, she visited Scotland for the first time and it has inhabited her imagination ever since.

Laurin writes bestselling and award-winning Scottish medieval romances and lives in southeastern Virginia. For more information about all of Laurin's books, please visit her at LaurinWittig.com.